THE UNMARKED FLOOR

LUKAS OSWALD

OVERCAST SUNDAY
PUBLISHING

The Unmarked Floor

Publisher: Overcast Sunday, LLC

Paperback ISBN: 979-8-9882012-0-5

Hardcover ISBN: 979-8-9882012-1-2

Cover Design: Natasha Brown

Editors: Kirsten Rees | Book Editor & Author Coach

Hayes J. Dufner

To all those lost among us.

1

FRIDAY EVENING

"Can we stop at the next gas station? I have to use the bathroom," said Aleeia.

As rain misted the front windshield, Marcus focused on the road. "Let's try and find one before this storm slows us down. We have to get gas anyway."

"Can you believe it?" Aleeia sighed. "Who would have thought, after all these years, we'd finally leave San Francisco?" She leaned her head against the window. "Who are we?"

"With you, I can imagine anything." Marcus reached over and gently squeezed her leg. "Moving out of the Bay will be healthy. I think we're both ready for this next chapter."

"Take this exit!" shouted Aleeia, pointing at a sign for a gas station.

"I got it. I got it." Marcus waved his hands and laughed. "My favorite co-pilot!"

When they pulled into the empty forecourt, Aleeia stared at Marcus's pant zipper and promiscuously raised her eyebrows. "I'll be right back," she whispered, dragging her hand down and unbuckling her seatbelt.

Marcus bit his knuckle as she opened the door and walked towards the store. As he stepped to the gas pump, he watched rain drizzle down Aleeia's blonde hair and soak her velour tracksuit from behind. He felt drawn to her like a magnet.

"Good afternoon, ma'am," said the store clerk.

Aleeia looked around the room. "Which way is the bathroom?"

"That way!" he yelled with a crooked smile and cheerful glow.

As Aleeia cautiously opened the bathroom door, a dank, musty smell flew up her nose and sent shivers down her spine. She winced and quickly rushed in and out of the stall. *Gross! Get me out of here.* Before washing her hands, she noticed a newly framed poster hanging on the cracked porcelain tiles.

NATIONAL HUMAN TRAFFICKING HOTLINE
GET HELP ~ REPORT TRAFFICKING

Hmm... Just like in the airports. Aleeia shook her hands out and used her shoulder to open the door. As she found her sense of smell again, she leisurely strolled through the aisles and eyed everything that drew her attention. Eventually, she found herself by the refrigerator and grabbed a Diet Coke.

"That'll be $1.99, ma'am." The clerk tilted his hat up and peeked at her dilated eyes.

Aleeia looked at Marcus through the glass door and passed over a $20 bill. As the clerk reached for her change, a bucket of individual Blow-Pop lollipops caught her attention. "I'll have one of these, too, please." Aleeia grabbed her favorite flavor, apple.

"You got it." The clerk picked at his gold tooth and itched his nose.

When Aleeia stepped out of the store, she found Marcus

analyzing the gloomy clouds hanging over the rundown awning. He was waiting for her next move.

"Hey, mister!" she shouted.

Marcus looked up and saw Aleeia in the distance. The twinkle in her eye meant one thing.

Aleeia confidently stepped up to him and sensually popped her lollipop in her mouth.

"Did you need help with this?" She gently touched his chest.

Marcus played dumb and looked at her with a helpless smile.

"Don't worry, I can help," she said, pushing her body in front of him.

"That would be amazing."

"Anything for a gentleman like you." Aleeia twirled her lollipop around her mouth with her tongue and slowly put the nozzle back into its holder. "Where're you headin'?"

Marcus tried not to laugh as Aleeia kept character. "A town about an hour away. I'm not from here. This weather is something else, isn't it?"

"My friends left me." Aleeia dropped her lollipop to her waist. "Can you give me a ride? I'm sure I can find some way to repay you." She looked into Marcus's soul and then down to his pants, where she clenched the top of his belt seam.

"I think we can work something out. After all, there's a storm approaching." Marcus opened the passenger door and watched her climb inside.

2

FRIDAY EVENING: II

While wiping her eyeliner in the mirror, Aleeia glanced at Marcus, pulling up his pants.

"How much longer until we're there? We still need to get the keys from the realtor. What's her name again?" said Aleeia.

"It's somewhere in my email. Can you look?" Marcus brushed his hair back and looked at the time. "That was another long detour, Aleeia! We said we'd be there by now."

"Oh, don't worry about it. They can wait." Aleeia slipped her panties back on. "I know you liked it."

"This rain is really starting to pick up, and I'm kind of nervous... I don't want to try and rush there." Marcus wiggled around in his seat and started the car. "Can you call the realtor and ask if she'll still be in? It's Friday night, and I don't know if people work late in this weather."

"Deep breaths, baby. It's going to be fine." Aleeia grabbed Marcus's phone from the cup holder and navigated his email. Her eyes perked open when she saw two messages at the top of his inbox about new jingle requests. She sighed and scrolled down.

"I can't find anything."

"Uh... Search for our address, 8372 New Heaven Road."

"Okay. Found it." Aleeia cleared her throat. "Lindsay Pilar... That's her."

As Aleeia turned the radio volume down and waited for the phone to connect, she watched Marcus anxiously rub his chest and neck.

"Leave a message," he mumbled, hearing the voicemail operator in the background.

Aleeia put a finger up and shushed him. "Hi, this is Aleeia Bynes. We're arriving within the next hour to pick up the keys to 8372 New Heaven Road. Please give us a call back when you receive this message. Thank you."

Aleeia's energy after any form of roleplay was always livelier than Marcus's. She knew he was stressed about the drive and the weather, so relieving his tension left her on cloud nine.

"I've never seen rain like this. Are you worried?" Marcus quickly readjusted his posture when he heard a lightning crack along the horizon.

"The rain is pretty, isn't it?" Aleeia watched the powerful raindrops slide down the passenger side window.

"If you like panic attacks!" barked Marcus.

"Don't be a baby. I know you like the rain. I made you fond of it." Aleeia put her hand on his shoulder. "It washes everything away."

"I guess, but this is a bit too much for me."

"Well, we better get used to it. Just keep your eyes on the road. We'll be there in no time. I'm going to look at some furniture." Aleeia pulled out her phone. "We have some stuff arriving from home already, but I'm thinking about mixing it with a little Southern charm... Still modern, though. Don't worry."

"Whatever you say. I love your style, and I think everyone

does as well." Marcus hesitantly took his eyes off the road and smiled at Aleeia. "I really think you should pursue some sort of career in interior design."

Aleeia rolled her eyes and put her feet on the dashboard. "I should, but let's start with this. Who knows, there's a few extra rooms for those little monsters we've always dreamed about."

Marcus hummed and put his hand on top of Aleeia's head. "I like the sound of that."

Deep down, Marcus knew he wanted a big family. Ever since their wedding six years ago, he'd been eager to have children. Aleeia, on the other hand, was a free-spirit and wanted to wait for the right time. After reevaluating their interests in San Francisco, Marcus and Aleeia knew it was time to slow down and build something by themselves. Their friendships and social lives didn't bring them the same satisfaction and growth as they once did.

"It says to take the next exit." Aleeia looked up. "I bet Lindsay's still in."

As they pulled up to a home with antebellum architecture, they were amazed by the posh-looking structure. The grand, white building was stuck in time but lost in someone's dreams.

"This is the start." Aleeia grabbed Marcus's hand and squeezed it three times. He smiled, but she could sense his growing concern about the weather. The way his sweaty palms tightly gripped her hand told her he was nervous to go inside.

"I love you." Marcus leaned away. "If you're just getting the keys, I'm going to hang back."

"Okay, no problem. I'll be just a second." Aleeia knew Marcus never did well meeting new people. She gave him a kiss and quickly ran up the moss-covered steps and knocked on the door.

Looking back at him sitting in the car, Aleeia waited by the door, but no one answered. "Hello! Lindsay... Lindsay Pillar?

It's Aleeia Bynes." She knocked again, waited a brief moment, and then impatiently gave the unlocked doorknob a shuffle. As she peeked her head through the doorway and quietly opened the door, Aleeia took a leap of faith. "Lindsay! Hello! It's Aleeia Bynes. I'm here to pick up our keys. Hello?" Her voice echoed through the empty house as her nose caught the smell of dust and antique furniture.

A heavy door closed in the distance, and footsteps approached from the back of the house.

"One moment, Miss Bynes. I'll be right there," croaked a distant voice.

Dressed in designer ripped jeans and a Victorian-styled shirt, Lindsay Pillar appeared from the hallway with a burning candlestick holder in her hand. "This damn storm has all our power and service out. I'm so sorry if you tried to reach me. Here, please come in." Lindsay grabbed Aleeia's hand and pulled her to the middle of the room.

Aleeia glanced up at the magnificent chandelier and grand staircase. "When was this house built?" The refurbished wooden bookcase and pink velvet sofa with matching chairs caught her eye.

"I'd say it was built sometime in the late 1800s. It's my family's home. No one wanted it after everyone moved West. I can't imagine leaving the South. It's got the perfect charm for every occasion." Lindsay was clearly proud of her home, and with a slight hand motion, she pointed Aleeia to a hallway on the other side of the staircase. As they walked through the dated but well-kept building, Aleeia couldn't help but keep her eyes on the gold-framed oil paintings hanging on every inch of the walls.

"To the left!"

Aleeia walked into Lindsay's office and admired the gigantic leather chair behind the rustic wooden desk. Her mind started to whirr with new ideas for their home renovation.

Lindsay stepped behind her throne and sporadically pulled out different envelopes from a metal file cabinet. "83... 7... 2 New Heaven. Here we are."

After banging a stack of envelopes on the table, Lindsay ripped open a manila folder and passed Aleeia an antique-looking key with a large circular end.

"It's a bit older, like I mentioned on the phone and during our FaceTimes, so the home needs a lot of work. However, once it's renovated and restored, it may be the most unique building in this town."

"Right, we already have so many ideas for it. We're so excited!" Aleeia squeezed the key in her palm.

There was a moment of silence between the two as Lindsay shoved the remaining envelopes back into the drawer. Aleeia couldn't help but appreciate Lindsay's office and outfit one last time. She caught herself daydreaming.

"I should be going now. Marcus is waiting in the car. This storm has really put us on our toes. We want to get there as soon as possible."

Lindsay shook her head and escorted Aleeia down the hallway.

"Sure thing, sweetie. If you need anything, please feel free to call me, and if I don't pick up, come on in. Mi casa es su casa."

"Right... Thanks again for everything. You're a lifesaver! We'll let you know if we need anything else." Aleeia studied the entranceway again, and as she stuck her hand out to say goodbye, Lindsay quickly swatted it away and leaned in for a hug.

"And be careful on these streets! This storm could change at any moment."

Aleeia nodded and slowly pushed the heavy door forward with all her might. A draft raged through the entryway, and like a leaf in the middle of a breezy fall day, she spun to the passenger car door.

"Let's go! We're only fourteen minutes away," said Marcus. "That tree just fell on that car!"

Aleeia looked over at the smashed rear end. "Don't worry, everything's going to be fine." She grabbed Marcus's hand and brought it to her lips.

"I love you," he said.

Aleeia batted her eyes. "Love you, too."

3

FRIDAY EVENING: III

After a short drive and a lifetime of worry for Marcus, the directions pointed them into a driveway on the right. "I think this is it." He squinted his eyes and tried looking past the windshield wipers. "I can't deal with this rain anymore."

"Hey, hey, hey. Remember what I said?" Aleeia slapped her hand on the dashboard. "This is a new chapter. Embrace imperfections."

Marcus took a sharp inhale.

"Isn't it pretty?" Aleeia pointed at their front porch.

"Yes, a lifetime of prettiness. Let's go!"

Aleeia laughed to lighten the mood. "Everything's going to be fine. I promise."

"I know. I know," said Marcus, waiting for her lead again.

"Can you grab everything from the back?" Aleeia tenderly squeezed his arm.

"Yes, but did they give us another set of keys?"

"Just one for now. We'll be okay."

Marcus cut the engine and dryly gulped. "Ready?

In unison, they catapulted their doors open.

"Be careful!" shouted Aleeia, running towards the front door.

Marcus jumped to the trunk and did his best to fill his arms and shoulders with their luggage. *Why does she always have so much stuff?* But, as he pivoted and lunged down the driveway, he tripped and dropped everything. *You gotta be kidding me!*

"Just a little shimmy more," mumbled Aleeia, feeling Marcus's energy shooting up the stairs. "It's a tricky one!" She kept fiddling with the lock as the wind roared from every angle.

"Here! Let me try," grunted Marcus.

"I got it!" said Aleeia, unlocking the door and stumbling into a black abyss.

As Marcus stepped behind her and threw their belongings on the floor, he quickly turned around and felt the thunderous wind pelting his body. With all his strength, he shut the door and said, "Where's the light switch? I can't see anything."

"Lindsay mentioned the storm caused her to lose power. I think we may be without lights tonight."

"Wonderful," he said sarcastically.

"I think I have some candles. You know how I always like to set the mood." Aleeia shined her phone light into one of her bags. "Ahh, here they are!"

Marcus rolled his eyes.

"Oh my gosh! This house is going to be amazing, Marcus!" Aleeia twirled her arms around.

"It's a mess in here." Marcus wiped his hand on the wooden staircase and looked at his dusty fingers.

"Just try and envision it for two seconds. And if you're lucky, you might see those little ones running around... Besides, I already scheduled cleaners and the moving crew to come tomorrow." Aleeia flung her arms around Marcus's shoulders as he moved their bags further into the living room. "This will be perfect for tonight. It's like camping," she said.

"And I've only just started to camp," grunted Marcus, rubbing his fingers on his hairline. He anxiously looked around the room.

"It's just for a night!" Aleeia sat on the old living room couch, taking off her wet clothes. "Come here. Come keep me warm."

Marcus approached her with the one blanket they always packed. It was something they couldn't travel without.

After giving in to Aleeia's love, Marcus leaned down and wrapped them in a bundle of lust.

As time burned out that night, so did the light in the candle. They fell asleep holding each other's warmth while hurricane winds battered the outside of their home.

4
SATURDAY

The high-pitched hum of a mosquito poked the insides of Marcus's eardrum until he woke up in a daze. As he gradually opened his eyes and regained his whereabouts, he saw Aleeia covered in their blanket, latched onto his arm. Every morning, he liked to take a moment to cherish her glow and calming aura. She made him feel at home.

Swatting the mosquito away from his arm, Marcus perched up from his slumber. As he tip-toed through the house, he dreamt about their family: two daughters, a son, and a Great Dane to play fetch with. He couldn't wait to start the day and the first chapter of their new lives. Before waking Aleeia, Marcus stumbled into the space that was to be transformed into his piano studio and favorite room in the house. It overlooked their marshland backyard, and in that moment, the morning sunlight quietly painted a rainbow through the tall glass windows.

After feeling his cheeks warm, Marcus stepped back into the living room and nuzzled his face into Aleeia's neck. "Good morning, love. I'm going to go see if there's a breakfast place nearby." He gave her a passionate kiss and waited for her eyelids to reveal the deepest parts of his universe. "Can I get you anything? Coffee?"

"Mmm..." Aleeia let out a loud but relaxing sigh that shot oxytocin through his bloodstream. "I'll have whatever you can find." She rolled over. "You know what I like... oat milk, not coconut or almond." Marcus rubbed his nails up her arm. "If they don't have that, just black coffee. I'll be up in a few minutes. The movers are due at eight." Aleeia reached for her eye mask.

When Marcus stepped onto their front porch, he took a moment to examine their yard; he saw more fallen trees, cloudy puddles, and a humidity he'd never experienced. It was wet and hot simultaneously, and by the time he got to the car, he was sweating underneath his sweatshirt. *Okay, let's do this. It's go-time!* He knew today needed to be perfect by Aleeia's standards, and that would start by bringing her coffee. As Marcus opened his phone, he noticed two red notifications on his mail and phone apps, and with temptation, he read the top message.

I GOT A NEW ONE FOR YOU. CALL ME.

Marcus began chewing his nails. *What does that mean, Penny?* His mind rushed to Aleeia, countering his headspace for a new project. He knew his best friend and agent wouldn't reach out if it weren't worth his time.

With a scattered brain and an upside-down stomach, Marcus scrolled through his phone until he found the only café with oat milk. It was called The Lodge.

I need to play and be creative. It's been so long. I think she'll understand. Marcus reversed out of the driveway. *I know she wants me to take a break, but I'm only half of me when I'm not playing.*

Before listening to Penny's voicemail, Marcus aimlessly stared through the windshield, thinking about Aleeia's reaction. After a moment, he shrugged and put his phone on speaker.

"Marcus, it's Penny." His voice sounded rough and tired. "Give me a call when you have a minute. We haven't heard from you in a while." Marcus could hear a girl talking in the background. "I have a new one for you. I think you're going to like it."

Penny's lack of details made Marcus scrunch his face, and to avoid thinking about whatever he had planned, he put on his favorite music: Piano Lounge. Marcus could get lost in any piano, jazz, soul, or classical music. It's where he found his peace and best moments of reflection. Ever since he learned to play the piano at nine years old, he never took a break from exploring the different sounds a baby grand could make.

As the smooth jazz chimes touched his heart, Marcus finally calmed down. However, as he found nirvana, the robotic voice from the stereo system caught him off guard. His eyes gazed up at the gigantic green spider webs hanging adrift. The spanish moss dangling from every inch of the trees above left him in a state of disgust and yet harmonious with life. *What is that?* He was fascinated by it.

As he continued driving down the tree-lined streets, Marcus's mind slowly spiraled and hyper-focused on their move. He loved San Francisco, his friends and family, and all the great food and entertainment money could buy, but they knew the city no longer served its purpose. Aleeia was the first to crack about their friendships and social lives, and he soon began feeling the same. They decided that to live the life they've always wanted, they needed to escape and build something that was only theirs.

Jumping out of his thoughts, Marcus glanced at the rearview mirror and made eye contact with the honking driver

behind him. He waved and quickly moved through the inter-
section.

When he arrived at The Lodge, Marcus's eyes bulged as he
realized he was a long way from overcast skies looking over
Marina Green. The old plantation-like building intrigued him
—the beaten but refurbished porch had a whimsical glow. He
took a moment to absorb its charm.

As he walked up the steps and looked back at the scenery,
he noticed a lone black, out-of-place suburban SUV in the
parking lot. He rolled his shoulders back and opened the door.

"How can I help you today, sweetie?" The waitress batted
her eyes and cross-examined Marcus's lean physique. "What
road did you take to get here? You sure ain't from here, are
you?"

Marcus froze. "No, I'm not from here." He couldn't take his
eyes off the waitress's top blouse button. It was nearly popping
off. "I just moved to town with my wife. We're from
California."

The waitress tapped her long nails across the counter.
"Well, welcome to town, darling. I'm sure you'll love it. We
have the best pecan bread and Georgia's *favorite* ice cream.
Would you like to try it?" She winked. "We have *all* the best
flavors, honey. You just tell me what you want, and we'll
find it."

Marcus knew he wouldn't find many juice bars and hot
yoga studios in town. "I appreciate the offer, but I think it's a bit
early for ice cream." He peeked over at the window with an
array of muffins, breads, and pies. "But I do need breakfast."

"You're a cutie, aren't you?" The waitress pushed her chest
out and smiled.

Marcus blushed. "You said the pecan bread is good?"

"A fan favorite." Bending over, the waitress grabbed a pair of tongs.

"I'll give that a try... And can I also have one vanilla latte with oat milk, one black coffee, and..." He paused and scratched his chin. "Is there anything else you'd recommend?"

"Sure thing, mister. Have you ever had grits? You'll have to give 'em a try. It's our Southern belle's secret to staying thick behind the waist." The waitress gently patted her backside and shuffled over to the espresso machine.

Marcus's mind spun to Aleeia. "Uh... Okay. Let's add one of those with the coffees and pecan, please."

The waitress smirked as the milk frother cut their tension.

"Ma'am!" shouted Marcus as if a ghost had bumped him from behind. The waitress giggled and continued preparing his order.

"Here you go, mister. And please don't forget to come and visit us every once in a while. We love men who are soft on the eyes." The waitress gave an innocent look and reached for a napkin on the counter. "How about I do this..." she said, swiftly picking up a pen, licking the ballpoint, and writing her number down. Marcus's instincts didn't kick in fast enough. An electric shock flew through his pants as he watched her tiny hands stuff napkins into his to-go bag. "If you need anything or want to come back for our *famous* ice cream... you give me a call," she said. "We can get *any flavors* you want."

Marcus timidly looked down at the counter but wandered to her chest again. Their eyes locked as the waitress stuck the pen into her mouth and waved Marcus out the door.

5

SATURDAY: II

Back at home, Aleeia started unveiling her hopes and dreams. She stepped into the living room's natural light and admired their backyard. With the imagination of a child, she danced around the house and gracefully opened all the doors and windows to air out the rancid and mildew smell left behind by years of neglect and weathering. Each room's unique flower wallpaper told a different story, inviting her to get lost in a new world.

Aleeia knew Marcus was ready for kids, but each time she thought about carrying something inside her for nine months, she would get queasy and need to distract herself. As she scurried out of their soon-to-be kid's room, she saw a colorful pattern shining from their bedroom balcony. Serenity rested on her heart and captured a feeling of home, but as she stepped further into the room, she was dazzled by a reflection from a wooden vanity desk. She held her hand up and moved closer. The sounds of creaking floors broke the room's silence. Life stood still as she felt the desk's rugged curves and years of stain. While opening the middle drawer, she found an old lipstick tube that reminded her of her mother. Feeling her stomach drop, she took a deep breath and slowly pretended to apply the tainted wax to her puckered lips. She gazed into her soul, looking for an answer.

"Muah," she whispered, kissing the space between her and the mirror. Images of her mother and their last memories played across the dusty glass.

"Aleeia! I'm back!" shouted Marcus from the front door with a sour taste in his mouth. His heart told him one thing, but his body said otherwise. The waitress's interaction left him craving intimacy, and to fight any temptation, he had crumpled up the napkin and thrown it away on his way out.

"Pie for breakfast? Marcus, we've been here for twelve hours." Aleeia laughed and watched him reach into the to-go bag and pull out their breakfast.

"I try, baby." Marcus leaned in for a kiss.

Aleeia loved poking fun at him because he would either take it as a joke or erupt in frustration. She liked both tempers because they flattered her in different ways. As a child, Aleeia didn't grow up with much, so Marcus's constant reassurance and co-dependent personality made her feel loved. To her, Marcus was a caring man, an anchor in her chaotic world, and a natural lover. Aleeia even saw a part of her father in Marcus. Although she was too young to remember spending time with her father, her mother told her stories of his kindness and taste for the arts.

On the other hand, her relationship with her mother was distant; she was an escort for as long as Aleeia could remember. Every night before her mother left the house with the TV on and a microwave dinner for one, Aleeia watched her mother purse her lips and put her red cherry lipstick on in front of the mirror. She'd blow a kiss to Aleeia as she walked out and would say, "I won't be back too late." That was never the case. From an early age, Aleeia learned to care for herself. She found it was easier not to rely on her mother because she was never there.

"It's grits! And that's what they recommended. They said it's a Southern girl's secret to a happy life." Marcus's mind raced to the waitress's gestures, but a knock at the door snapped him out of his daydream

"They're here," said Aleeia, taking a quick sip of her coffee and grazing Marcus's backside with her nails.

Marcus bit his tongue as his eyes followed her to the front door, watching the crease between her tracksuit bottoms move from side to side.

How they planned to turn their home from a soiled antique mess to a restored historic family dwelling was beyond Marcus. He left all the planning and décor to Aleeia—she was naturally gifted with creativity in the home. She'd always dreamed of having a house with charm, character, and X-factor. In San Francisco, she twisted her modern style with a touch of Western design, or as she'd say, "like cowboys."

Back home, the Bynes were known for their exquisite taste, which gave way to their many connections around the Bay. From architects to the most expensive estate sales, they were well-versed in every category. But there was one promise throughout their different abodes and move across the US— Marcus would have his baby grand piano. It was a work of art and a bit of magic when he played.

The first time Aleeia met Marcus was at an art exhibit in Haight-Ashbury. He played the smoothest jazz, and Aleeia knew right then and there that she wanted his sound trickling throughout her body for the rest of her life. After the show, Aleeia confidently presented herself to Marcus. Her allure and innocent seduction left him flustered beyond his worst nightmares.

Fumbling his words, Marcus glanced at his watch and realized he had another gig downtown. He looked at Aleeia's eyes and knew there was something about her that would have him suffocating in pleasure until his last breath.

Before he could say he needed to leave, Aleeia asked where he was going next as if she were his number one fan. Marcus was stunned but said he needed to be downtown by 9:30pm for another party—it was 8:37pm. Aleeia looked up at Marcus's chest and smirked, "I'm heading downtown as well. Would you mind if I joined you for the ride?"

When they got into Marcus's car, Aleeia asked if he was ready to perform again after such a dreamy show. Marcus took a deep breath and played it cool. He mentioned he was more stressed about the next exhibit because it was for an upcoming artist who had the potential to be the next Picasso—the guest list was unworldly. Aleeia took note and asked Marcus if she could help him relax before the show.

As they started to drive, she placed her hand on his chest and began moaning in his ear. Marcus watched her slowly drag her hand down to his zipper. She opened it and relinquished a sigh that would forever be ingrained in his memory. Zooming through the streets, he watched in awe—Marcus couldn't believe what was happening. While pulling into the parking garage for the next venue, Aleeia finished him with her mouth. Both taken aback by the casual but everlasting experience, Marcus leaned across in his seat. "You're sitting front row tonight," he said, putting his arm around Aleeia and kissing her lips as if a meteor were about to strike the Earth. At that moment, time stopped. They'd been searching for the perfect combination of each other. Marcus didn't have a guest pass to the venue, but he didn't care. He had his everything by his side.

And, like a man out of a spiritual awakening, he marched into the venue with her on his waist—confidence glowing in each of their eyes. There were no questions or hold-ups, only a night filled with Marcus playing next to his forever muse.

"Wonderful! It's nice to meet you as well." Aleeia reached out to shake hands with the head mover. "Can we remove all the old furniture and take it away? I think I made a note that we're getting rid of everything."

The lead mover smiled and whistled to his crew. "Of course, ma'am. We received your furniture last week, too." He looked back at the truck. "And we also brought our cleaners, per your request. We are happy to help."

Although most of the cleaners kept to themselves, they seemed mesmerized by Aleeia's caring confidence. "You're doing such a great job. Thank you!" She directed everyone like they were her best friends, which made the day go by faster. But as the minutes and hours passed, the weather began to take a turn. Gray clouds and gloomy skies soon encompassed the afternoon sun.

As Aleeia oversaw everyone's assignments like an orchestra conductor managing their band, Marcus anxiously walked through the house, waiting for the most important part to arrive.

"And you can put that in the kitchen. Thank you!" said Aleeia, feeling the workers' wandering eyes. "Oh wow! Marcus is going to be so happy... Ask him where he wants it. He's inside."

"Sure thing, ma'am!" said one of the movers as they ran to find Marcus.

"Mister, we have something for you."

Marcus's heart skipped a beat as he lunged for the front door to find his prized possession: his baby grand piano.

Five movers in mixed baseball caps looked at him for more instructions.

"Let's bring it around the house. It'll be easier to get in that way."

The workers nodded and went straight to the piano to haul it towards the back.

Marcus held his breath, watching men he didn't know hold his livelihood in their hands. He nervously guided his crispy pearl white wood and swanky keys along the mucky path to the back patio door.

"Help! Help!" cried one of the men. Marcus saw his leg go out. Rushing over to take his place, he couldn't help but think of the worst. Over the years, he'd seen a few pianos take a tumble.

Marcus gestured to the door and asked another worker, "Can you open the sliding door?" Sweat began sliding down his face. He knew the piano needed to be moved, or he'd drop his end. "One, two, three," he shouted as they lugged up the slippery wooden steps. "Gently. More to the left."

"C'mon! Move it!" said one of the movers.

"Perfect. Perfect. Okay... now to the right... easy, now. Yes... okay... right... here!"

The men softly dropped the piano exactly where Marcus wanted it.

"Perfect, friends!" He grinned and held up a high-five.

The movers charismatically smiled and touched his hand with encouragement. They still had half a house to unpack, but they'd moved the only item Marcus cared about.

Sitting on the piano bench, Marcus carefully swiped his fingers over the soft ivory edges, admiring its natural beauty like a father looking at his child for the first time. Every few seconds, he started playing a new key, some high and some low, and over the next hour, he created a background noise that left all the movers intrigued as to who the Bynes were. "This feels right," Marcus said, looking above the piano and into their backyard.

"Ma'am, the total will be $3,500 for the day," said the lead mover, walking up the front door steps.

"Wonderful, thank you so much. You all did a lovely job. Can we pay with a check, yes?"

"Yes. A check is good."

"Okay, one second. Let me get Marcus. Stay here."

"Ah, fuck!" yelled one of the workers from the side of the house.

Aleeia could hear an inaudible conversation. "Does he need anything? I think we packed a first aid kit."

"No, we are good. I appreciate your kindness. Thank you, ma'am."

"Marcus!" Aleeia walked in and found him sitting on his piano bench. "Can you pay the movers? She rolled her eyes around the room. "It's perfect, isn't it?"

"It is. Even more perfect with those little ones." He kissed her head and walked outside.

"How much is it?" Marcus pulled out his checkbook.

"$3,500, sir." The head mover grinned and slumped back on his right leg.

"Here you go."

"Thank you for your business, sir." The head mover nodded.

Marcus stuck his hand out and watched them pile into three moving trucks.

6

SATURDAY EVENING

"What do you think?" asked Aleeia, holding up a piece of lingerie from her suitcase.

"I like it. I can't wait to see you in it." Marcus fell back onto their bed and closed his eyes.

He was tired, and the day sucked his energy dry, but in contrast, Aleeia was ready to go. She never lost her spunk—she was always ready to adventure and love. She got her non-stop liveliness from her father: a man of his word and a dedicated husband and teacher.

For almost ten years, Aleeia's father, David, taught Music Theory at New York University until he died of a sudden brain aneurysm—it shocked everyone. David was a gifted musician and had passion when he played; his art was the first glimpse of sunshine Aleeia's mother, Emilee, felt since moving from London. Even though David was her teacher, she couldn't stay away from him and wasn't shy about doing extra credit assignments or attending his late-night office hours. All the female students adored David, but his eyes and heart were set on Emilee.

Not long after their semester with each other ended, they started dating and kept it a secret from the school because Emilee would eventually have to take another class taught by David. Between early morning coffee runs and private tutor sessions, David and Emilee did their best to hide their love story until Emilee found herself pregnant with Aleeia. They were hopelessly in love for years, but in the fall of '91, Emilee received a call that something had happened to David during one of his lectures.

As they got to the hospital, Emilee wept in pain. Tears came like a tsunami. The lack of closure with her lover made her numb to the world. David, being who he was, meant the school helped Emilee and Aleeia as much as possible, but when Emilee's addiction to cocaine got the best of her, they cut her off. With nothing but a broken heart, her dreams were empty and consumed by white powder. Sometimes, she'd forget she even had Aleeia.

In a world where sexual actions can feed an addiction, Emilee took her chances and was a star. She was a functioning junkie and supported Aleeia just enough. She fed her every day, took her to school most mornings, and would be there when the bell rang to walk home. Her mother worked all night while Aleeia dreamt of the man she was too young to remember. Her mother slept all day while Aleeia learned to find peace with the loss of her father. They were a dynamic duo, but Aleeia grew up too quickly. Seeing drugs, alcohol, sex, and money at a young age made her emotionless. She thought of it as evil and knew she needed to leave.

Marcus stretched out on their white duvet in exhaustion as Aleeia continued to admire her clothes in their closet.

"I'm going to play." Marcus puttered off the bed.

"Play my favorite, would you? I want to hear it from here." Aleeia poked her head out from their closet.

Marcus loved her song; it brought him back to a place he'd only dreamt of as a kid. It was a riff that he made the night they met.

As the sun began to melt below the marsh, Marcus pulled up his chair and sat down. He took a deep breath and sparked the piano with his energy. His music reached the insides of the old screws keeping the doors together. It jumped inside the porcelain bathtub and stretched inside Aleeia's mind as she sat on the perch in their bedroom and lit a cigarette.

Aleeia didn't think of herself as a smoker but loved a drag or two in the right mood. She craved the head rush and the faint smell of her mother. She didn't know where the woman was and didn't want to know the truth. The last image she had of her was shooting heroin on the couch. She told her mom was going to a friend's house to study, but instead, she took her books and got a one-way bus ticket to the Golden State.

"I love the sound of it, Marcus," said Aleeia, wrapping her arms around him. "I'm going to run out and get dinner. I'll be right back." She kissed him on top of his head.

Deep in a trance, Marcus barely heard her hazy goodbye; he wandered deeper into his imagination.

7

SATURDAY EVENING: II

Almost always, Aleeia liked to go with the flow of life, and tonight's drive was precisely that—an escape from the realities that existed around her, only she was on an adventure to find dinner for two. And, like Marcus, she also enjoyed music that awakened her soul. Aleeia grabbed her phone and played *Oh Honey* by Delegation.

For Aleeia, their sleepy neighborhood was a refreshing feeling. The storm's wreckage had her putting the landscape's pieces together like a puzzle. Between the flooded streets and broken tree branches scattered across the wide roads, she couldn't help but think about their future. Before her mind skipped chapters, Aleeia was interrupted by heavy raindrops pounding the sunroof. As she looked into the cotton candy skyline, her vision was blocked. Rain poured from the sky like a broken faucet on a hot summer day. *What is this weather?*

Coming to a halt, Aleeia cautiously pulled over and called Marcus. As assumed, he didn't pick up. She knew he was amusing and losing himself in his Steinway sounds. Interrupting a session was nearly impossible; only thigh-high boots and a trench coat could stop his train of thought.

While Aleeia soaked in her alone time, she continued reevaluating whether their move was the right decision. She knew moving across the country was her idea and came with the promise of starting a family. *What if I don't want one right now?* Aleeia stared into the distance, sucking on the diamond necklace Marcus had bought her as an anniversary gift, until she was awakened by quiet raindrops kissing the hood of the car. *Finally, time to find dinner.* She looked up with a confused smirk and watched the evening sun glow from the tiniest crevasses in the clouds.

As she steered the car back onto the road, Aleeia was greeted by a gust of fog clouding her view. Unfamiliar with driving in rain and humidity, she shuffled around the different climate settings until she could see out the window again. As the fog dissipated, a tiny shopping center appeared alongside the road. She looked up at a sign: Captain Cooks Fish & Southern Eatery. *That's the one.*

Turning down the radio, Aleeia jaggedly pulled into the parking lot and rammed her car into the only open space. The restaurant looked packed from the outside, and when she got out of the car, she could hear talking and loud music. It sounded like a party.

"Hi there," she said, stepping inside and smelling a green and skunky aroma. Everyone turned to her as if she were a musician opening the curtain of their first global show. One person in the back corner even whistled.

"Hello. How are you tonight, ma'am? Table for one or take out?"

"Take out, please," responded Aleeia, feeling uncomfortable but in all the right ways.

"Is it your first time here?" The host gazed at Aleeia's blonde hair.

"Yes, it is! What should I get?"

"Well, welcome in. I'd recommend our Flounder, Fried Green Tomatoes, and Fried Mac and Cheese," said the boy in a Southern strum.

Aleeia politely nodded. "Is it fine if I take a seat and order there?" She pointed at the bar.

"Please, ma'am. Right this way," The host towered over Aleeia's short stature and led her to the only open seat at the bar.

"What can I get you to drink, Miss?" asked the bartender.

"I think I'm going to order some food to go if you don't mind."

The man grinned and continued cleaning a glass. "Sure thing, ma'am. Let me know when you're ready, and I can start your order."

Looking down at the menu, Aleeia smiled cheek-to-cheek. From the names and ingredients of each dish to the price, she wanted to order one of everything. Aleeia basked in her freedom. She knew she had plenty of time to relax in her new world because Marcus was drowning in his B and C chords. "Actually, can I have a double vodka martini on the rocks with lemon and orange wedges, please?"

Everyone at the bar turned their heads and looked at Aleeia again.

"You got it, ma'am. Is well-vodka okay?" The bartender grabbed a shaker and filled it with ice.

"If you have Belvedere or Ketel One, that would be lovely."

"How about Deep Eddy? That's the best we got."

Aleeia batted her eyes in agreement.

"Now, miss, you sures ain't from here. We all knows that...

What brought you into Captain's tonight?" slurred the man next to her.

"My husband and I just moved here from California," Aleeia said, twisting her body to look at him.

"Wow, California. Yous a long ways from home, Dorothy. How bout I buys you this fancy drink so I can say I drank with a Hollywood celebrity tonight?" The man crowed and smacked his leg. He was missing all but three front teeth.

Aleeia blushed. "That's so sweet... sure, mister. That would be okay with me."

The bartender placed Aleeia's drink down and waited for her reaction.

"Call me... Mister Peaches, like 'em Georgia Peaches. Ay Don, put them pretty miss's drinks on mine!" He took a big whiff at Aleeia. "I appreciate your sweet scent, miss... I never gots your name."

"It's Aleeia," she said, sipping her stiff drink.

"Ahh, so there it is... Miss Aleeia. Well... welcome to the original Captain Cooks. My mama over there was once married to Captain himself." Mr. Peaches pointed to a stout older woman with slick black hair and an infectious cackle. "She had the sweetest love for my pa. Rest his soul." He toasted his drink and slugged it back.

Aleeia felt mixed emotions, thinking of her parents. "I'm so sorry about your father. He must have been great. He probably left a nice story to tell... I mean, look at how many people are in this restaurant." Aleeia looked down into her drink and played with the fruit wedges. "I'm excited to try the food."

"Yes, Miss Aleeia, the food is what brings them peoples in the doors—sweet, home-style Southern cooking. You best try our famous Flounder and Collard Greens. It's my mama's specialty."

The bartender placed another drink in front of Mr. Peaches without hesitation.

"I'll have to try them all. I appreciate the tip, Mr. Peaches."

"Anything for a sweetheart like yous."

Aleeia gave one more look at the menu and knew exactly what she wanted. "Excuse me, sir. Can I put my order in, please?

"Sure thing."

"Can I please have one order of the Flounder, Fried Green Tomatoes, Mac and Cheese, Collard Greens, Cornbread, and the Apple Cobbler?"

"That's my girl!" Mr. Peaches turned and lightly tapped Aleeia on her back. "You even gots my favorite dessert. You gon' like the South misses."

While Aleeia waited for her order, she began to people-watch. She took in all the different aromas of the room, voice inflections from the surrounding tables, and the clothing styles of everyone around her. She saw a birthday party, family dinners, and a group of men wearing all black sitting in the back of the restaurant. They were yelling and laughing in what she thought might be Russian. Everything was different. She felt at home again.

"Okay, Miss Aleeia, here you are." The bartender gestured to the food that the waiter had brought out. "Now, you take care now. We hope to see you again soon."

Aleeia's eyes lit up when she smelt the soul food seeping from the to-go boxes. She turned to Mr. Peaches. "It was a pleasure meeting you, mister. I'll have to bring my husband in next time." She placed her hand on his shoulder and smiled. "And thank you so much for the drink. I'll have to buy the next round."

"Oowee!" Mr. Peaches shimmied his body and watched Aleeia grab her food. "We'll be seeing ya, Miss Aleeia!"

8

SATURDAY EVENING: III

The evening felt young and alive as Aleeia opened the driver's side door and placed the to-go boxes on the passenger seat. Her mind finally relaxed after basking in the new scenery and the town's liveliness. When deciding on the home of their dreams, Aleeia wanted it to be in the countryside but close enough to town, and now, to her surprise, Captain Cooks. *Marcus's morning grits won't stand a chance after he tries this.*

Aleeia turned on her headlights as the evening sky faded into the horizon. Her interaction with Mr. Peaches had put a smile on her face.

"Fuck! What was that?" she shouted, steering off the road. She was stunned. Every drop of happiness and relaxation evaporated from her body like a black hole swallowing a planet. Her mind went blank. She could see a flinching body with fur and four legs on the right side of the road. She timidly covered her mouth and turned off the radio. The ominous silence of the deserted highway pierced her eardrums. Her heartbeat and the deep breathing of the distressed deer were the only sounds for miles.

Stepping out of the car, Aleeia knelt and looked at its black, pained eyes that showed her reflection against the night sky. She choked up and knew its life would be shortly ending. She didn't know what to do, so she went back to the car and called Marcus. By the luck of it, he picked up.

"Marcus?" Aleeia dryly swallowed.

"Hey, where are you? Is everything okay?" Marcus could hear her sniffling.

"No, not really. I don't know what to do."

"What happened?"

"I don't know... I was driving home with dinner... and... one second, I was enjoying the drive... and the next... I hit a deer... There's blood... everywhere... and it's still alive. It's in so much pain. It's still breathing, Marcus."

"It's going to be fine. Where are you?"

"I don't know." Aleeia's voice choked. "Can you look at my location?" She paused, seeing a car's headlights approaching. "Wait, Marcus, there's another car. I'm going to see if they can help. I'll be home as soon as possible." Aleeia stepped into the middle of the road and started waving her hands.

"Are you sure? I'll look to see where you are." Marcus pulled up her location on his phone and saw she was only half a mile away. "Hello! Aleeia!?" He shook his head and put on his running shoes.

"Please! Please! Help!" she shouted, watching the car's headlights blind her as they slowly pulled up next to her.

"Hello, Miss. Are you okay?" The woman driver was hidden by the darkness of the night.

"No, I hit a deer... and... I'm not sure what to do." Aleeia pointed across the road. "It's still breathing. I can see the pain in its eyes."

"Okay, slow down, hon." The woman put her hand up and

turned off the car. "This happens all the time. It's quite normal."

Aleeia wiped her tears as she saw the woman come to her side and rub her shoulder. "Thank you for stopping." Aleeia froze after making eye contact with the driver's light green eyes. The woman's olive skin and black hair glimmered in the moonlight.

"Let's have a look at your car." The woman grazed Aleeia's lower back as she passed by. "It looks okay, but the deer." She shrugged her shoulders. "They're going to have to be put down." She pulled out her phone. "I'll call my husband. He's the sheriff in town."

Aleeia could tell she had an accent but couldn't pinpoint it. "Thank you," she said, wiping her eyeliner and staring at the woman's all-black outfit.

"Donnie, can you look at my location? I stopped for someone on the road that hit a deer." She waved at Aleeia. "Yes, baby. That's why I'm calling. We need help." The woman paced around the flinching deer and eyed Aleeia from head to toe.

"Aleeia! Aleeia!" shouted Marcus as he got closer. His breathing was heavy as he went to her side. "Is everything okay? I came as fast as I could."

"Yes..." Aleeia closed her eyes. She struggled to find the right words to explain her situation and who the woman on the phone was.

"Izabelle. I'm Izabelle. It's nice to meet you," the woman said, sticking her hand out and hanging up the phone. "My husband should be here soon. He's coming from the station downtown."

"It's nice to meet you, Izabelle. I'm Aleeia," she said, pushing away from Marcus's hug. "And this is my husband, Marcus."

"It's nice to meet you both. Are you new here?"

"Yes, we just moved from San Francisco." Aleeia fixed her hair as Marcus went to look at the car.

"What a move for you both!" Izabelle looked at her phone. "We should have dinner sometime. It's been so long since Donnie and I have met anyone new."

"Really?" Aleeia smirked. "I mean, that sounds lovely." A flush of embarrassment colored her cheeks. "We would love that. We don't know anyone right now." She brushed her hair behind her ears and gestured to Marcus, stepping back from the car.

Izabelle smiled.

"It looks alright," said Marcus, grabbing Aleeia by the waist and looking at Izabelle. "Thanks for stopping."

"Of course. It's a small town. I'm sure the favor will come back around." Izabelle paused. "But the deer took quite a beating. Your car is lucky." She pulled a tiny mirror from her purse and applied lipstick as another car approached.

"Who's this?" Marcus cupped his hand over his eyes to see.

"My husband," said Izabelle. "He's also the town sheriff."

Slamming the car door and pulling his pants higher on his waist, a heavier-set man stepped onto the road. "How are we doin' tonight, folks?"

Before Marcus and Aleeia could respond, Izabelle butted in. "Donnie, baby. They hit a deer." She pointed. "Aleeia said the deer popped out of nowhere. That is what happened, right?"

"Yeah, that's what happened. I just picked up food from Captain Cooks, and when I pulled onto this road... I just couldn't react in time. I'm sorry."

Marcus leaned over to hug her.

"There you have it, angel... And then her husband, Marcus, just ran from home?" Izabelle said, a little confused.

"What a gentleman. I like this guy!" Donnie moved behind Marcus and patted him on the back. "Okay, no need to worry anymore." Donnie walked towards the deer and knelt by its head. Ending the life of a crippling animal had become a spiritual ceremony for him. Between hunting and small-town sheriff duties, he had plenty of experience with a blade.

After sharing a moment with the deer, Donnie stroked its face and began to hush it to sleep. He pulled a knife from his side belt and then jabbed it through its neck. The action made a gushing noise. They all pictured the deer's soul rising from its body and galloping into the distance.

Getting up and wiping the tiny blood spots on his pants, Donnie said, "I'll go ahead and take care of this. Y'all can get out of here."

"Thank you so much, sir," said Marcus, sticking his hand out.

"And Donnie, these two just moved here, so I invited them to dinner tomorrow."

Donnie nodded, wiping his hands with a spare towel from his trunk.

"Tomorrow? Tomorrow's perfect!" Aleeia's eyes lit up. "What should we bring?"

"Just yourselves and a smile will do," said Izabelle, raising her eyebrows.

"We'll bring some of our favorite champagne for a toast." Marcus could feel something between Aleeia and Izabelle.

"Perfect. Why don't I give you my number?"

Aleeia passed her phone to Izabelle.

"There you go, hon! I'll text you our address, but let's try for 7:00pm. You can text or call me when you're on your way."

43

"Sounds wonderful. We'll see you then." Aleeia turned to Marcus and kissed his cheek. "Thanks for coming."

"They were nice." Marcus laughed, looking at Donnie from the rearview mirror, putting a blanket over the deer.

"Yes, they were. I guess everything happens for a reason." Aleeia laid her head on the passenger window and gazed into the endless marshlands.

They were silent for the longest second, decompressing what happened.

"I can't wait for you to try this food. I hope it's not too cold." Aleeia could feel Marcus's mind swirling with anxiety.

9

SUNDAY

Like the 88 keys on a piano, Marcus could use his tongue to play a symphony on Aleeia's tight lips. With enough oral stimulation and preaching fingers, Marcus made her sing a relaxing lullaby most mornings.

"Right there."

Marcus looked up at Aleeia, tugging on their linen sheets. "Do you like that?" he asked, gently exploring her almond-scented curves.

"Don't stop, Marcus." He felt her dig her nails into his hair.

For them, mornings were an adventure into each other's intimate cravings. The more passion and stimulation they created together, the higher the climax.

After orgasming together and falling in and out of a trance that left their ears ringing, Marcus popped up from the bed and went to the bathroom. "Shower?"

"Give me a second," said Aleeia, out of breath.

Marcus kissed her neck and looked at the red hue creeping through their window. They were morning people and loved waking up as the sun rose. Their new bedroom had a lovely view that overlooked their backyard, a large walk-in closet, and a high-ceiling chandelier.

While Marcus was in the shower, Aleeia continued to play with herself. She could always get off and would try to take advantage of her body's peak orgasm state—she could never get enough.

As Aleeia sensed Marcus finishing up his shower, she quickly ran to him and threw herself around his wet body. She touched his chest like it was their first time. She loved living fully present and embracing each other's love. Nothing could stop her from making her sexual fantasies a reality.

After another timeless connection, the steam from the shower told them it was time to start their day.

"Are you still planning on shopping?" Marcus scratched his head as he sat on the bench by their bed.

"Yeah, I need to buy more décor. We still have a long way to go." Aleeia stood naked in their bathroom hallway, applying lotion to every inch of her tan body.

"What do you think about a few houseplants? I think it would look great next to the piano." Marcus always felt timid when suggesting new ideas.

"I'll think about it. You know I love it when you help me style. You have such good taste." Aleeia was only kidding. Before they'd met, Marcus wasn't nearly as artistic with his home design or fashion. He was a simple man, and Aleeia liked that. She turned him into her ideal husband, and he had no complaints.

Marcus stepped closer to Aleeia. "I checked my phone and saw that Penny left me a voicemail about a new project." He paused. "I know we said I'd take a break, but I'm going to see what it's all about. Are you okay with that?"

Aleeia stopped what she was doing—she could hear the nervousness in his voice.

"Like I said, I think you need to take a break for a bit. We know how worked up you can get with a new project, but... I know we also had a six-week road trip where you didn't play or work on anything." She looked into Marcus's eyes. "So, I agree. You should see what it's all about." She wrapped her arms around his shoulders. "You know I love you, Marcus, and I want the best for you... and your well-being. So please tread lightly with it."

Marcus admired her stretch marks in the bathroom mirror's reflection. Her words went through his ears and down his pants. Deep down, he knew she was right. He always over-worked himself, and Aleeia would be the one to fight his demons when his music didn't perform or he was stuck.

"I know, you're right... but Penny has my best interests at heart, too. He's my best friend... And he's one of the few people we told about expanding our family and getting out of the Bay. He's looking out for me... I promise." Marcus's hands gently cupped Aleeia's butt cheeks. "I love you."

"I love you too," she whispered in his ear. "Go call Penny."

"You're the best." Marcus let out a relaxing sigh and ran down-stairs, thinking about his relationship with Penny and how it had changed over the years. From middle school sports to their first prom and college roommates, they knew everything about each other. When Marcus's career skyrocketed, he trusted Penny with all his auditions and communication. They made for a dynamic duo and lived their best years together until Marcus met Aleeia. Almost immediately, their relationship grew apart. They still communicated like best friends, but deep down, Marcus was wary about Penny's business ventures because he didn't have any other clients. He was Penny's main source of income and livelihood.

Marcus sat upright on his squishy velvet piano bench, ready to create a new sound for whatever Penny had in store. He closed his eyes and took a grounding breath. As he pulled out his phone, he felt Aleeia touch his neck.

"Okay, well, I'm going out for the day. I'll let you know if anything will be delivered. And I promise... if I find those plants you're dreaming about, I'll be sure to turn your piano area into a forest." Aleeia scratched his arm.

"I'll let you know about the project. I promise. I'll be better this time," he said, watching Aleeia walk out of the room in a black co-ord tracksuit.

Marcus rested his hands on the top of the piano and let his head fall. He waited a few minutes after he heard Aleeia close the front door to call Penny.

"Guey! How you living? It's fuckin' early, man." Penny's raspy voice made Marcus smile.

"Hey, brother. How are you? Long time, no talk. It's been a minute."

"It has. How was the drive out there?"

"It was something else. I mean, super pretty, but some parts were so boring. I think Aleeia got a picture at every state border we crossed.

"That sounds like her."

"Yeah. But the house is different. It needs a lot of work, but you know Aleeia. She's always got a vision."

"That she does, that she does."

Marcus could hear a female voice talking to Penny in the background.

"Are you with someone?"

"A girl from last night. We haven't gone to bed." Penny laughed.

"Just like old times." Marcus reminisced on their years together.

"Yeah. Yeah. But let me tell you about this new gig." Penny cleared his throat. "I tried calling and emailing you, so I'm happy you got a hold of me. It's for an upcycle vintage brand. They're looking to have a fashion show in SF in two weeks... and they want some background noise for their models. I talked with the owner, and she's familiar with your work." Penny chuckled. "She's also smoking hot. But that's beside the point. She wants it to be authentic—she's giving you full control. I know that's something you'd love... I can send pictures of the models and clothing if you are interested. It's 3k for five 60-second riffs. You got it?"

"She's familiar with my work? I haven't gotten that in a couple of years." Marcus felt alive.

"I know. She went to USF, too... so we've got that connection."

"Alright, well... Aleeia's out for the day... and she gave me the green light to explore the project if it feels right with me... I can get you some ideas by early next week. Does that work? I figure we have a few days of revisions."

"I like it, man! Let's do it. I gotta go. This girl doesn't stop, though... I'll call you later."

"Enjoy it! Send a pic? Is she a keeper?"

"We'll see. We'll see... I just forwarded you the email with all the outfits and backdrops."

After their conversation, Marcus quickly opened his inbox and scanned the project's details. Before recording anything on a keyboard or other instruments, Marcus liked to work on his baby grand as much as possible. Ever since his first piano lesson, Marcus was a natural. He was a student of classical music, but his grandfather was his real maestro—he loved playing and teaching Marcus different jazz marks.

At a young age, he watched his grandfather's chunky fingers skip patterns on different black and white keys. The diverse sounds and songs his grandfather would perform left him craving more. After showing Marcus different chords and rhythms, his grandfather would tell him stories of when he was younger, playing at different shows and hanging around people like Chet Baker and company. His grandfather had all the freedom a young musician could ask for.

But as the years went by, so did his best friend. Marcus didn't play for some time after he passed; he took a break—his passion left him, as did the last breath of his mentor and idol. He only played the piano and performed in different venues for about a year before meeting Aleeia. Her feminine energy and beautiful mind gave him everything anyone could ask for. He had his inspiration again and acquitted most of his success to her. If she hadn't come into his life then, he would have never had the confidence to put his music out there and create content for some of the hottest brands.

Marcus sat for the next few hours, ruffling the piano, writing notes, and singing aloud. He liked to work alone but didn't mind a few people in his study. In the beginning, he loved covering other artists, but eventually, with the help of Aleeia, he started to come out of his shell and perform original pieces.

"And a one... and a two... and a one, two, three."

Marcus always recorded as if he had his grandfather there with his metronome.

That's perfect. Penny's going to love this one. I think I'm on to something.

As Marcus wrapped up his session, his creative gene

wouldn't let him rest. Part of him was drained, but the other was elated from discovering a new world.

10

SUNDAY: II

Aleeia gently stroked Marcus's back. "That sounds so pretty."

"You're home, already? How long were you gone?" he asked, leaning back into her breasts.

"You're so cute! Have you been here the whole time?"

Marcus let out a gigantic stretch. "I have. What did you get?"

"You have to guess!" she teased, running her fingers down his chest.

"Plants?" He released his hands from the piano.

"Yes, I did get plants. They'll arrive by tomorrow or the next day... but I got one of those sex swings we've always talked about. There was an adult store in one of the plazas, so I decided to stop by." Aleeia gave him a seductive gaze.

"Really? I love the sound of that."

For the most part, their sex drives were equal, but sometimes, Marcus felt like Aleeia could never get enough. Everything seemed to turn her. Even though he loved her with all his heart, he felt guilty when they weren't on the same wavelength.

In some unfortunate instances, Aleeia had acted out of temptation and had a few one-night stands with women. Between couples therapy and gaining Aleeia's trust, they'd put everything in the past. Nevertheless, Marcus could always see a little twinkle in Aleeia's eye when another woman caught her attention.

"I'm almost done." Marcus played a few random high notes.

"You don't seem excited."

"What? I am excited. I... I'm just in the middle of the new project Penny sent me."

"Oh... well... how is it?" Aleeia put her hand on her waist.

"It's going well. I think the next couple of parts will be even easier to compile. You'd love the catalog—let me show you."

"I'll look at it later. There's a lot in the car. Could you help me?"

Marcus put his head down. "Uh, yeah. Give me a second. I need to finish this last part."

"Okay, I know what that means." Aleeia stomped away.

By the time Marcus called it quits, the sun had set. *Fuck.* He tip-toed up to their bedroom, holding his breath. "You up here?" he said with a contorted face. "There you are!" Marcus poked his head through their bathroom doorway.

"Did you say something?" Aleeia stopped blow-drying her hair and glared at Marcus.

"I was saying... You look pretty... I'm excited for dinner. Are you?" Marcus lied. He wasn't exactly the social type unless he had a few glasses of champagne.

"Oh. Thanks. Did you finish your thing?"

"I did... or close to it. Thank you for understanding... You know," he said, moving closer. "I couldn't do this without you... Does the car still need to be unloaded?"

"What do you think?" Aleeia scowled.

Marcus knew he needed to fix their woes before stepping into unfamiliar waters. Aleeia was always his anchor amid his social anxiety. "I'm sorry."

"Sometimes, I think you'd choose the music over me." Aleeia laid her head back against his chest.

"Aleeia, you're the reason I make music!" Marcus raised his voice. "You gave me the green light to work on something today, and I couldn't lose my mojo."

"I know. I know. I just worry... I love you so much." Aleeia turned to hug Marcus, but as she twisted her body, her towel dropped to the floor. "Make it up to me?" She stuck her hand over his zipper.

"I... I think I could do that." Marcus grabbed her butt and lifted her onto the bathroom counter. "Will this work?" he asked, slipping his head between her thighs.

"Fuck... That'll do..." Aleeia clawed her hands into Marcus's hair. "Right there... Keep going. Please... Ple..." Her body flinched with his every tongue movement.

After a few rounds of the alphabet, Marcus felt Aleeia losing control. Her breath sped, her moaning became louder, and as he incorporated his fingers, he noticed her toes curling.

"I'm about to come," she announced.

Marcus immediately stroked his fingers deeper and watched her come. "I love that," he confessed, stepping forward and sticking his dick into Aleeia. While he pushed, she pulled, and over the next few minutes, they whispered into each other's ears until they climaxed together again.

"We need to get going," shouted Aleeia from their closet.

"I know. I'll be quick. Do you have everything picked out?"

"I do, but I want your thoughts on something else. Hold on."

As Marcus emerged from the shower, toweling off his wet body, Aleeia appeared in their bathroom doorway wearing black stilettos, a cropped white tank top, faux leather pants, and a matching black jacket.

"Wow! This one is perfect. It has my vote!" Marcus smiled and dried his face.

"Really? It's not too much?" Aleeia eyed herself in their full-length mirror. "What do you think Izabelle is going to be wearing?"

Marcus rolled his eyes. "Who cares? You look gorgeous! You don't need to compare yourself to her." He kissed her cheek. "I'm going to change real quick, and then let's go?"

"Fine. You win." Aleeia looked at her outfit in the mirror again. "I'm going to have some champagne. Do you want any?"

"Always... But can't you wait until we get there? I'm the one with social anxiety, not you!" Marcus pulled an olive green sweater over his head.

"I can never wait for champagne, and neither can you."

"Okay, twist my arm."

Aleeia left Marcus in their closet, deciding on his cologne. "Wear the Jo Malone, Myrrh & Tonka. You know I love that one."

The noise from Aleeia's stilettos banging on the staircase ran goosebumps down Marcus's spine. "Okay. I'll be right there."

Downstairs, Aleeia poured two glasses of champagne and mindlessly floated into Marcus's studio. It was clean as usual.

"You have to see the natural light during the day," he said, creeping into the room and admiring his kingdom from afar.

"Here's your champagne, My King." Aleeia inhaled his sensual scent.

"Cheers!?" Marcus awkwardly smiled.

"Everything will be fine. Don't worry... I'm right here."

"We should get going, ya?"

Aleeia toasted another sip of her champagne. "To us and our new chapter."

11

SUNDAY EVENING

"I'm going to text Izabelle and ask for the address." Aleeia looked at herself in the passenger-side vanity mirror and straightened her necklace.

"Whatever you say, I just need another glass of something to calm these nerves."

Aleeia watched Marcus push his lips together. "Don't worry, everything's going to be fine."

"You know how I get with these things." His eyes looked worried.

"I know," she said, reaching for his hand. "I'll be right next to you." The veins crawling up his forearm were raised. "Well, I just..." Aleeia felt her phone vibrate. "That was quick. She just sent me it."

"Is it close?" Marcus pulled away, itching his neck.

"One second..." Aleeia looked down at her phone. "Go that way!"

"Whatever you say."

"How about some music?" Aleeia turned on the stereo.

With an estimated 24.9 million victims
worldwide at any given time, human
traffickers prey on adults and children of
all ages, backgrounds, and nationalities.

Get Help Today ~ Report Trafficking.

"Is this stuff on the radio now?" said Marcus.

"I don't know." Aleeia pinched her nose. "Isn't trafficking more and more popular these days? I saw a poster in the bathroom at the gas station... I don't think it's anything to joke about. I'm pretty sure Atlanta is one of the bigger cities for it."

"Aleeia." Marcus shook his hands out and flattened them on his chest. "I have no idea. I'm just trying to exist."

"Do you need to take your medication?"

"No, I just need a drink," he snapped.

"It says it's only a nine-minute drive. Will you be okay?" She could see his leg moving up and down. "Take the next right."

"Got it," he mumbled, staring down the dark street.

"I mean left. I'm sorry." Aleeia covered her mouth and heard him scoff.

"I should just start going the opposite direction."

"You should." Aleeia laughed, trying to lighten the mood. *Why does he get like this?* "I can't believe we're having dinner at the sheriff's house tonight. Who would have thought?"

"Look at you already making new friends!" Marcus's tone was off-pitch.

"And Izabelle..." Aleeia tilted her head. "I wonder what she does. I'm sure it's something creative... I loved her outfit last night."

"How much longer?" Marcus loudly gritted his teeth. He couldn't sit still for longer than a few seconds.

"It's a little further down. Chill out..." She raised her hand. "Are you sure you don't need to take your medication?"

"Yes!" yelled Marcus. "Is this it?" He slowed the car and furrowed his eyebrows at the large steel gate. "Um?" A black modern house with a quarter mile long driveway froze his forehead. "This isn't what I was expecting. Is that a fountain in the middle?"

"Right? It looks like Tia and Sebastian's house in PV." Aleeia sat up.

"Do you want to let her know we're outside? I don't see a buzzer anywhere." Marcus looked around at their fenced yard. "What do you think it'll be like inside?"

"There's no more keeping up with the Joneses out here, Marcus... Try pulling up more."

Marcus inched forward toward the gate, but nothing happened.

Aleeia took off her seatbelt and faced him. "Don't worry, I'll call her."

"Hi, sweetie! Are you here?" Izabelle picked up without a second ring.

"Yes!" Aleeia's face lit up. "We're outside, but the gate isn't opening. Is there a passcode or something?" She looked through the front windshield and twirled her hair.

"Donnie! You didn't turn the sensor back on." Aleeia overheard Izabelle yelling across the room. "Sorry about that. Try pulling up again, hon. Park anywhere."

"See?" Aleeia said with a smirk as they watched the gate swing open.

As they turned into the gravel loop driveway, Aleeia said. "It reminds me of the Filoli Gardens." White marble statues and abstract geometric shapes were spread across acres of green grass.

"It does." Marcus scratched his chin. "But it's confusing, right? You'd think they would be living in an older home. It's so modern and new for being in a small town." He rolled his eyes. "They should see where we're from."

"Oh, calm down, Marcus! This is a new chapter, remember?"

"Fuck! Look at all those cars." Aleeia heard a tremor in his voice. "Do you think it's just us?"

"By the looks of it, I'd say no." Aleeia marveled at the sharp-edged architecture as she felt the car move into park. "Just go with the flow tonight... it'll be fun! I'm right here if anything happens, Marcus. I love you." She moved across the center console and kissed him. "Ready?"

Marcus followed her up the front steps, and as they stood beside each other, he leaned over and asked, "Hold my hand, will you?"

Aleeia squeezed his hand and looked through the living room windows. "This is our new life. We can be anyone," she whispered, reaching for the doorbell.

Each second that passed, waiting outside the door, felt like an eternity. Aleeia looked down at Marcus, tightly clenching the champagne bottle in one hand and wiping his forehead with the other.

"To new beginnings," he mumbled, feeling his hand slip away from her grip.

"There they are! You made it!" Izabelle shouted, opening her arms for a hug.

Aleeia's pupils expanded when she made eye contact with Izabelle's beaming, big eyes.

"I'm so sorry about the gate entrance. Donnie's doing this new thing." Izabelle gave each of them a cheek kiss as she welcomed them inside.

"What're you wearing? You smell great!" asked Aleeia, feeling the scent from Izabelle's neck warm her chest.

"Some secret essential oils." Izabelle lightly tapped Aleeia's shoulder and winked. "I can't kiss and tell, but I can show you one day." She placed her hands on Marcus's lower back as he passed by. "I love this color on you, Marcus!"

He awkwardly raised the champagne bottle and moved further into the doorway. "Thanks. We brought champagne!"

"Aren't you an angel?" Izabelle looked at Aleeia. "You're one *lucky* woman." The soft olive skin tones popping from underneath Izabelle's cropped ripped shirt made Aleeia's cheeks flush. "Let me give you the tour."

"Wow," said Marcus, looking at the black marble staircase. He scratched the top of his head and tried his best to keep a smile.

"I love this, Izabelle!" The dining room immediately caught Aleeia's attention. "Everything is stunning."

Izabelle stepped into the dining room. "Donnie's family left us with a lot of collectibles and family heirlooms." She paused and looked at the six place settings on the table. "Unfortunately, they passed away two years after we married."

"I'm so sorry to hear that," interjected Aleeia.

"It's fine. It's been some time since it happened." Izabelle threw her hands together. "I love this jacket, by the way. Where'd you get it?"

"I don't remember. I've had it for so long." Aleeia took a large mouth breath.

"I hope you don't mind," Izabelle said, pointing to the table. "We invited another couple. The more the merrier, right?"

Marcus moved his neck from side to side.

"Even better. More new friends!" said Aleeia, scanning the room's antique wooden furniture and gold-framed oil canvas paintings. *Just like Lindsay's house?*

Izabelle pointed to a deer on the wall. "Donnie and his dad's prized possession." Aleeia caught Izabelle looking her up and down. "They loved to hunt together."

"I guess last night was nothing new for Donnie?" Marcus laughed, half-joking, half-serious.

The deer's enormous antlers froze Aleeia. *I'm sorry. I didn't mean to kill your friend.* "I'm lucky you stopped last night."

"You know, boys!" Izabelle put her hand up. "Here, come this way! I want to show you this."

Through the doorway that connected the dining room to the kitchen, Marcus saw another man walking around. He wiped his hands on his pants and followed Izabelle and Aleeia.

"And over here..." Izabelle guided them to the other side of the hallway. "Is my art room." She watched them enter into her gallery of Renaissance-style paintings.

"Another artist!? I make music for a living." Marcus moved further into the room. "You painted all of these?"

"For the most part. I trained in Rome for many years. This is more of a hobby now."

"These are fun." Aleeia raised her eyebrows and looked at the multicolored lazy couches.

"Don't look at those!" Izabelle cackled and pointed them down the hallway. "Shall we go meet everyone else?" Aleeia noticed Izabelle flirtatiously bit her lip. "Marcus, take all the time you want. I can tell you have a taste for the finer things in life."

Marcus's mouth dropped as he looked at a painting of a whale swimming beside Noah's Ark. "I mean, you don't see this every day." He spun around and saw a half-finished painting of an open elevator with hands crawling beneath it. "Your style, Izabelle." He paused. "You know, I wish I could paint like this. I compose musical pieces for various commercials and movies."

Aleeia shook her head and butted in. "You should stick to music, baby. I think Izabelle's got you beat on the brush strokes."

As they made their way down the hallway, Aleeia felt her inner thighs tingle. Izabelle's tiny hips swaying from side to side piqued her interest.

"This way, you two! Come on in." Izabelle looked back. "Don't be shy. We're all waiting for you."

Each step Marcus took down the hallway was in slow motion. On the right side, underneath the staircase, he noticed an elevator. He furrowed his eyebrows and tried not to think much of it. *An elevator? That's pretty wild.* "Where should I put this champagne, Izabelle?" he shouted, shaking off his nerves and stepping into the living room. "Can we put it on ice?" He looked across the room and saw Donnie and another couple sitting in a dark purple conversation pit. *You have to be kidding me.* The same waitress from yesterday morning sat in between Donnie and another man. Marcus focused on the dozens of house plants scattered across the room to distract himself. The ceiling-to-ceiling windows behind the couch over-looking their backyard were a brief oasis for his scattered thoughts.

"Hey! They're here!" shouted Donnie as he stood up.

"Yes, they made it!" Izabelle walked over and kissed his head. "Time to party!" She grabbed Aleeia's hand and pulled her down into the conversation pit. "Let me introduce you to our best friends, Colleen and Derek."

Aleeia put her hand out. "It's so nice to meet you. I'm Aleeia."

"It's a pleasure to meet you, Aleeia. I'm Derek. Donnie's better half." He laughed and slapped Donnie's knee.

"Oh, you two!" said Izabelle, turning around and seeing

65

Marcus looking at a tall snake plant near the kitchen. "Do you like that one? That's been my baby for a few years now."

"I love it." Marcus gulped and rushed over to everyone.

"And I'm Colleen," said the other woman, pulling her hair behind her ears. "I love your pants. Where'd you get them?"

"Thank you! I feel like I've had all my clothes for so long. I was telling Izabelle that I don't remember where I got this jacket either."

"That doesn't matter, you're stunning, girl!"

Marcus awkwardly stepped up to the conversation pit.

"And this is Marcus." Izabelle put her hands on his shoulders. "He's a musician."

Aleeia could see a slight tremor in his hand as he raised the bottle and widely smiled.

"We brought champagne! I can't wait to get to know you all," said Marcus.

"Izabelle, I can help him put it on ice." Colleen got up from her seat and climbed out of the conversation pit. "Here come sit, Iz."

"Aleeia and Marcus just moved here," said Donnie. "And by chance, Izabelle was driving by and stopped to help Aleeia last night. She hit a deer."

"Oh my gosh!" Derek covered his chest. "I'm glad everyone was okay. I've hit my fair share of deer..., and I know how it feels."

Aleeia pursed her lips. "I've never hit anything before, so it was a lot, to say the least." She gulped. "And Donnie, I really can't thank you enough for your help. I owe you."

"What're friends for?!" He grabbed his drink and raised a toast.

"He's someone you can always rely on," said Derek.

In the kitchen, Marcus couldn't take his eyes off Colleen's short, lime green bodysuit and high white boots. "Funny seeing you here, huh?" Colleen pulled an ice bucket from a cabinet and closed it with her hip.

Marcus laughed to cut the tension. "Your accent sounds different."

Colleen smirked. "I only use it for the ones I *really* like."

Marcus's eyes wandered to her chest. "Aleeia loved the grits. Thanks for that recommendation," he said.

"Anything for you... Stop by anytime... And give me a call about that *ice cream*... Don't worry. It's our secret." Colleen went to the refrigerator. "Oops!" An ice cube dropped to the floor.

Before she could bend over, Marcus ran around the kitchen island and picked it up.

"Always a gentleman, I see."

Marcus felt a warm flood of energy from his pants. "I'll take it from here," he said, grabbing the ice bucket from her.

Sensing his temptations, Colleen grazed his hand and used her eyes to direct them back towards everyone.

"And last night, I went to Captain Cooks to pick up dinner. Have you been before?" Aleeia's eyes were sparkling as she warmed up.

"We love Captains! It's my favorite spot," said Derek.

"It's an amazing place. I met the owner's son or something. Mr. Peaches?"

Donnie laughed. "Mr. Peaches is the town drunk. Everyone is his father, mother, brother, or sister. He's got a story for everything."

Aleeia raised her eyebrow, taking note of his comment.

"Can I get you two anything to drink while we wait for the

champagne to chill? What a sweet surprise, Marcus!" said Izabelle to the group.

Aleeia quickly looked around at everyone's drinks. "I'll have what everyone else is having."

"Well, Donnie and Derek enjoy their scotch, but Colleen and I drink a gin martini. Will that do? We also have vodka."

"A vodka martini sounds wonderful."

"With a lemon wedge?" asked Izabelle.

"Lemon is perfect. Do you have any oranges as well?"

"I knew you were a little diva." Izabelle snarled. "Marcus? Anything for you?"

"Um... I'll have the same as Aleeia. Let's keep it simple."

"Nothing simple about a lemon-orange wedge vodka martini, hon!" Izabelle walked towards the kitchen bar area. "Ladies, do you want to help me?"

Aleeia and Colleen quickly stood up and followed Izabelle.

"So, Marcus, since you're a musician, feel free to change the music tonight if the playlist isn't your style." Donnie poured more scotch from a decanter. "I've got two left feet." He snorted. "What kind of music do you play?"

"Uh, I record music for commercials and movies, but I love to play jazz. I can play the piano, bass, trumpet, and guitar." He shrugged and rubbed the back of his neck.

"Wow, I've been looking for a guitar teacher. If you have any free time, I'd love to learn from a master of the arts," said Derek, sitting back and crossing his legs.

"Yeah, maybe we could work something out," Marcus mumbled.

"Is it live recordings or concerts?" Derek leaned closer.

"Mostly recordings. Jingles. Soundtracks. The fun stuff." Marcus rubbed his hands together. "I'm working on a fashion project right now." He looked back at the champagne chilling in its bucket on the kitchen counter.

"I'm jealous! I've always wanted to play an instrument... You better watch out now. Donnie and I are coming to you for all our music needs!" Derek lightly nudged Marcus's shoulder.

12

SUNDAY EVENING: II

Gathered around the kitchen island, Aleeia and Colleen watched Izabelle concoct their martinis.

"So... how do you like it so far?" Colleen leaned over in her seat, showing off her breasts.

"Well, we've only been here for forty-eight hours, so it's coming together. The town is super cute, but our home needs a lot of work. We plan to restore it."

"They bought that old home over on New Heaven," said Izabelle.

I never said anything about where we lived. How did she know that? Aleeia gave a twisted face.

"Word travels fast. They've been trying to sell that property for as long as I can remember."

"As long as you can remember?" asked Aleeia.

"Was that Lindsay's property?" Colleen tapped her nails on the counter.

Izabelle nodded. "Well, ever since we moved here, it's always been on the market. It was owned by a guy named

Mikal... Mikal Wallace. He was a charming man, *actually*... I met him in passing once."

"Easy on the eyes." Colleen grinned and looked back at the boys.

"Hmm." Aleeia bit on her thumbnail.

"But he just couldn't stay out of trouble... Arrest warrants for robberies, grand theft auto, drunk and disorderly, you name it. If only he had his shit together... His parents gave him everything."

"But... why did no one want to buy it?" Aleeia hesitantly laughed.

"I don't know. I think as the house got older, more and more work needed to be put into it. And people in these areas don't have much... a home makeover isn't on everyone's budget these days."

"That would make sense." Aleeia felt like something was off.

"And here you go." Izabelle slid her martini across the counter.

"Colleen, can you take this one to Marcus?"

"Sure thing."

Colleen and Aleeia walked back to the conversation pit.

"Marcus," said Colleen, handing over the martini.

"Ah, thank you so much."

"You better drink that one quickly!" Donnie padded Marcus on the back. "By the end of the night, young man, we'll have you drinkin' scotch. No more martinis for you."

Marcus's first sip ran chills down his spine as he felt himself coming alive. He began to inspect the see-through glass coffee table. *Interesting vibe.* There was a small wooden square box, a collection of colorful crystals, and an open book that displayed a black-and-white drawing of a detailed third eye and a death-themed merry-go-round.

Izabelle walked back to everyone and plopped down into the conversation pit.

"Is that clear quartz?" asked Aleeia.

"I didn't think you were the crystal type." Izabelle pushed her hair out of her face.

"Hasn't everyone had a crystal phase?!" Aleeia shifted closer to Izabelle, watching Marcus across from her.

"Touché." Derek's big, toothy smile brought Aleeia to a sudden stop.

"How about a quick game?" said Izabelle. "This is one of my favorite games to play with new friends—it's a classic..." Everyone paused. "You might know it... Truth or Dare!" Izabelle wiggled in excitement and waited for everyone's reaction.

"I love truth or dare!" said Aleeia, rearranging her legs.

"Good. I'm glad. I'll go first." Izabelle leaned forward and grabbed a deck of cards from a tiny drawer at the bottom of the coffee table. "This one's for you, Donnie." She took a moment to read it to herself before rolling her head back. "Do you have a favorite friend? Ah! That's not a good one!"

"That's easy!" Donnie let out a deep belly laugh. "We all know that one. It's Derek."

"Ding, ding, ding. That's me!" Derek ran his hand through his thick black hair.

"Another one!" said Izabelle with a pouty face.

"No, no, no. You know the rules." Donnie put her card back down on the table.

"Alright, alright. Donnie, you're up then. You pick the next card," said Izabelle.

"Okay, this one's for my new favorite friend, Marcus."

Aleeia chewed on the inside of her cheek and glanced at the terror etched on his face.

"This one is a Dare." Donnie winked and looked at Derek. "Can I get a drum roll?"

Derek lightly tapped his knees.

"Marcus." Donnie paused and looked around at everyone. "You must leave the room, and every player will pour you a shot. Then, when you come back into the room, you have to pick one of the shots to take. Whoever's shot you take, you have to sit on that person's lap for the next round."

"I love incorporating a few drinks into the game," said Colleen. "Where are the shot glasses, Donnie?"

"I can get them," Donnie stood up. "But my new friend," he pointed at Marcus, "you have to leave the room now."

"And that's my cue." Marcus made his way to the hallway.

"Aleeia! Does he like gin or vodka more?" roared Donnie, bringing over five shot glasses and placing a bottle of gin and vodka on the table.

"I'm pouring a big one!" blurted Colleen.

"Oh, man." Aleeia felt her cheekbones burn from laughter. "That's too much for him!"

"I can hear you guys!" Marcus tried playfully interacting with everyone from the hallway but was caught off guard when he saw his reflection on the shiny metal door underneath their staircase. *I don't get it. And he's a small town sheriff? It sounds like he came from money, but still.*

"Okay, you can come back now," shouted the group.

Marcus walked back into the room and gestured behind him. "That's an elevator?"

"Not just an elevator, but a man cave with a giant aquarium," said Derek, elbowing Donnie.

"I'll show you after dinner," Donnie said, helping Marcus climb into the conversation pit. "It's where all my greatest ideas come from. It's my think tank. No pun intended."

"Right." The five water-looking shots on the table made Marcus nauseous.

"Which one are you going to choose?" Izabelle smiled at Marcus's blank face.

Pick one!" she shouted, readjusting her legs and gently grazing Aleeia's thigh.

Aleeia felt her face warm. A tingling sensation funneled up her legs.

"This one?" Marcus hesitantly held the shot to eye level and looked around at everyone.

"Good luck," said Colleen with a twinkle in her eye.

"Here we go." Marcus quickly coughed his prized response. "Gin!" he squealed. "Who takes shots of gin?"

"I don't think anyone!" Izabelle threw her head back.

"Who poured it?" asked Derek.

"I did." Aleeia scrunched her face in sympathy and reached for Marcus's hand. She could feel his personality teetering.

"Okay, Marcus, it's your turn now." Izabelle wasted no time moving to the next round.

"Okay." He shook his head. "This one's for Aleeia." He pulled a card. "What is your favorite female body part?"

Without hesitation, Aleeia exclaimed, "Boobs! Who doesn't love them?!"

Everyone peeked at Izabelle's chest.

"Enough! Don't be jealous now." Izabelle swiped a section of her hair behind her ear and glared at Aleeia. "I'm glad I know what gets everyone going."

Aleeia immediately felt tingly, feeling Izabelle's words slither into her panties.

"Alright, alright, one more before dinner, kids." Izabelle got up and went to the kitchen. "Everything is just about ready."

"Do you need any help?" said Aleeia, in a trance, trying not to imagine her fantasies in reality.

75

"No, you sit and play, hon." Izabelle winked.

Marcus rolled his eyes as he saw Aleeia push her knees together.

"Okay." Aleeia paused. "This one's for Derek, then." She pulled a card and read it to herself.

"What does it say, Aleeia? I can't hear you from here," shouted Izabelle.

"She hasn't said anything. Calm down. She's getting to it," said Donnie.

Aleeia rubbed her chest. "I'm a little nervous to read it because it's a deeper question than I anticipated."

Everyone was on the edge of their seats.

"Derek, what has been your favorite version of yourself, and does it coincide with a relationship?" No one said anything.

Derek sat and analyzed the question and then grabbed Colleen's hand. "My favorite version of myself is who I'll be tomorrow, the next day, and the next year. My favorite person is the one I wake up to every morning. Without her, I'd be incomplete. I'd perish. I'd rest in pain." He kissed her on the cheek.

"Oh, Derek, you're such a hopeless romantic," yelled Izabelle, pulling plates from the cabinets.

Aleeia's stomach fluttered.

"What a response, kid. I need to read more of that poetry you've sent me," said Donnie before getting up and gracelessly walking to the kitchen. "Bella, Bella, what can I do to help?"

She rolled her eyes to the oven, and instinctually, Donnie started loading dishes onto a pushcart.

"You better get ready for a meal of a lifetime," said Derek.

"Really?" Aleeia's eyes sparkled in the dim light. "I'm excited!"

"It beats my cooking any day, but that's not saying much." Colleen stepped in front of Marcus's face and made her way to the kitchen.

Feeling restless from Colleen, Marcus downed the last of his martini and then confidently grabbed Aleeia's hand. "Shall we see what it's all about?"

Aleeia allowed Marcus to help her climb out of the conversation pit.

"You got it?" Derek raised his hand and gave Marcus a friendly smile as his eyes wandered up and down Aleeia's backside.

13

SUNDAY EVENING: III

"Marcus, sweetie, do you want to pop the champagne before we eat?" Izabelle sat down and put her napkin on her lap. "I think we'd all love a little taste of California."

"Of course. I'd love to." Marcus reached across the dining table with a fierce grin and grabbed the ice-cold bottle. He unwrapped the top and popped the cork off with ease. For whatever reason, champagne was his elixir to life, his muse before Aleeia, and his emptiness before he had any thought of true love.

Aleeia, sitting across from him, made eye contact with the deer above his head again.

"This is one of our favorites—Salmon Billecart. Have you had it before?"

"Champagne is champagne, right?" Derek looked around the table with a clueless smile.

"Not all champagne is champagne. It's gotta come from the Champagne region in France. Otherwise, it's sparkling wine," said Marcus.

"Don't worry, guys. Over the years, he's taught me a thing

or two about champagne and wine. I thought the same thing." Aleeia placed her hands between her legs and smushed them together.

"Well, I can't wait to try it." Donnie clapped his hands. "A master of music. A master of wine." He toasted his scotch to Marcus. "What else can this guy do?!"

"You'll enjoy it. Trust me." Marcus's eyes were like that of a child on Christmas morning. "Izabelle, could you help me with some flutes or glasses?" He palmed the bottom of the bottle in one hand.

"Oh my gosh." She flung her hands up. "Of course, hon. One second!"

Marcus watched Aleeia's eyes follow her through the doorway. *Really? I guess Izabelle does look a bit like her first girlfriend.* Immediately, he cleared his throat and made eye contact with Aleeia.

"This is stunning!" Aleeia exclaimed, her fingers gently caressing the vibrant rose and alstroemeria arrangement in the center. The gold-plated cups and high-quality China surrounding the table brought a much-needed distraction.

"Here we are!" grunted Izabelle, rushing through the doorway with six champagne flutes and a remote control in her mouth.

"You're the best, Bella," Donnie said, helping pass them out and reaching for the remote.

For Marcus, champagne reminded him of the late holiday dinners at his grandfather's house, the sour and sweet drink he'd sneak as everyone was busy conversing in the other room. It gave him a nostalgic feeling of home and a melancholy thought of his childhood. "Thank you, Izabelle." With a gentle wrist, he poured each polished flute to the brim and watched the tiny bubbles float to the top and tickle the atmosphere.

"Look at that!" shouted Donnie.

After passing everyone their drink, Marcus raised his glass. "To new friends!" He fell back into his seat like an addict after their first hit.

"Aleeia," said Donnie. "Does he always get this big of a grin with champagne?"

She giggled and waited for the bubbles to settle down her throat. "He does, but I like to think he loves me more than the bottle."

"Donnie!" Izabelle bumped his arm. "You can be such an ass sometimes. Why don't you show our guests some respect?"

He rolled his eyes and pointed the remote control behind his head. A calming opera tone emerged from the baseboards. "Surround sound—ever heard of it?"

"Donnie! Enough!" Izabelle rubbed her forehead. "Sorry about him."

Marcus put his hand up as the beginning strings of an opera composition faintly escaped from the speakers.

"It's quite lovely," said Colleen, looking at Marcus and Aleeia. "I remember the first time we had dinner here. I was confused as to why such a man as Donnie would be obsessed with fine music. I mean, look at him!" Colleen laughed and pointed at Donnie, who grabbed his belly and brushed his hand through his thinning hairline.

"This body is the peak male physique." He gestured his hands up and laughed.

Aleeia and Marcus smirked at each other when they recognized the song playing in the background. Aleeia couldn't help but hum along. "*O mio babbino caro*—Giacomo Puccini. Am I right?" she said.

Donnie's mouth dropped. "I'm sorry, Izabelle." He slammed the table. "But I'm leaving you for her. Aleeia, will you marry me?"

Izabelle lightheartedly hit Donnie's arm again. "You're a true ass, Donnie."

"Marcus is the one that got me into this type of music. Just ask him!"

"I knew I'd love this guy!" Donnie pinched his fingers together and shook his hand.

With another glass of champagne, Marcus was finally content in a void that would only be diminished the second he opened his eyes the next morning. "I love opera. Who doesn't, right?"

"A true gentleman!" Donnie raised his arms and played with his hands as a conductor would with their band.

"And I think that's the cue for our food!" Izabelle threw her napkin at Donnie and disappeared into the kitchen.

"Get ready." Derek rubbed his hands together.

"I hope you like it," said Izabelle, timidly walking through the doorway with a pushcart of dishes hidden underneath silver domes. "I was torn between this and a nice piece of fish."

"Whatever it is, I'm sure it'll be great," said Colleen.

Marcus's eyes immediately lit up when Izabelle placed the roasted rosemary pork chops in front of him.

"You did all of this?" Aleeia pushed her hands together. Izabelle looked angelic as she floated to each corner of the table. Her movements were mesmerizing, like a ballerina completing the final recital of her life.

"A green salad... creamed spinach... mashed potatoes... and, to finish us off... crispy cornbread. Yum!" announced Izabelle.

"As usual, Iz, it looks amazing." Derek scooted his chair in and began serving himself.

"I'm impressed! My gosh. Please show me how to cook like this," said Aleeia.

"You come over anytime, and we'll really get into it... No

82

boys allowed!" Izabelle winked and encouraged everyone to start eating.

The chilled lemon vinaigrette dressing on the fresh salad awakened Marcus. *Just like mom's.* He took another bite and leaned back in his chair. "This is incredible, Izabelle." He reached for his drink and asked, "So, how long have you lived here? I mean, this house is something else."

"You're too sweet, Marcus." Izabelle rubbed her shoulder and tapped Donnie's wrist above the table.

Donnie looked up with hazy, bloodshot eyes. "I think I was in a trance... This food, Bella... We started building three years ago... so we've been here for about two years." A piece of creamed spinach flew from his mouth. "But we've been in the area for as long as I can remember." His glass of scotch became a microphone. "My family had a home about thirty minutes from here, so we built this property a safe distance to do our own thing... You know how families can be, right?"

Marcus nodded.

"And Derek and I moved here... What..." Colleen eyed Derek from across the table. "I think about a year. Everything's gone by so quickly. It's been awesome to have met these two, though. They've helped us through so much."

"You know you're family when you're with us. Mi casa es su casa!" Izabelle tried reaching her hand to Colleen.

"You know." Colleen moved up in her seat, gently placing her hand on Marcus's thigh below the table. "We should all go to one of those rodeo shows soon."

Marcus felt a bulge growing through his pants. *What the fuck?!*

"Have you all been to one?" said Colleen, looking at Aleeia.

"I don't think we have," she said as she sipped her wine. But it sounds like a great plan."

"That it does." Marcus coughed and rearranged himself in

his seat until Colleen dropped her hand away. "Just let us know when, and we can put it on our calendar."

There was a moment of silence before another song slowly played from the speakers.

"Here we go," mumbled Izabelle, folding her napkin over her thighs.

Derek and Colleen sat back in their seats. "Watch," mouthed Derek.

Marcus was confused by everyone's sudden reaction, but as the song picked up, Donnie stood up and started singing *Libiamo ne' lieti calici* – La Traviata in the crispest accent and deep Italian voice. Marcus's jaw dropped.

After watching Donnie escape to another time period, he bowed and said, "One of my favorites. Cheers, everyone. Divertiti!" His flushed red face was beaming with happiness.

"Where did you learn to sing like that?" Marcus couldn't hold back a smile.

"His father. He was always singing, that man." Izabelle shook her head. "Donnie grew up listening to old Italian records. I guess they never left his soul... It was a romantic quirk that didn't take much time for me to get used to." She reached for her necklace and mindlessly played with it while she watched Donnie lose himself in the duet's voices.

As everyone continued salivating over Izabelle's cooking, Aleeia couldn't help but compliment her culinary skills again. "Izabelle, when is our date to cook again?" She giggled. "I need to be this good of a chef before I die!"

"Oh, hush, now. I learned it all from Donnie's mother and Nonna. They were the bosses."

"And I guess you're following in those footsteps?" Derek chuckled.

Izabelle scowled at him and turned back to Aleeia. "I'll tell

84

you what, you name the date and bring the wine. I'll supply the rest."

Aleeia took her last bite of pork chop. "Sounds like a plan to me."

"So, do you two have any contractor leads for the house? I'm sure there's a lot of work to be done." Derek chimed as he pushed his seat out.

Marcus moved his eyes at Aleeia. "You got this, baby." He wore a carefree smile.

"Well, we felt like the house was so magical in the pictures and videos." She reached for Marcus's hand. "It was breathtaking, actually. Especially with the models after a renovation. After that, I knew it was perfect." She swirled her finger over her wine glass. "You all will have to come over when it's relatively finished. We'd love to have you there for dinner... Marcus can show you his piano skills. I'm sure it would be a lovely night."

"That it would be. If you can play anything like this, Marcus, I won't be leaving your house for quite some time... Play for me, monkey!" Donnie's veins popped from his neck as he smacked his leg.

Marcus reached for more wine. "I was classically trained, so I'm sure there would be a few songs I could play for you. How about I play, and you sing?"

Donnie put down his silverware and gave a chef's kiss. "Bellissimo, bellissimo."

"And Lindsay Pillar sold you the home?" Colleen raised her eyebrows.

"Yes, yes, she did," said Aleeia.

"Lindsay's great. She used to be a good friend of mine, but ever since her divorce, she hasn't been the same. She's been cooped up in her home, living off her family's wealth and

selling a house or two a year. You helped her out, I'm sure."
Colleen said as she crossed her legs.

"She was so sweet when we showed up." Aleeia rested her
hand on her chin. "It was in the middle of that darn storm a few
days ago. I don't know what we would have done if she hadn't
been there." Aleeia played with her hands above the table.

"Well, if anything happens, you should know you aren't a
stranger... and like Izabelle said, mi casa es su casa."

Aleeia smiled and leaned forward.

"How is it? Or should I say how was it?" said Izabelle. No
one's forks and knives had moved for a few minutes. "Derek, it
looked like you enjoyed yourself."

"As always, Izabelle. You know I love your cooking." He
patted his stomach. "Colleen's got to up her game."

"Hey, I'm not going to argue that. It's always a treat having
dinner here." Colleen reached for her purse behind the chair
and pulled out a Capri cigarette. "Oh, darn. Does anyone have
a lighter?"

Derek reached into his pocket. "Here."

"It's still okay if I smoke in here, Iz?"

"Of course, hon." Izabelle blew a kiss and put her hands on
Donnie's shoulder.

Aleeia's eyes lit up. "Colleen, you wouldn't mind if I had
one?"

"Please! Colleen passed her a metal cigarette holder
engraved with the name, 'Ivanna.' "My mother," she said,
feeling Aleeia's incoming question. "Here." Colleen leaned
over and lit the cigarette for her. They inhaled together and
watched the smoke overcome the dining room.

"Cigar?" Derek raised his eyebrows at Donnie. "We can do
better than this!"

"You know me too well!" slurred Donnie, turning his body

and pointing his finger at Marcus. "And whether you smoke cigars or not, you'll smoke a celebratory one with us tonight, Marcus."

"What're we celebrating?" he asked.

Derek walked behind Donnie. "Life!" They posed together as if someone was taking a photo of them.

"Alright. Alright. Let's get to it." Donnie raised his drink to everyone and stumbled back a few steps.

"I love you, Bella," he mouthed before kissing the top of her forehead and wobbling to the kitchen with Derek's assistance.

"Those two!" Izabelle shook her head at Aleeia. "They invested in some super-secret investment last month and tripled their money."

Colleen blew out a fat drag and fell back into her chair.

"That's amazing!" Aleeia quietly placed her elbows on the table.

"They won't tell us what it was, but we can see the money in our accounts. I'm not gonna ask questions when I can buy all these new clothes." Colleen gestured down at her outfit.

"They're celebrating life, those two." Izabelle picked up her drink and swirled it around.

"I guess that means I'll be smoking tonight," said Marcus with a sniffle.

Colleen wagged her head. "Just keep an eye on them, Marcus. Their bromance can switch up ya at any second."

He chuckled and hesitantly looked at Izabelle. "Is there anything I can do to help clean up?"

"He really is a keeper," said Izabelle, waving Marcus towards the door. "Don't worry about it. Everything's going in the dishwasher. I like cleaning; it helps me clear my mind anyway." Izabelle caressed Marcus's hand while he walked out of the room.

14

SUNDAY EVENING: IV

Remembering the last time he smoked a cigar, Marcus felt his stomach quiver with knots. Reluctantly, he put on another smile and walked through the kitchen doorway. *Is that Russian? What are they saying?* Marcus cleared his throat and interrupted Donnie and Derek's conversation.

"Ahh! There he is!" Derek patted Donnie's back and rushed over to welcome Marcus with open arms.

"Cigars?" Marcus blew raspberries. "I haven't smoked one of those in years."

"You'll be fine." Derek showed Marcus to the hallway. "If you don't like it, you don't like it. No hard feelings."

"Right." All the drinks from dinner started to make Marcus feel dizzy. "I take it you two smoke them often?" Donnie's heavy footsteps clunking behind him made him nervous. *That isn't good.* Marcus pulled his sweater collar out.

"Whenever we get the chance. You'll learn soon enough." Derek winked but was caught off guard when he saw Donnie dipping his head into his chest.

"Just you wait, young man," Donnie rasped, pausing to

catch his breath. "Just you..." he mumbled before reaching his arm to press the elevator button.

"He goes from zero to sixty really quick." Derek grabbed Donnie's elbow. "Trust me. He'll be fine."

Marcus took a step back, letting Donnie stumble to the corner.

"Floor 1!" Donnie's glassy eyes closed with the elevator doors. His loud hiccupping made Marcus worried.

"Have you ever seen a home with an elevator before?" Derek clicked a circular button labeled '1' and pinned Donnie on his shoulder. "Stay."

"Not in a long time." Marcus picked at his fingertips to distract him from being locked in a small space.

"Well, you're in for a treat then. Donnie's man cave is something else."

Marcus looked down at the four elevator buttons as they dropped to the next floor. *Floor 3 must be upstairs if we just came from Floor 2. What's the last one?* There was an awkward silence before the door opened. "Is Floor 3 upstairs?" asked Marcus.

"You got it." Derek gestured for him forward. "After you... I have to get this guy inside. Make yourself at home."

When he entered the room, glowing aqua lights blinded Marcus's eyes. "What in the world..." he gasped and stood with his mouth open.

"Pretty neat, right?" Derek flung Donnie onto an oversized dark leather chair. "That was my first reaction when I saw it." He pointed to Donnie snoring. "It looks like this guy is already calling it a night."

"An aquarium?" Twenty feet of saltwater ripped through Marcus's eyes, shooting adrenaline through his bloodstream. Rainbowfish, angelfish, eels, and tiny sea creatures colored the entire tank. It felt like a little slice of the ocean. "Wow!"

Marcus smiled at the different-sized tiki huts, realistic pebbles, and sand covering the bottom floor. "I'm just... I'm just... Donnie did all of this?"

"Yep. Every time I come in here, I'm at peace. It's like nothing I've ever seen before. It's like a zoo." Derek rubbed his hands together and then crossed them over his chest. "We gotta give it to him... For as drunk of an ass as he is, Donnie sure does know what he likes."

"It's inspiring." Marcus glued his hands to the glass. "How many fish are in there?"

"I have no idea, but he's got names for all of them." Derek walked over to Donnie's desk and pulled a small humidifier from the bottom drawer. "It feels like bliss, huh? It's where he comes to get away from everything."

"I want to play the piano down here!"

Derek laughed. "I'm sure he'd love that." He opened the humidifier on the coffee table. "We'll start you with this one." The finger-length cigar in his hand looked small. "Here."

Marcus took a step backward. "Did you see that?" A tiny clownfish swam through dark kelp. "This is amazing." He grabbed the cigar from Derek. "Thanks."

"And a lighter..." Derek shook his head. "Colleen has mine," he said, rushing back to Donnie's desk.

"You weren't kidding when you said man cave." A bookcase in the corner turned Marcus's head. "This is beautiful," he said, reaching for an old leather book.

"Hey! Hey! Hey!" shouted Derek. "What are you doing?" His face wrinkled as he lunged across the room. "I mean..." He pushed Marcus away. "Donnie wouldn't like that."

"My bad?" Marcus put his hands up. "I didn't know. Are they from his family?"

"Family?" Derek's face twisted as he brushed his hair back. "I mean, yes." He put his hand on Marcus's shoulder and guided them back to the couch. "They're very special to him. He's the only one that touches them."

Marcus felt the hesitation in his voice. "I'm sorry again," he said, touching the cigar to his dry lips.

"You know the one I gave you, I think, is from Cuba." Derek crossed his legs. "Here... nice and easy now." He leaned over and lit Marcus's cigar. "Just like that."

"Oh my God!" Marcus coughed. "Just like I remember." His eyes immediately turned red.

"That's it!" Derek howled. Marcus's virgin lungs made him giggle. "I should turn the fan on, huh?"

"I don't know. What would Donnie do?" Marcus quickly put the cigar down on the coffee table's ashtray. "That's strong."

"Give it a second." Derek patted him on the leg, and as he got up, Marcus saw a key card fall out of his pocket.

"I think you dropped this." Marcus grabbed the card and held it up in the air.

"Oh my God!" Derek barely skipped a beat as he ran back to the couch. "Thank you."

"No problem." Marcus, unfazed, turned and faced the aquarium.

Derek sat next to him again and pointed at Donnie. "You think this guy will ever wake up!" He shook his head and jerked his body forward. "You know, I kinda like the quiet. What about you?"

"I mean... I guess." A lightheadedness crunched Marcus's skull as he imagined life in Donnie's fish tank.

Derek hummed in agreement.

The noise from the fish tank filter was the only sound funneling through Marcus's mind before he fixed his posture and asked, "So, where are you from, Derek." He grabbed his cigar and took another puff.

Derek took a few short breaths. "Ukraine. I've been in America for the last six years." He opened his eyes and looked at Marcus. "I grew up in Kyiv if you know where that is."

Marcus nodded.

"My dream since I was a boy was to live in the United States," Derek said, putting his hands up. "And now look where I am. Anything is possible!" The gold chain on his wrist glimmered in the light.

"Wow, was the visa process or whatever you had to do hard?"

"Hard? I think I got lucky. My uncle has friends in New York who helped me out." He put his cigar down. "Once I got to the city, I spent the next year learning English and doing anything I could to survive." Marcus watched him crack his knuckles. "It's one of a kind, right? I can't wait to go back soon."

"I know. We love New York." Marcus put his cigar on the ashtray.

"No more?"

"Just taking a break. It's not like a joint, I'll tell you that." Marcus turned his attention back to the aquarium.

"I bet you're a little lightheaded. Do you want anything to drink?"

"A little would be an understatement."

Derek walked over to the wet bar. "Looks like we've only got gin or scotch."

"Oh, man." Marcus shook his head in defeat. "I don't know. Scotch, I guess." He paused. "I sometimes drank it with my grandpa. I've had enough gin for the day."

Derek reached into an ice box, pulled out a few ice cubes with a scooper, and placed them into a glass cup. "You know the secret to drinking scotch is watering it with an ice cube. Then, over time, you'll build a tolerance and won't need it anymore." He poured the height of two fingers stacked and walked back to the couch. "Here."

Marcus took the glass and swished the liquid inside. The smell of it ran chills down his spine. "When in Rome?" He hesitantly took a baby sip. "Holy fuck!" Trying his best not to make a face, he blew a heavy hue out of his mouth.

"You're getting the hang of it," Derek tapped his knee. "So, how'd you and Aleeia meet? She's gorgeous, by the way."

The sour acid lining Marcus's stomach was ready to shoot out of his esophagus. "Thank you," he said, clearing his throat. "She's... one of a kind." He tilted his head back. "We met at a piano show years back, you know?" The more he talked, the more saliva lubricated his mouth. "I knew there was something about her that was different." Marcus pictured her blonde hair bouncing up and down in his driver's seat.

"Isn't it always like that? I remember the first time I saw Colleen." Derek happily sighed. "She was a dancer at my uncle's club in Manhattan." He put his hands up and pretended to show her body in front of him. "The way her eyes drifted as she danced to the music." He whistled through his teeth. "I knew she was the one."

"Oh, she was a dancer?"

"By night a dancer, and by day a waitress. She hustled as hard as anyone in that city."

"What does she do now?" Marcus rolled his shoulders back. *Does he know how flirty she can be?*

"She works at a café called The Lodge. We were over the non-stop party, so we moved here."

Marcus held his breath and pressed his fingers on his pants. *There's no way I'm going to tell him she gave me her number.* "I'll have to check it out. We want to try all the local spots."

"It's a spot for sure. She loves it, and it makes her happy. That's all that matters, right?"

"Right." Trying to distract himself from the large amounts of saliva he was swallowing, Marcus continued his cross-examination. "And what do you do?"

Derek took another drag of his cigar. "I'm in foreign affairs with some friends from back home. Export-import. Boring stuff."

This dude is a man of mystery, like everything else in this house. "Interesting. How long have you done that?"

Derek put his scotch glass down. "Did you know a fish's lifetime in an aquarium is only three to five years? And they're here stuck in Donnie's aquarium." He cackled. "I mean, what a life! He treats them like a mistress. If I were ever reincarnated, I'd want to be here."

Marcus marveled at the tank again.

For the next fifteen minutes, they sat in silence, watching the fish create endless patterns until Donnie's snoring broke their trance.

"It seems to be that time of night." Derek slowly raised a finger to the clock in the corner.

"Yeah. It's late." Marcus fixed his ruffled shirt. "Thanks for this," he said as he stood up.

"Any time, my friend." Derek pointed him to the elevator. "Shall we?"

15

SUNDAY EVENING: V

"I still can't believe you spent all day cooking for us." Aleeia rested her back against the counter and watched Izabelle elbow-deep in the sink cleaning dishes.

"Hey," Izabelle looked back, "When everything's paid for, it's the least I can do... Can you help me?" She tried blowing wet strands of hair out of her face.

"Of course!" Aleeia's eyes perked up. "Like this?" she said, moving to Izabelle's side and pulling her hair behind her ears. The lavender scents floating from the sink made her calm.

"Perfect, hon." Aleeia watched her soapy fingers slide in and out of a wine glass. "But to your point... things are a bit different in the South. It's how Donnie grew up, you know." She placed the last glass on the sink and flung off her gloves. "I kinda like it. Playing house and all. I never thought it would have been for me, but after all these years, there's something sexy about it, right?"

The way Izabelle shimmed her body shot goosebumps between Aleeia's legs. "I get it... A MILF vibe, am I wrong?"

"True, but I'd still need someone to want to fuck me."
Izabelle winked and bent down to a lower cabinet.

Aleeia's panties felt wet.

"So, sweetie, San Francisco? What's all that racket about?"
slurred Colleen. She'd been chain-smoking cigarettes since the
end of dinner.

"Hmm." Aleeia took a moment before responding. "It's a
beautiful place," she stuttered, making eye contact with Izabelle;
her suggestive eyes rolled towards the dining room. *Is she saying
to go in there?* "If you haven't been before, I mean." Aleeia
looked across the room and rapidly blinked. "The food, the
bridge, the views, the beaches." She sighed. "I already miss it. If
you ever go, let me know, and I can tell you the best places."

"I went years ago, but I've never understood the infatuation
with it... Being from Queens, there was never any appeal to live
on the West Coast." Colleen swirled her wine.

"You're from Queens? I grew up in Brooklyn—Park Slope
near Prospect Park." Aleeia saw Izabelle move her eyes to the
dining room again.

"No, kidding? I lived in Ridgewood with my mom until I
could finally leave home. It was a time I'll never forget."

"That area will always have a piece of me," said Aleeia,
doing her best to keep eye contact with Colleen.

"Do you still have family there?"

Family? Aleeia thought about the last image of her mother
basking in her high. "No, my parents passed away years ago,
and I don't have any siblings. It's just me now."

"I don't have any siblings either. My dad's somewhere in
Eastern Europe. Military." Colleen squished her cigarette into
an ashtray and lit another. "And my mom and I butted heads. I
haven't seen them in years."

"You know, we should all plan a trip there soon. Wouldn't

that be lovely?" Izabelle pulled her hair back into a ponytail and walked to the other side of the island.

"That it would," blurted Colleen.

"You know how Donnie's schedule is, though." Izabelle squatted below the sink in Aleeia's direct peripheral and looked up, tempting her to look at the skin showing just above her pants.

Aleeia stared at her tiny lace thong from her waistline. *Now I want to see it all.* A warm, tingling sensation pulsated through her body.

"Come on, he can barely take off a Friday night," said Izabelle, pulling out a bottle of surface cleaner. "I'm surprised they didn't call him in tonight. This town." She placed the cleaner in front of Colleen with a rag. "Can you?"

"Of course, babe." Colleen rearranged another cigarette in her mouth and stood up to spray the counter.

"If we plan it, couldn't we make it happen?" Aleeia played with her necklace, trying not to give all her attention to Izabelle.

"Who knows? This town is a mystery." Izabelle put her hand on Aleeia and pushed them to the dining room. "Can you help me grab a few more dishes?"

Aleeia let her body melt into Izabelle's grip. "Sure, whatever you need," she said, soaking in her touch.

"Thanks for helping me," said Izabelle. "It was great having you and Marcus for dinner."

"It was. We'll have to do it again." Aleeia stacked the last of the dirty plates from the table and pulled them to her waist. *I want her, but Marcus. I promised him.* Falling into a daydream, Aleeia's hand flinched, and she dropped the stack of plates. *Oh fuck.*

"Are you okay in there?" Colleen hollered.

"We got it." Izabelle looked down at the shards of porcelain covering the floor.

"I'm so sorry. We can pay for it." Aleeia's puppy eyes shot up at Izabelle with remorse.

"Don't worry about it. They were from Donnie's family, and I know he doesn't keep track of what he inherited. As you saw tonight, he's a man of other arts." Izabelle crouched down and gingerly touched Aleeia's backside. "Maybe there is something you can do," she said, running her nails up Aleeia's spine.

Aleeia felt an arousing sensation curl between her thighs. *It's been years since a woman touched me like that. I can feel it. My body. That feeling again.* Izabelle's touch awakened something inside her. "What did you have in mind," she whispered.

Izabelle softly shushed Aleeia. "This," she said, leaning in for a kiss.

Within the silence of the room, they felt each other's souls colliding at cosmic speeds.

Adrift to her temptations, Aleeia's heart danced with passion. Izabelle's kiss erupted a feeling of ecstasy: the emotion of knowing how wrong and freeing something is at the same time. Aleeia felt Izabelle's wet tongue exploring the inside of her mind. As she felt her new admirer reach for her inner thigh, Aleeia let out a high-pitched moan.

Izabelle pulled back. Aleeia felt her sensually inhale her scent. With every poisonous breath Izabelle blew into her ear, Aleeia wished for her warmth between her legs. She imagined her tongue exploring the most sensitive parts of her clit. *Marcus is here.* Aleeia jumped back to reality. *And Colleen is in the next room. What am I doing!?*

"I knew you were a kinky one," said Izabelle, wiping her lips.

Aleeia didn't say anything. She sat on the floor in confusion. *What just happened?*

As Izabelle walked back into the kitchen, Aleeia couldn't take her eyes off Izabelle's straight black hair and tiny waist. *Fuck. I'm so wet.*

"I can take it from here, hon." Izabelle barged back into the room with a broom and pan.

"Is there... Is there anything... anything... I can do to help?" Aleeia's face was white. "I feel awful."

"No, hon. Just stay you." Izabelle winked and started sweeping up the tiny pieces of clay and feldspar. "Don't play too much. Go talk to Colleen and make this normal."

Aleeia pulled herself up from the floor and walked into the kitchen.

"You look like you saw a ghost. Is everything okay?" said Colleen.

The very thought of Colleen seeing what happened sank Aleeia's stomach. "Yes. Everything's fine." She brushed her hair back and sporadically looked around the room. *Did she hear or see anything? How do I even play this off?* Aleeia cleared her throat. "It's just when you asked me about my family, it brought back a lot of emotions." A tear dropped down her face. "My dad passed when I was young, and my mom was a junkie. I don't know if she's alive or..."

"Oh, you poor thing." Colleen opened her arms to embrace Aleeia. "I didn't mean to bring anything up from the past. Come here."

"What did I just miss?" said Izabelle.

"Aleeia was just feeling a bit sad about..." Colleen paused.

"About my family..." Aleeia let out a sigh.

"Oh. You poor thing." Izabelle pulled them in for a group

hug. "We're always here for you, hon," she mumbled into Aleeia's ear, wandering her hand to her lower back again.

For a moment, they sat there like old friends.

"Everything okay, ladies?" shouted Derek as he entered the kitchen.

Marcus quickly became sober when he saw tears dripping from Aleeia's face.

"Aleeia, is everything alright?" he said.

She shook her head and let Marcus wrap his arms around her.

"We were talking about where we are from, and Colleen is from Queens." Aleeia pushed her face into Marcus's chest. "And she asked about my family, and now we're here. I think I've had too much to drink now."

Marcus furrowed his eyebrows and put his hand on top of her head.

"I think it's been a long night for everybody," said Derek, stepping behind Colleen and rolling his head to the hallway. "And Izabelle, we left your loving little teddy bear downstairs in his cave. We couldn't wake him up."

"What a fun night for me! I was hoping to get lucky," she said sarcastically.

"There's always the morning," said Colleen. "We should get going, though, Derek. Are you ready?"

"Yes. It's that time." Derek hugged and kissed Izabelle goodbye. "As always, Iz!"

"And we'll see you two next time?" Colleen went to Marcus's side and scratched his back. She was playing with fire as much as Izabelle.

"We'll see you all soon," shouted Derek as they headed for the front door.

"Izabelle, is there anything else we can do before we

leave?" Marcus loosened his grip on Aleeia after she pulled away.

"You can leave this little one to help me with all my cooking," she said with a playful snarl.

Marcus smiled. "How about next time? I know she'd love to learn something new in the kitchen, especially after this meal. It was incredible! Thank you again."

"He's a keeper," said Izabelle to Aleeia.

Marcus laughed. "I only try. Aleeia keeps me in check."

"Oh, I bet she does." Izabelle showed them to the door. "Well, we should do this again. You two are welcome here anytime. Feel free to pop over whenever."

Does that really mean whenever, whenever? Aleeia thought about her wildest fantasies. "We'd love that. Thank you again for everything. It was amazing. We'll be seeing you soon." She politely smiled, trying her best to make their hug transactional. *No touching this time? That's not fair.*

As they were driving home, Aleeia's mind was elsewhere. *Izabelle turned me on so much.* She cleared her throat. "Baby," she whispered, unclicking her seat belt.

"Yeah?" Marcus rolled his eyes to her. "What're you doing?" he said, watching Aleeia slowly unbutton her pants.

"I missed you all of dinner." Aleeia's breath was heavy. "I want you," she said in her sexy voice.

"Fuck..." Marcus felt his pants grow tight. "We need to pull over."

"Mhm," Aleeia mumbled, slipping off her stilettos and pants.

"Should we just wait until we're home?" Marcus slowed the car.

"Shut up and fuck me," commanded Aleeia, sticking her wet fingers between her thighs.

Marcus swallowed and cut the engine.

"Do you want me?" Aleeia stretched her legs on the dashboard. "Tell me you want me." Her voice got higher with every moan.

"I want you," Marcus said, reaching over and edging his fingers into her tight pussy. He could feel her pulsating with her heartbeat.

"Just keep going like that," said Aleeia.

"You're so wet." Marcus smiled, watching her body rise and fall.

"Just keep going like..." Aleeia pursed her lips. "I think you're going to make me squirt."

"Yeah?" Marcus made a pulling motion with his fingers.

"Right there," She mumbled, tensing up. "Oh my God, Marcus!" Aleeia reached for the back of his head and let out a high-pitched sigh. "I'm coming! I'm coming!" she shouted, releasing her hot, watery explosion on the passenger seat.

"Holy shit, that was a lot." Marcus was speechless. "Where did that come from?"

"I wanted you all night. I love you so much, baby." Aleeia threw herself on top of Marcus's hard cock and rode him until he finished inside her.

It was the perfect ending to their eventful evening.

16

MONDAY

"Aleeia?" The taste of cigars still roasted the insides of Marcus's mouth. "Baby, can you hold me?" He reached his hand across to her side of the bed. "Where are you?" he mumbled, opening his eyes and feeling the aftereffects of last night puncturing his chest. *Things got blurry.* His anxiety ate at his self-worth. *Donnie has an aquarium. Derek's from Ukraine. The elevator. What?* Aching in pain, Marcus rushed to the bathroom. "Aleeia!" He shouted again.

"Over here," came a voice from the patio.

Walking through the doorway with pillow marks on his stomach and face, Marcus hunched over and asked, "How're you feeling?" Aleeia didn't respond. The dark sunglasses, full champagne flute, and half-living facial expressions said enough. "I feel the same," he said as he squinted his eyes, walked across the cold patio tile, and sat beside her.

Aleeia turned her head and mouthed, "I'm dead."

"Cremate me." Marcus laid back into her breasts. "I don't want an open casket anymore."

Aleeia put her hand on his chest and whispered, "I'll be right there with you."

"I hope," he mumbled, feeling her scratching his chest hairs like the first time they slept together. Her cold hands sent shivers down his spine and turned him on.

"Does that feel good?" Aleeia slipped her fingers into his mouth and watched him suck on her forest green nails.

"Yes," he hummed.

Aleeia could feel Marcus's heart beating faster and faster. "I want you," she whispered, dropping her wet fingers down his stomach. "I want you inside of me," she pleaded, spreading her legs.

"Fuck." Marcus felt his torso tremble as he leaned down and seductively kissed her neck like cheating on your significant other for the first time. "Oh my God." He watched her tiny hands squeeze his hard cock and flop it out of his boxers.

Aleeia pushed her sunglasses up. "Someone's happy to see me."

Marcus unbuttoned her top. "Always." Her dry hand rubbing only made him harder. "You're going to make me come," he said, pushing her away and sliding down her belly. He tried to keep his composure, but her body was like sugar.

"Marcus," she sighed, digging her hands into his hair. His tongue was painting a picture with her clit.

"I love it down here." He watched her eyes roll back.

"Keep going." Aleeia kicked her legs back as tiny raindrops started falling on them. "I'm so wet."

"I want to feel you," said Marcus, quickly sticking his cock into her vagina and rubbing her clit with his thumb. Thunder cracked in the background.

"Don't stop," shouted Aleeia, releasing her frustrations about last night. Without a moment wasted, she pushed

Marcus off and threw herself against the balcony. "Fuck me here."

Marcus dryly swallowed. "Fuck," he mumbled, clenching her hips. "Do you like that?" He pulled out and shoved his face between her thighs.

"Marcus!" Aleeia stood on her tippy toes. "Just fuck me."

As he removed his face from her vagina, Marcus saw a wooden bunker on the far end of their property.

"I'm so close, baby. Pull my hair."

Marcus slowly stuck his cock back inside. "You feel so good." He brushed his hair back and looked up into the sky. "I'm close," he muttered, syncing their movements to the ever-changing thunder shocks until they both finished.

17

MONDAY: II

At least my headache is gone. Fuck. What time is it? Marcus found himself alone in their bed again. *Where did the day go? Aleeia?* Leaning to his bedside table, he saw it was 4:21pm. *What am I doing with my life?* His inner critic stabbed him in the gut and forced him to get up. "Aleeia! Aleeia! Where are you?" He stumbled down the stairs in his boxers. "Aleeia!" he howled, walking into the kitchen. There was no response. *Weird.* He grabbed a glass of water and sat at his piano. *Something to relax us both.* The sound of a fine-tuned Steinway always helped Aleeia's mind wander to a place of euphoria. As he began to play, he could feel the house awakening from a foggy haze. Each sound allowed his worries to dissipate into the horizon.

When Aleeia finally heard her favorite E-flat chord, she caught herself in an empty stare. She stopped what she was doing and sauntered to the sounds she heard from across the house. Every step she took toward the piano room felt like the end of a movie. Marcus's heart was calling her. The creaking floorboards in their hallway told Marcus she was close, and with one final chord, he tailed off the sounds that brought a smile to her face.

"Feeling better, I see," said Marcus.

"You could say so. I've been up for a few hours." Aleeia had a twinkle in her eye as she stood in the doorway.

"Oh, yeah?" Marcus locked their hands together as she approached and pushed his face into her stomach.

"Did you know there's a basement?"

"A basement?" mumbled Marcus, making kissing noises around her waist. "I don't remember Lindsay mentioning anything like that. Did you find it?"

"I don't think she did," Aleeia pulled his chin up. "But I did find it." She grabbed his hand and led him down the hallway. "There's a lot of junk in it, but it's interesting."

"What, are you a dumpster diver now?" Marcus laughed. "An extra room in the house? We got a steal with this price."

"Always calculating something." Aleeia shook her head and pulled him closer to the staircase. "See?" She pointed to a small knob.

"How did I miss this?"

"Don't worry. I did, too. My shirt got caught on it when I came downstairs this afternoon." Aleeia pulled the door open. "Spooky, right?" Darkness swallowed their view.

"You went down there?"

"Don't worry. There are lights." Aleeia turned on her phone flashlight and slowly submerged into a black abyss. "See! All better."

Marcus straddled his way down the stairs and asked, "You've been down here for how long?" As he dipped his head into the dim light, he saw paperwork scattered across the floor and articles from various newspapers hanging around the room.

"Maybe an hour or so. Here, check this out." Aleeia passed him a cut-out news article.

Another Bank Robbed; Another Hostage Taken

Marcus gave the room a dirty look. "Aleeia, what the fuck is this?"

"What do you mean?" She sat crisscrossed on the floor and picked up more pieces of paper. "Izabelle and Colleen said the guy who used to own this house was a troublemaker or something."

"Troublemaker?"

"Yeah, I don't know." She shuffled more news articles in her hands. "I think his name was Michael Wallace. I'll have to ask them again."

Marcus held his breath.

"Look! All this stuff is from the seventies and early eighties." Aleeia spread the papers across the floor. "It's been so long."

"Aleeia." Marcus raised his voice. "I don't like having this in the house. I'm calling Lindsay. After that, we should give it to the police."

"Baby, don't be silly." Aleeia stood up and wrapped her arms around his neck. "It's from decades ago. And besides, the articles don't make any sense." She bent down and picked one up. "Here. Look at this one."

Ellis Bros Circus visits with 20 Star Acts.

"I think this guy was just a weirdo. See, here's another."

Gunner Wins Mayor!
Enacts Underground Permit

"There's no correlation between anything." Aleeia poked his nose. "It's just old newspapers. He was probably going crazy." She rolled her eyes. "You know how old people get."

The more Marcus looked at the articles, the more nothing made sense. "I don't know. The fact Lindsay didn't tell us about it, and now there's all these random news cutouts." He paused. "I just have a bad feeling. Can we go upstairs and talk about it later?"

Aleeia looked around at the floor with her hands on her waist. "Sure, but I think this would make a perfect wine cellar?"

Marcus's face softened. "Really?" His eyes lit up. Everything about the room's creepy feelings floated away. "You're right. A little project for us."

"How about a little present from me to you? You deserve it!" Aleeia batted her eyes. "You do so much for me."

"You're joking." Marcus looked around the room. "I mean, I'm not going to say no." The room instantly became a canvas of imagination.

"Just you wait." Aleeia played with her necklace. "Hungry?" she said, changing the topic. "What's for dinner?"

"Let's get out of here first."

When they were back upstairs, the sun's orange skies were beyond the marshes in the piano room. From the evenings they spent together at Baker Beach, sunsets held the perfect amount of romance and peace in a singular photo.

Aleeia stood near the large windows and stared into the yard's red and pink patterns. "Hey, a bunny!" she yelled. "Did you see that?"

As if he was expecting a call, Marcus walked into the other room as his phone rang. "I didn't, but this is Penny." He shrugged. "Let me take this, and then let's talk about dinner."

Aleeia opened the doors outside the piano room and then went to the kitchen to open a bottle of white wine.

"Hey, bro." Marcus picked at his nails.

"Yo! Did you see Bitcoin's price skyrocket?"

Marcus could sense something in his voice. "I didn't, but it is still the best investment of our lives to buy it at $100."

"Right? You've got a hunch for this crypto stuff, dude. What're we doing next?"

"I think it was just a bit of luck," Marcus said as he checked his Bitcoin balance on his phone. "But I'm glad you called. I think we'll be throwing a housewarming party soon. I expect you here."

"I wouldn't miss it. Just give me the dates, and I'll be there. How is everything?"

"A little rough. We went to a new friend's house last night, and it was..." He looked around for Aleeia. "Interesting to keep it short. They're nice. I think Aleeia really hit it off with the other couples."

"Are you hungover?"

"I don't know what I am."

"You'll be fine. But I'm glad you two are settling in." Penny lowered his voice. "How's the project?"

"It's coming along. I have some rough ideas but plan to finish them by Friday. It should be pretty straightforward."

"That's great." Penny cleared his throat. "I hate to do this, but they're postponing the event... The budget fell through."

"Did it?" Marcus crouched down.

"Yeah. They're putting a 120-day pause on it." Penny waited for his response. "But, hey, the good news is that they still want your music. We just won't need it rushed anymore."

"I see." Marcus started walking back to the kitchen. "Are you doing alright? Something in your voice seems off?"

"Yeah, I'm fine. Everything's great. Just trying to work with new people, you know." Penny laughed. "They aren't as talented as you. You're easy, man."

Marcus pursed his lips. He felt like he wasn't telling him something. "Okay, well, if anything good comes up, you know how to reach me."

"Of course. I gotta run, but tell Aleeia I said, 'Hi'!"

"You got it. Stay safe, brother." Marcus hung up the phone.

"How's Penny?" Aleeia was sitting on the kitchen island, drinking a glass of wine.

"He's Penny." Marcus went to the cabinet. "Sometimes I worry about him. I think something's goin' on with his mom again. You know how he gets." He pulled his hair behind his ears and poured himself a glass of wine. "And he said the music I was putting together isn't needed for another four months or so now."

Aleeia's eyes narrowed. "Well, could you still work on it with your timetable? We both know how you get when you overwork yourself."

He shrugged his shoulders and chugged his drink. "Yeah. I'll figure it out." An awkward silence filled the room as he stared past Aleeia and changed the topic. "Is everything okay with you after last night?"

"Of course! Why wouldn't it be?" Aleeia flipped her hair on the other side of her shoulder and twirled her finger on the top part of her glass.

"I don't know. I didn't expect to come into the kitchen last night and see you crying."

"Oh, right," she stuttered. *I can't let him know about Izabelle.* "I think I may have had a bit too much to drink. They can party, right?" She smirked. "After Colleen brought up my parents, a whirlwind of emotions came up. I don't know. I just couldn't hold back my tears. It was probably just a lot to drink. We haven't talked about them in a while, ya know." *That's right. I was mostly crying because of my family, not Izabelle. That's right, it was for my family.*

"I'm sorry." Marcus walked over and hugged her. "You know I'm always here to talk." He placed his head on top of hers. "I know this move has us under all sorts of stress," he said, kissing her forehead. Aleeia somehow felt distant. He couldn't place it. "But they were fun," Marcus said as he made a funny face.

How do I play this? "They were!" she shouted. "Colleen and Izabelle were both so sweet. We should get together with them again. How was Donnie's man cave?"

Marcus slammed his drink down. "Donnie is not the man I'd take for being an aquarium buff, but God almighty, he knows what he's doing. It was the most spectacular thing I've seen in a while. I couldn't believe it." He shook his head. "The elevator, too. Who would have thought? There was another floor below the aquarium, but I didn't see it."

I'm glad he's distracted. I don't know what would have happened if he had come upstairs sooner. "I'll have to check it out next time we're there."

"You need to. Derek showed me everything. Donnie dozed off as soon as we sat down—it was like seeing a passed-out bear!" Marcus reenacted Donnie's stalky shoulders, sleeping in a chair.

Aleeia looked for a way out of the conversation.

"And Derek told me he's from Ukraine. Did you know that? I don't think I've met anyone from there. Maybe that's why I couldn't get a read on him."

"I thought he was nice... And Colleen and him seem happy together."

"They do. He told me they met in New York. That's where he learned English and came to America."

"It sounds like you two had some good conversations," Aleeia said as she played with her necklace again. "I'm glad you made a new friend."

"I wouldn't go that far. Let's see how the next time we see them goes." Marcus playfully grinned. "And I think you topped Izabelle with your outfit. How about that?"

Aleeia choked on her drink. "What?"

"Oh, come on! You didn't see how she was looking at you." Marcus tilted his head. "Even Derek was checking you out when you got out of the conversation pit. I saw his eyes... That's my girl!"

"Really?" Aleeia blushed.

"Yes, I know you know it, too." Marcus poured another glass. "Do you want to order pizza for dinner?" he said, walking down the hallway.

Aleeia spun around in her chair. "That sounds good." *Can he tell something is up? Be normal. You've been down this road before. Don't hurt him again.* "I can order it for delivery." Her mind wandered to last night as she pulled out her phone. *I can feel it in my chest and my...* Aleeia put her hand between her thighs. *I have to stop. You have Marcus.*

After playing battle royal with her heart, Aleeia quickly placed their order. "Okay. The food should be here in about an hour," she shouted.

"Okay, thank you! Come here and sit," said Marcus on the couch.

Aleeia took another deep breath and put her hair up in a ponytail, but as she placed her phone face down on the counter, she heard it ring. *The pizza can't be here already.*

```
Donnie's going to be out of town this weekend
if you want to get together again. I can show
          you how to cook! Maybe Friday?
```

Izabelle's message made butterflies dance around her stomach. *What will I say to Marcus? We're just cooking, right? It's no big deal?* Aleeia's heart raced with guilty pleasure. "I'll be right there!" she said, closing her phone and going to sit with Marcus.

18

TUESDAY

Donnie's leather boots echoed down the historic hallways of the police station, and with every click of his back heels, his officers knew he was slowly approaching.

"Here are those recent crime reports for you, sir," said York, laying a pile of papers on his desk.

"Thanks for that." Donnie glared at his waist. "No gun again?"

"That's right, sir. I made a promise." York cleared his throat. "Every problem can be solved with words or God's faith... I hope it's something we can work together on."

"Yeah, yeah, yeah. I've heard it. I get it, kid." Donnie dropped his newspaper and folded his hands on his desk. "I approved your time off for this weekend."

"Really?" York's eyes shot open. "I mean, I appreciate it. Thank you, sir."

"Where're you going again?" Donnie watched him shake his head in disbelief.

"Down south to Tallahassee. My niece is getting baptized."

"Beautiful!" shouted Donnie with a wide grin. "We'll hold the fort down for you."

"I know you will, sir," said York, smiling as he turned away. "Thank you again."

"Wait a second, would you?" Donnie waggled his finger. "Close the door. I need to tell you something."

"Of course," said York.

"Please." Donnie opened his hand. "Take a seat."

"Is everything okay?" York asked.

"Kid. You're doing great." Donnie loudly scooted his chair forward. "As you know, I'm going to be moving on in the next year or so, and I've seen many men and women come through this station and piss away our reputation. But since you've been here." He pointed at York's blushed face. "You've helped turn our name around. I've already spoken to my boss and others involved in the decision process, and your name has come up quite a bit."

"I'm flattered." Sweat faintly slid down York's temples. "I wasn't expecting this type of compliment... I'm simply doing my duty with God's purpose." He pulled out his cross necklace. "It's a pleasure to work with such a great..."

"And that..." Donnie slammed his desk. "Is exactly why your name has been floating around everyone's minds. You can instill a new brand of officers." He looked out the window for inspiration. "When I announce my retirement, I'd like you to submit your application to take my spot. Your leadership is needed, and I want to know that my city and people will be safe."

"Sir, I would be honored with such loyalty to continue your legacy and..."

"But!" Donnie interrupted. "It would require you to always carry a firearm... I know this is a tough spot for you, but you need to know that you have the power to pick and choose when to use it."

"You know why I don't use them, sir."

"York... How could I forget? It was the most tragic hit and run this side of the Mississippi." Donnie looked away. "We're still praying for your missus... But, hey, at least the bad guys are where they're supposed to be."

"I appreciate your input." York twiddled his thumbs. "I'll have to consider this with my family over the weekend. Thank you again for your insight."

Donnie sat back in his chair as York closed the door. "You don't know what's going to hit you, kid... You have no idea."

The faint sounds of birds chirping outside Donnie's window disrupted his daydream about his retirement. "And good morning to you," he said, mimicking their whistling. "Everything's perfect." Reaching for his coffee mug across his desk, Donnie took a heavy whiff of his lukewarm java and sang, "Time to make some money!" As he stepped towards the door and opened the blinds, an off-beat hum escaped his mouth after seeing empty hallways. "Let the games begin," he mumbled, running back to his desk and picking up a flip phone hidden underneath a manila folder. "We're in the clear. Let's get started!"

19

TUESDAY: II

Even after spending the night together, watching a movie, and falling asleep in Marcus's arms, Aleeia couldn't shake Izabelle from her thoughts.

For most of the morning, she paced around the house, taking inventory of everything they needed to make their home feel more organized. As she stepped upstairs, Aleeia heard Marcus's emotions playing through the piano. A gleeful C chord rubbed her heart when she admired their guest bedroom. Contradicting thoughts about becoming a mother and feeling everything about Izabelle put weights on her chest. Eventually, she craved to numb something and went to their patio to smoke a cigarette. *I know this isn't the best vice.*

"Baby!" Aleeia shouted, stepping into the piano room. *Huh?* Marcus was hunched over, playing a somber tune. She looked at the foot pedal and saw a half-empty bottle of red wine. *That's not good.* "Marcus," she whispered again, touching his back. "I'm going to the store. Do you need anything?" He barely moved. "Are you drunk?"

"I'm... I'm..." Marcus mumbled.

"Hey, hey, what's wrong?" Aleeia tried sitting him up. "Marcus! Can you hear me?" She pushed his hands down as he attempted to play an eerie chord.

"I don't know. I think I drank too much," he hiccupped. "And too early. I'm sorry."

Aleeia looked around the room for an answer. "Talk to me!" An emptiness pierced her stomach. *Does he know?* "What's going on, Marcus? You can tell me anything."

"I don't know!" Tears erupted off his cheeks. "I'm overwhelmed with the move." Aleeia let him bury his face into her stomach. "You know I don't like to see you cry. What was all that about?" Snot built up in his nose. "I miss home... and on top of it, Penny didn't sound right. I know it's his mom. She's had cancer three times before this."

Aleeia stuck her necklace in her mouth. "I know she's like a second mother to you."

"I just want to be there." He wailed.

The pain in his voice made Aleeia's heart wrench.

"And I know those tears, Aleeia. I know what they were about." Marcus rubbed his eyes. "Did you do anything with her?"

"What?" Aleeia's soft, wrinkled forehead jumped back. "What did you just say?" She raised her voice.

"You know what I mean," shouted Marcus.

"I can't believe you." Aleeia squeezed her fists. "We haven't even been here a week, and you think I'd put our relationship in jeopardy again. I can't have girlfriends now! Would you rather me hang around a bunch of guys?!"

"I saw the twinkle in your eye... You know how much all of that still affects me." Marcus covered his face. "I'm sorry. I'm sorry. I'm sorry."

Aleeia waited for him to calm down. An old lullaby

vibrated from her throat as she stroked his hair. *How does he know? I can't tell him. I can't.*

After letting Marcus shed a few more tears, Aleeia delicately pulled his head up. "I'm going to go to the store... Why don't you nap while I'm out? I think rest will do you good." She wrapped one of his arms around her shoulder.

"I'm sorry... I love you."

"I love you, too." Aleeia held her breath. "Let's get you upstairs. Everything's okay. I know how stressful it is right now." She watched Marcus stumble next to her. "You can do it... There you go... Almost there," she muttered, dropping him onto their bed.

As she closed their bedroom door, Aleeia could already hear him snoring. *I haven't seen him that drunk since Mexico last year.* She sighed and walked out the front door to the car. *I guess that's when he caught me in the hot tub with that girl. We didn't even do anything but kiss. Why did you turn to the bottle instead of me? Am I the problem?* Guilt punctured her chest. *What should I tell him about dinner? Izabelle's just a friend, right?* Aleeia sank her worries into the empty roads and followed the directions to the store.

20

TUESDAY: III

Aleeia had hot pants when she pulled into the grocery store parking lot. Glimpses of Marcus and her making love skipped pictures through her mind, but like an old film camera, everything looked faded. Her darker side was thinking about sleeping with Izabelle.

"List. List," Aleeia said aloud, looking at different phallic vegetables. *Focus.* The mist sprayer in the produce section cooled her warm body. Each thick, long cucumber she placed into her basket made her push her legs together. *Will she have toys?* Aleeia could feel her panties getting wetter. "I have to stop daydreaming," she grunted, scanning her shopping list.

"Aleeia!" a voice said from behind her.

A flickering sensation funneled through Aleeia's body and rhythmically prickled her clit. She recognized the voice. *It can't be her.* Turning around, she found the petite, black-haired woman she'd been half peaking to for thirty minutes.

"Izabelle!" Aleeia's inner thighs quaked. "What're you doing here?" The tiny lips below her waist began to dew like wet grass in the morning.

"I'm just getting a few things for the house. Did you get my text last night?"

"I did!" *I also read it a million times.*

"And so? Can you make it? I wanted to make homemade pasta!" The tone in Izabelle's voice was fiery but mysterious and inviting.

"I think it should work. I just have to check with Marcus." *Having an evening away from him might be a good thing. It's part of a healthy relationship.*

Izabelle grazed the top part of Aleeia's hand. "Perfect! I'll have everything, so just bring yourself." Her plump lips and wide grin made Aleeia's heart race. "And wear something cute —or nothing at all," she said with a wink that meant a million things.

The hairs on Aleeia's arms rose.

"And don't forget, it's a girl's night only. Let's say 6:00pm on Friday?" Izabelle leaned in for a cheek kiss.

"Yes, that sounds... great... I mean, perfect." Aleeia stood stiff and clumsily gave her a half-hug.

"Don't look so shocked," Izabelle shouted, pushing her cart towards the exit.

"I'll see you then..." Aleeia waved goodbye. *Don't look so shocked.* She winced. *6:00pm on Friday. Marcus knows she's a good cook. I know he'll believe me.* A euphoric wave cuddled around her pussy.

After loading the car, Aleeia melted into the driver's seat. "She turned me on so much," she whispered, looking through the open sunroof. The warm sunlight beat down on her chest and invited her hand into the seam of her pants. *Just something quick.* After seeing nobody nearby, Aleeia quietly slipped off her shoes and pulled her polyester yoga pants and red panties to her ankles. Her breathing was hot and heavy. With nothing but her bare butt touching the driver seat, she positioned her left leg just above the air-conditioner near the driver's mirror. *I'm so wet.* She wrapped her mouth around her middle and pointer fingers, then dropped them to her clit. "Fuck," she moaned, leaning forward and spitting onto her hand. A trance laced with adultery made her finger movements move like a delusional artist, finger-painting circles. "Oh, right there!" Aleeia heard a car pass by as she orgasmed. She could see her leg shaking near the mirror. Immediately, she pulled her pants up and drove home.

As Aleeia pulled into their driveway, thick raindrops pelted the windshield. The aftereffects of her afternoon delight were slowly wearing off. *What am I doing?* She dropped her head onto the steering wheel. *What am I doing to him?* Flashbacks of Izabelle's smile, her orgasm, and their future dinner date capsuled her mind. *Act normal. Don't say you saw her at the store.* The innocent and guilty side of her subconscious was battling with her heart.

"I'm home," Aleeia shouted, entering the doorway with a hollow grin.

Marcus met her halfway and grabbed as many bags from her arms as possible. "Let me help you with those... How many more are there?"

"That's all of it, baby."

Before Aleeia could ask how he felt, Marcus quickly reached into the bags and began placing everything on the counter.

"Feeling better?" she asked.

Marcus awkwardly smiled and then stopped unpacking the bags. "I think. But before you say anything, I want to say I'm sorry about earlier. I was stressed about so many things, but now that I've had some rest..." He turned and placed the orange

129

juice in the refrigerator. "I thought it would be a good idea if I went back to San Francisco for the weekend to check on Penny."

Gone for the weekend? That would make everything a lot easier. Aleeia tilted her head and frowned.

"I know something's off with him... Besides, a little space apart might ignite something for us to come back to."

Aleeia stayed silent, examining Marcus's body language. "Alright, I guess... But it's just for the weekend... and you can't see anyone but Penny... That wouldn't be fair to me."

"Deal!" Marcus pumped his hands. "I was hoping you'd be okay with it—I already booked a ticket to leave on Thursday." He kissed her forehead. "I'll be back Sunday evening."

Aleeia tensed up. "Whatever you need to do."

"You sure it's okay? You aren't saying much."

Aleeia felt her spine shiver. "I'm sure. And you're right. We need a little something to ground us. Distance makes the heart grow fonder."

Marcus rubbed his tiny mustache stubble. "Are you sure?"

"I'm sure." Aleeia pushed his arm away and continued unpacking their groceries. "Don't worry about me. It'll give me some time to work on that special little project."

"The wine cellar? I thought you were joking."

"That was no joke, mister." Aleeia playfully smirked. "I'll have help, don't worry. Izabelle invited me to hang out this weekend." She saw Marcus hold his breath. "I was going to see if she wanted to lend a hand."

"Right. Izabelle." Marcus's knees buckled as he passed her a piece of fish wrapped in brown paper. "About that."

"About what?" Aleeia glared. "We're just friends."

"I know you said she's just a friend, but something tells me there's more." Marcus cleared his throat. "I'm sorry. I just know what's happened in the past. I'm working on it, but you can't blame me. Therapy only fixes so much."

"She's just a friend," Aleeia said, putting her hands around his neck. "I promise. You don't have to worry about anything. I'm not going to hurt you again. You're my rock." She pushed her head into his chest. "I'm not going to hurt you again."

Marcus squeezed her tight.

He's buying it. "Go call Penny and tell him you're coming to visit. I know how happy he'll be," she said.

As Aleeia watched Marcus leave the room, she pulled a bottle of wine from the refrigerator. *He can't know about any of this. It will be my secret forever. Besides, all those other times were when he was around. This will be much easier.*

"Penny! How are you?" Marcus's voice boomed across the hallway. "I got a surprise for you! I'm flying out to San Francisco on Thursday. Can you grab me from the airport?"

Aleeia heard Marcus say, "Only the weekend. I wanted to come and see you."

There was a long silence before Marcus walked back into the room, pinching his nose. "Alright. Well, I'll send you my flight information, okay? Love you, man."

"Everything okay?" Aleeia furrowed her eyebrows.

"It's his mom." Marcus flexed his throat. "She's not doing well again... I was right... She was diagnosed with stage III colon cancer last week."

"Marcus!" Aleeia shouted, covering her mouth. "That's terrible. I'm sorry."

"I know." The innocent boy in Marcus silently sat at the kitchen island.

"Well, it's good you are going out there." Aleeia went to his side. "I'm sure Penny can use all your support."

"I know," he mumbled, burying his face into his elbow.

"If you need to stay longer than the weekend, I completely understand." Aleeia looked at his back, moving up and down. "I can come out there after the weekend, too. Whatever you think is best." *Just let me have the weekend to myself. We both need it, Marcus.* "Penny will get through this. We'll all get through this... I'm going to start dinner. Why don't you go relax? You've had a long day."

Marcus palmed his eyes and then poured himself a glass of wine. "Thank you," he said, walking into the other room and turning on the TV.

After waiting a moment, Aleeia pulled out her phone. Izabelle's conversation was her top message.

    6:00pm on Friday sounds great.
    It was good seeing you today.

Aleeia smirked, feeling her vision and decisions clouded by a blanket of lust and trust. *It's just this one time. I won't do it again. I promise.*

21

WEDNESDAY

As the Southern humidity roasted Marcus on his mid-morning run, he found himself floating in and out of a meditative state. "Why?" he yelled at the sticking gray clouds covering the blue sky. Pink magnolias and the smell of pollen filled the air as he opened his lungs. *I have to forget about the past. She's not going to do anything to hurt me. She promised.* The rows of oak trees and dangling spanish moss became his new therapist. "You can do this," he screamed, licking the salty sweat from his mouth. *Trust her. Everything's going to work itself out. You two just need a little time apart.* The heat popping off the asphalt turned Marcus's jog into a sprint, and the more he felt himself detoxing from his mind games, the happier he became. *I love this.* He smiled. *I'm free. No phone. No music. Unplugged.*

Out of breath, Marcus pulled off to the side of the road. *Sleeping porches? Isn't that something?* Along the horizon was a black top with basketball hoops, a giant grass field, and rows of orange lockers. Marcus's face lit up as he remembered his time in high school.

"Inside now!" shouted one of the teachers.

They have so much ahead of them... And so much to learn. I miss volunteering. I had fun teaching music... I need to do that again, even if it's for an hour. I made a difference. I know I did.

While the rosy sun tanned his body, Marcus imagined an after-school program. *Mr. Bynes, the music teacher.* As he ran closer to the school, everyone slowly disappeared inside. A slight, calm wind drifted in the palm trees above his head. *I need water. This isn't like running by the Bay. What is this heat?*

Marcus walked around the school's perimeter, keeping a safe distance, while looking for a water fountain. *Please, God, help me.* After searching for his hidden oasis, he finally saw an old metal faucet near the edge of the closest building. *Make it quick.* He gulped and jolted across the field, but out of the corner of his eye, he saw two girls rushing off campus and looking back to see if anyone saw them. *Skipping class? Those were the days.* Marcus hesitantly ran towards the water fountain and pressed his lips against the stream. An ice-cold wiggling sensation flowed through his body. *I need to get out of here before anyone sees me.* Like a barbarian replenishing his body after battle, he took a deep breath and sprinted away from the school.

As he got back to the road, Marcus stopped his jog and looked around. Every house he passed looked outdated. The chipped paint and rusted metal gates kept him on his toes as he followed a sign leading to downtown. *Aleeia. I know something needs to change. Maybe we need to have a kid. That's the answer.* A screeching cry interrupted his daydream. *What was that?* Marcus backpedaled and looked down the street he just passed.

"No! Stop it! Help!" A girl yelled in the distance. "Please! No! Help!"

Marcus's heart dropped. *Are those the girls from school?*

"Hey!" he shouted, running towards them. "Stop! Don't do that!"

Two men dressed in all black picked the girls up by their waists and shoved them into the back seat of a black SUV.

"Get off!" screamed one of the girls as she kicked her feet. "Please! Help!"

"Hey!" shouted Marcus again, waving his hands. Sweat from his forehead ran into his eyes and blurred his vision. *Am I seeing something?* In a split second, he watched the two men in all black jump back into their car and sped off.

"Hello! Anyone!" he yelled, looking around the streets. *Did no one see that?*

His head moved from side to side, searching for any answer. *What just happened? Was that a kidnapping? Is that what an abduction is? Why didn't I bring my phone?* Marcus huffed under his breath. *I have to get to the police station. I have to tell Donnie.*

"Fuck," he grunted, scanning the streets for anyone to help.

22

WEDNESDAY: II

Aleeia crept down the basement stairs. *Where do I even start?* The smell of dust lurked in the air. *I'm in no mood for this, but a promise is a promise.* She bent down and aimlessly stared at the newspapers covering the floor. As she prayed for a spark of inspiration, her eyes fixated on an old city utility map above the wooden desk in the corner. *What was he planning?* Tiny yellow and red pins with stretched rubber bands filled the blue and black dotted map. Aleeia followed each band with her fingertips and moved closer. *New Heaven? That's our street.* After counting each dot and pretending to know her new city, she looked around the room again. *Is this what Marcus wants? Is this what I want?* Pressing her fingers into her temples, she squatted down and covered her face. *I know this move was my idea. I'm not ready for kids. I still have so much I want to do.* The dark hues in the room started blurring together. *Why do I do this to myself? A promise for kids. Fuck. I wonder what Izabelle is doing.* Aleeia buried herself in broken promises and sat on the bottom step of the staircase until she heard a door close upstairs.

"Marcus!" she yelled, jolting up the stairs. "Are you home? How was your run?"

The silence of the house ate at her already fragile state of mind. *Weird.* Aleeia stepped into the kitchen. It was much sunnier than the morning. *I wonder how he's doing.* She looked at his phone charging on the kitchen counter and envisioned him yelling at the sky, looking for an answer. *I can't hurt him again.* She sighed and walked upstairs. *I need to take the edge off.* Passing by their empty, soon-to-be kids' bedrooms made her heart twitch. *What am I going to do?* She shook her head and pressed a crisp cigarette tip to her lips as she stepped onto their patio. Burnt cigarettes in the daytime reminded her of the afternoon Marcus caught her in Mexico. *He won't find out this time. He won't.* Aleeia watched the red ember burn next to her fingertips.

"You can do this!" she shouted, rushing back inside and throwing the cigarette bud in the toilet. *It's just cleaning. Throw everything out and worry about the fun stuff later.* She went to the kitchen, grabbed a few trash bags, and ran down the basement stairs—she was organized chaos.

WEDNESDAY: III

"Excuse me." Marcus stopped his jog and glared at the elderly woman sitting in a rocking chair on her front porch. "Do you have a phone? It's an emergency."

"Mhm," she mumbled, pondering his wrangled appearance.

"Can I please use it?" Marcus's bloodshot eyes and oiled skin made him look like a lunatic asking for a favor.

The older woman put her hand up to her chin. "Nows you sures ain't from here, pretty boy. Where you from?"

Marcus rolled his head back. "I'm from California. I really need to use a phone to call 911. I just saw two girls get kidnapped." He pointed down the street and waited for her reaction.

"Mhm," the woman said again.

A soft wind grazed his back and cooled him down for a split second.

"Bailey!" yelled the woman with a cackle before picking up a cigarette from her side table. The creaking sound of her chair in the hot afternoon sun sent shivers down Marcus's spine.

"Please, it's an emergency." Marcus put his hands on her metal gate.

"I don't know you," she shouted. "Step back, boy!"

Marcus put his hands up. "I'm sorry. I'll just..." A young boy opening the front screen door interrupted his train of thought.

"Bailey. Can you help this man? He on our property!" The older woman attempted to stand up but was dragged down by her frail bones.

Marcus stood outside their front yard and watched the boy in an oversized striped shirt shuffle down the steps and walk up to him.

"Hey, I was asking your..." Marcus put his eyes on the older woman. "For a phone. I saw a kidnapping, and I need to call the police."

"Police?" yelled the woman. "Boy, we don't need any trouble here today. Bailey, get back inside! May God bless you, sir."

The boy rubbed his fingers together and looked up at Marcus with squinted eyes.

"Hey." Marcus bent down to be at eye level with him. "Can you tell me where the police station is then?"

The boy furrowed his eyebrows and looked back at the porch. "It's on State. Two blocks that way, and then it's all the ways down there."

Marcus clapped his hands together. "Thank you."

"Bailey! Come here," yelled the woman again. "Don't talk to strangers, or we'll have to call the police!"

Marcus shook his head at the older woman and continued down the street.

24

WEDNESDAY: IV

A stomach-emptying headline caught Aleeia's attention as she ripped a black and white newspaper article from a bulletin board on the wall near the desk.

Three missing from Georgia State Fair

Three children—two boys and a young girl—are missing after the 1988 Georgia State Fair. Authorities say they were last seen at 7:00pm with their grandfather, Charles Benn. If you have any information regarding the whereabouts of Miles and Caleb Benn, and Ann Boe, please contact your local authorities. Miles was last seen in a blue T-shirt, Caleb was last seen in a black sweatshirt, and Ann was last seen in a floral dress.

Missing? Why would anyone save this article, let alone post it here? What did Izabelle and Colleen say about this guy?

Michael? Aleeia pulled her eyebags down. *Marcus can't find out about this. I know he'll want to stay the weekend if he's worried about anything. I need to ask Izabelle about this again.*

Aleeia crumpled the news article in her hand and walked upstairs to grab her phone.

It's just a question about the house. Nothing more. That's not breaking a boundary, right?

With each monotone-sounding dial tone ring, Aleeia waited for Izabelle to pick up. "Three missing from Georgia State Fair," she read aloud until Izabelle's voicemail cut in. *Of course.* She sighed and shoved the news article to the bottom of the trash.

25

WEDNESDAY: V

"Hey! Which way is the police station?" asked Marcus, passing by a man walking down the street.

"Huh?" The elderly veteran jumped back and caught his breath as he heard Marcus's raspy voice slip up his neck. "It's..." He paused. "You scared me!"

Marcus politely grinned. "Which way is it?!"

"It's on the next block, I think." The man's finger shook as he pointed down the street.

"Thanks." Marcus waved his hand and felt a knot growing in his leg. *C'mon, where are you?*

As he moved his head from side to side, searching for a clue, he noticed more than half of the town was boarded up with flimsy pile wood sheets nailed onto the front windows of each building. *Where the fuck is the police station in this tiny ass town!* His breath was the only sound he heard for minutes. *I don't see it. I'm at the next block.*

Finally, Marcus's eyes glued to a white building. *There it is.* He looked up at knee-high steps leading to the police station and felt his mood suddenly shift. A dark feeling swept up from his feet as he clutched his throat. *Just breathe. Stay calm and tell them exactly what happened.*

The heavy metal doors made a noise when he pushed them open. An arctic mist blew into his chest and instantly dropped his body temperature. *Just what I needed.* Marcus took a second to let the chilly air dry his body. With a swift movement, he threw his shirt back on and walked down the long hallway.

"Excuse me," he said, touching the front counter and clearing his throat. "I'd like to report a kidnapping I saw less than thirty minutes ago." The loud, ticking clock behind the desk made each second feel longer than it should. "I'm not sure of... I saw two men grab two girls from the sidewalk and throw them in the back of their car." He caught his breath. "It was a black SUV." The officer behind the counter tilted her head. "I tried to stop them, but I wasn't close enough. I'm sorry. I ran here as fast as I could. I didn't bring my phone with me."

"A kidnapping?" The black-haired woman raised an eyebrow and wrote the date and time on a notepad. "Where'd you see this?"

"I don't know." Marcus turned his body and put his hands in the air, counting how many blocks he ran. "I didn't look at the street names."

"Do you remember anything else?"

"Yes!" he shouted. "I saw them at a high school before it happened."

"A high school? What were you doing there?" The officer's tired eyes studied Marcus's sweaty body with confusion.

"I was on a run. It's not like that. Trust me."

"Okay, well, fill out this paperwork here." She slid over a clipboard. "And we'll have someone talk to you in a bit."

"No!" Marcus raised his voice and slammed his hand on the counter. "We need to do something right now. Do you realize what just happened?" Fear and hesitation covered his voice as he felt his arteries constricting.

The woman blankly smiled and tapped the clipboard on the counter again.

"Look, is Donnie in? I know he's the sheriff." Marcus prayed with his hands. "I had dinner at his house a few nights ago. I know him. Maybe he can help."

"He's in a meeting right now."

"Is there anyone else I can talk to? I need to tell someone about this right now."

"Everyone's in a meeting right now, sir." The officer shook her head and blew a big pink bubble gum bubble.

Marcus angrily shook. "I can wait."

"I'll let him know," she said, removing the clipboard from the counter. "You can wait over there. It should only be a few minutes."

As he stepped back, Marcus felt the police officer's bug eyes penetrating him. "Please," he mumbled with a final attempt. "We need to do something right now. We don't have time. It was a black SUV. Are there any street cameras in town?"

"Sir, I'm going to need you to lower your voice or step outside." The officer stood up and pointed her hand toward the entrance.

"It's a fuckin' kidnapping! Are you serious?" Marcus flailed his hands. "I'll be waiting outside for Donnie. Tell him it's urgent or whatever the fuck that means in this town."

"Please, sir." The officer sat back down and scooted her chair in. "I'll have them be with you as soon as they can."

Am I overreacting? I know what I saw. This is bullshit. Marcus furrowed his eyebrows and turned down the hallway. "Help me out, Donnie. What are you training your team to do?" he said, passing by a large portrait of him on the wall.

Outside the police station, Marcus leaned on a ledge near the steps and chewed his nails. *I know they would have done something if I was in San Francisco. They would have been better.* He knew each second that passed meant the girls would be more lost. After some time alone, the humidity wrapped around his cold, dry body, and he began to calm down. Twenty minutes later, Donnie stepped out into the sunlight with a man shadowing behind him.

"Marcus! What can I do for you? They told me you saw a kidnapping or something?" Donnie picked up his belt buckle and pointed to the man behind him. "And this is my colleague, York. He's a bright young fellow."

York reached his hand out to introduce himself.

"Nice to meet you." Marcus brushed his hair back. "Yes, I did. I tried explaining it to the officer inside, but they wanted me to fill out a bunch of paperwork." He began talking with his hands. "While I was on a run, I stopped to get water at a high school and saw these two girls walking in the distance." Donnie crossed his arms and turned to York. "And then when I was running down the street, away from the school, I saw two men in all black grab them and throw them into a black SUV." Marcus shook his hands together. "They were crying for help. I know what I saw!"

Donnie proceeded with caution. "Hold on now. Hold on. I know it's hot out there. You know how high school boys can be sometimes."

"No, no, no! It wasn't like that. You have to believe me. They were screaming for help, and then the car sped away." Marcus looked at York, taking notes on a clipboard.

"How far away from the high school was this?" said York.

"I don't know. I just moved here. I'm not too familiar with the city yet."

"And following high school students?" Donnie glared down at Marcus with authority. "I know it's hot out there, buddy. Why don't we get you home, and we'll look into this?" He crossed his arms again. "York, would you mind taking Marcus home and talking to him about anything else he can remember?"

Marcus shook his head in disbelief. "You have to believe me. Please," he begged.

"Look, Marcus." Donnie put his hand on his shoulder. "We haven't heard anything from the school or anybody's parents. Once we hear something, we can conduct an investigation. It's how things work in my town. I don't know how they do it back in California." He held up his hand in a shaka sign. "But we do it differently here. We have to use our limited time and resources wisely."

Marcus shrugged and watched York push up his glasses. "I don't fucking get it. Come on. Something just happened! Let's do something about it!"

Donnie's eyes lit up. "Marcus, Marcus, Marcus. Did you hear me?" He adjusted his shirt. "We don't have the *time* or *resources* to be the Hardy Boys... York, take him home and see if he can tell us anything else about these missing kids." Donnie looked down at Marcus again. "Do you know what the age of consent in Georgia is, Marcus? Would Aleeia like that you were following two minors?"

"That's not..." Marcus spun around. *Fucking prick. It's not like that.*

"Get him home, York. Maybe some water for you, too, Marcus. It's hot out there."

"Of course, sir," said York, guiding Marcus down the stairs.

"Please, listen to me," shouted Marcus again.

"We are." Donnie paused. "And now you're telling me how to do my job. I'll take it at face value, but I don't barge into your

work and tell you how to play music... Play for me, monkey!"
He raised his hands and laughed. "He's a goddamn Sherlock
Holmes, York! What's your hourly rate, kid?" Donnie patted
Marcus on the shoulders once more. "I promise, if anything
comes up, you'll be the first person I call. Get home and get
hydrated."

"So that's it? I just ran all the way here from the crime
scene to report it, and that's all we're going to do?"

"York." Donnie glared at Marcus again. "Give Marcus here
a ride. I know it's a long run back home for him. It'll be too hot
for this California boy."

"Yes, sir," said York.

Marcus looked at Donnie with despair.

"Right this way, Marcus." York gestured his hands down
the front steps again and watched Marcus aggressively shake
his head.

26

WEDNESDAY: VI

"What's your address, sir?" asked York, strapping his seatbelt and turning on the air conditioner.

"It's 8372 New Heaven Road." Marcus sighed. "It's off Highway 8."

York looked at him and smiled. "Got it."

"What do you think of this whole thing?" said Marcus, pushing his hands up to the cool air flowing out of the new Ford Charger police car.

"I mean." York pulled his neck skin. "I believe you. A lot of stuff happens under the radar here, but since it's such a small town, we can't do much most of the time."

Marcus agreed and looked out the window.

"Do you remember what these girls were wearing?" York cleared his throat as they approached a stoplight.

"Yes?" Marcus put his fingers on his temples. "They were wearing... One was wearing a white tank top with black shorts, and the other..." He started humming. "The other had a yellow T-shirt and white shoes." He opened his eyes and looked through the dashboard. "I think one of them had a blue back-pack. I was so far away, though."

"Okay, okay. That's a start. How old do you think they were?"

Marcus blew raspberries. "I don't know, man. They were at that high school, so I assume they were sixteen or seventeen. They both had blonde hair. I think."

"Do you know which high school it was near?"

"Fuck." Marcus sighed. "I don't know the name, but I could show you."

"There are only two high schools in town. Webster and Bankwood. Were you close to a skatepark?"

"Skatepark? I didn't even know this town had one."

"I bet it was Webster then. Was there a big field?"

"Yeah, and there were orange lockers and basketball hoops." Marcus looked out the window. "Can I show you?"

"That's Webster. Let's go see if you can remember anything else."

Marcus raised his fists. "Finally. I mean. I hope you don't take offense to that, but I thought Donnie would have done something more back there."

"You're telling me. I want to solve these cases, too... We hear about them all the time, but usually, the kids show up back home in a few days."

Marcus looked at York's big glasses and seventies mustache. "This happens all the time?"

"Not all the time," said York. "Maybe a few times a quarter. For the size of this town, I'd say it's a high number. Some-times it's kids, sometimes it's people visiting. It's hard to say. I haven't been able to figure out a pattern yet. I'm usually out of the office when it happens."

"Take this right!" shouted Marcus. "Right there! Down that

street! That's where I saw them." His booming voice startled York as he turned down the street.

"Just as I thought." York parked. "You see all these houses here?"

"Yeah?" Marcus looked around.

"Someone bought most of them a few years ago. I don't know what they're doing with it. Kids come here to party a lot since the houses are vacant. The real estate group that bought them is just waiting on their plans before they start building."

"Interesting... Well, this is where they were. I promise."

York pulled out a little notepad. "Okay, that's E Babylon and Third Street." He paused. "If any more details come back to you, don't hesitate to reach out. Let's exchange numbers when I drop you off."

"Good idea. Thanks for doing this."

York chuckled. "Sure thing. I could tell you wanted us to do something more. Donnie always seems to be under a lot of pressure."

"Why's he under so much pressure?"

"Well, if you can't tell. The city is going through gentrification, so he's spearheading the cleanup. You know? Meth labs. Cook houses. People getting drunk and starting fights. Homelessness. It's a long list."

"Sounds like a lot."

"It's just the start," said York, clicking on the radio and passing Marcus his phone. "Put your number in and send me a text. That way, I can let you know if I hear anything else. I know it'll give you peace of mind."

"Right." Marcus grabbed his phone. "Thanks for that, York. I appreciate you."

"Anytime, anytime."

27

WEDNESDAY: VII

A trembling, vibrating noise flew down the basement stairs. *That must be Izabelle.* Aleeia shoved the last news articles into two bags and ran up the stairs. She placed the trash by the door and grabbed her phone.

"Izabelle!"

"Hey, hon, I saw you rang. What's going on?"

"It's nothing..." Aleeia looked through the glass window in the piano room. "It's just some stuff I found in the house. I wanted to ask you about it before I told Marcus."

"What did you find?" Izabelle's high-pitched voice made Aleeia's shoulders jerk.

"I don't know... Lots of news articles. What did you say about that guy that used to live here? I think his name was Michael."

"Oh, no." Izabelle sighed. "It's Mikal. Was this in the basement?"

Basement? How does she know about that? "Yeah," Aleeia mumbled, "I got my shirt caught on the doorknob the other morning... We didn't know it was even there."

"No wonder Lindsay hasn't been able to sell the house. No one should have seen what he had down there... I'm so sorry. Can I come help you? I'll have to have a word with her."

Aleeia squinted her eyes. "It's fine. It's just weird... What's going on? Is there something I should know?" She gulped.

Izabelle grunted. "Mikal was charming... but a weirdo. He was a massive hoarder and liked to keep up with all the news around the town. He thought he was doing some justice for everyone." She paused. "He was just a drunk at the bar telling everyone he would save the day."

Save the day? With all that stuff? "So, he wasn't a creep? I thought you said he was a criminal or something?"

"He was all of the above. Please, let me help you."

Why is she making a big deal about this? "No, really, it's fine, Izabelle. I've already cleaned everything. I just want to tell someone, I guess... I'm going to turn it into a wine cellar for Marcus.... I just wanted to make sure it's nothing to worry about."

"Of course, you don't need to worry. You shouldn't have to deal with any of that... I know how stressful moving can be." Aleeia heard her voice go static. "Are you sure you don't want my help, hon? I'll still stop by and make sure everything's good."

Aleeia hummed. "Maybe another time," she said, thinking about her feelings after grocery shopping. "Marcus should be home any minute, and I don't want him to stress out." *But I also don't want him to see us alone.*

"Is that it? Is there anything else on your mind?" Izabelle laughed to lighten the mood.

"No, I mean." Aleeia sat on the piano bench, feeling her stomach flutter with butterflies. "I don't know." She tapped her forehead. "I gotta go. I'll talk to you later," she said, pushing her thighs together. "Marcus can help me when he's home. I just have to throw everything out... You don't need to stop by or anything."

"Alright. Well, you know you can tell me anything." Aleeia felt her smile through the phone. "And your special project sounds fun. Don't hesitate to reach out if you need any help. I love a good home renovation."

Aleeia heard a car pull into the driveway. "Hey, I think he just got home. I'll talk to you later," she mumbled, throwing her phone on the kitchen counter. *Why do I feel like this?* She dragged her hand to her warm chest.

"Huh?" Aleeia opened the front door and saw Marcus stepping out of the passenger seat of a cop car. Before she had a second to greet him or ask a question, a police officer popped out from the driver's side door.

"Hello, ma'am. My name is York." He tipped his hat. "I was giving your husband here a ride home. Seems he was trying to help us with a local crime in the neighborhood. You've got a true gentleman, ma'am."

"Thanks, York," said Marcus, looking up at Aleeia standing in the doorway. "I sent a text to myself, so I've got your number. I'll let you know if anything else comes to mind."

"You got it, sir... And I'll call you with any update." York nodded, then drove away.

"Marcus! What is going on? Where have you been?" She rushed down the front doorsteps and swung her arms around his shoulders.

"I can explain."

"Tell me everything," she said, looking up into his chest. "Are you okay?"

"I'm fine now." He kissed Aleeia's forehead as he walked them inside. "I'm still wrapping my head around it."

"What happened, Marcus!"

"Slow down..." He gulped. "Well, when I was on my run... I somehow saw these two girls get kidnapped. I think..."

"What!?" Aleeia stepped back and pushed Marcus from her side. "What? Start from the beginning. You saw what?"

"Right?" Marcus scratched his head as they walked through the doorway. "I was by this high school and stopped to get water because of how hot it was."

"Marcus! You can't just walk onto a school's campus." Aleeia raised her voice.

"I know, I made it quick. I don't think it's that big of a deal. I was just getting water." He shook his head. "But before I found a water fountain, I saw these two girls walking away from campus."

Aleeia pouted her face.

"And after I got water and started jogging away, I saw the same two girls a few blocks from campus screaming for help."

Aleeia pushed her hands into her chest.

"I was..." Marcus paused. "I'm not sure how far away from the school, but I know it was the same two girls. They were screaming for help while these guys in all black threw them in the back of a black SUV."

Aleeia held her breath.

"And because I didn't have my phone, I had to run to the police station for help."

"You need to bring your phone with you!" She smacked his hand. "Was Donnie there? What did he do?"

"Nothing." Marcus filled a cup with water and leaned against the sink. "He didn't do anything... York, that guy that dropped me off, was more helpful than Donnie."

"But everything's fine now?"

"I guess so. I'm not entirely sure. York said he'd call me with an update if he hears anything."

"Well, I'm glad you are okay." Aleeia squished her eyes with her fingers. "I was starting to worry about you."

"Were you?" Marcus grabbed Aleeia's hand and dragged it up to his cheek. "And how's your day been?"

She tilted her head from side to side. "I started cleaning out the wine cellar." *I can't tell him about the basement now. He's already so stressed.* "It's a work in progress. You're in charge of filling it with wine, mister." She smirked and turned around.

"Deal," mumbled Marcus as he playfully reached for Aleeia's butt as she walked away. "I can't wait to see it."

28

WEDNESDAY: VIII

Donnie calmly walked back into the police station and gestured to his officers as they passed him in the hallways. Before going to his office, he took his time in the breakroom and mingled with his counter partners. "This coffee is something else," he said, grabbing the hot pot and smiling. "You have yourself a day, Matilda!"

As he slid into his office, Donnie pressed his back against the closed door and sighed. "A black SUV!" he mumbled, stepping behind his desk and ripping open the bottom drawer to grab his flip phone. "Two men in all black!" He reached for a pencil on his desk and snapped it in half. "Goddammit! I can't fucking believe it. He's going to get all of me."

Donnie spun his chair around and anxiously tapped his foot, hearing the phone connect. "You had one fucking job! One job, and now I've got the new guy in town wondering what the fuck happened to those girls today." Donnie chugged his cup of coffee and smashed the paper cup in his hand. "Please, let me go ahead and save the fucking day... again!" He grunted. "You fuckin' moron!"

Anger was rushing through his bloodstream. "I don't care if you didn't see anyone—someone saw you!" Donnie paused. "I don't care what Wally says. I'll handle whatever he wants."

After rubbing his eyes awake and feeling his blood pressure drop, Donnie swirled behind his desk, flung open his cabinet, and pulled out a bottle of Glenlivet 12. He scooped up a cup from the bottom shelf and poured himself a heavy drink. "A black fuckin' SUV. Fuck you!"

29

THURSDAY

Marcus stood in their bathroom doorway. "Aleeia," he mumbled. "Are you up?" He saw her feet underneath their covers moving side to side, searching for his warm body. The gentle moan she made when she stretched in all directions made him smile.

"Yeah... Are you ready for your trip?" Aleeia pulled their duvet over her head.

"I'm excited!" Marcus crawled across the bed and touched her hip. "I can't wait to see Penny." He paused. "Are you going to be okay for a few days without me?"

"Mmm..." Aleeia muttered, half-asleep.

Marcus stared toward their bedroom patio and then walked into their closet, "It feels like it's been so long... I miss the ocean. The hills. The fog." He began placing an assortment of neatly folded pants, t-shirts, and sweaters into a carry-on bag. "How many pairs of shoes do you think I should bring?" The three rows of designer sneakers made him tilt his head.

"When do you leave?" Aleeia murmured, rearranging her eye mask and trying her best to doze off again.

"My flight's at 12:55pm." Marcus gently poked his head into their bedroom. Aleeia was hidden between their pillows and blankets. He felt her holding her breath, waiting for his question. "Could you drive me to the airport?" he asked.

"Marcus!" Aleeia scoffed. "Really? It's an hour-plus drive each way." Her tone made him anxious.

"Please?!" Marcus whispered, slowly pulling her eye mask to her forehead.

"I guess it's better than you taking the car for the weekend... Sure," she said quietly. "Now let me sleep a minute more."

Marcus shook his fist. "I love you," he sang, sitting by her side and waiting for her light brown eyes to stir his soul. "You're the best." As he watched Aleeia gradually un-cocoon herself, he used his fingernails to raise goosebumps on her arms. The hairs on her warm skin invited him to quote her favorite line from Sleeping Beauty. He knew any romantic idea from the film would awaken something inside her. As a kid, it was the only VHS her mom had in the house, and in some way, it became a part of her.

Aleeia barely opened her eyes, but the twinkle in her smile told Marcus to make a move.

"Sleeping Beauty, is that you?" His harmonious voice ignited a flame inside her.

"It is I," she said in an English accent. "I've been expecting you." She paused. "Only a kiss will break the curse." Hearing Marcus's heavy breathing above her face, she opened her eyes and wrapped her arms and legs around his body. For a slight second, she hung onto his lean shoulders and waited for him to lay her back down onto her pillow.

"My princess," Marcus mouthed, dragging a finger down her chapped lips. He held their mouths together like a true Prince Charming, awaiting their fairytale ending. "Aleeia..." Marcus said, moving his head beneath their covers and slowly pulling off her pajama bottoms. "I want a little of this before I go..."

"Mmm," Aleeia moaned.

"I think this is better than coffee, right?" Marcus spread Aleeia's legs apart and ran his tongue in circles. "Faster or slower?" he asked, letting saliva fall from his mouth like warm honey onto her vagina.

"Slower." Aleeia twisted her hips.

"I can do that." Marcus pulled their covers back again and watched Aleeia's toes curl out the side of his eye. Each time he ran his tongue up and down her wet lips, it reminded him of the first time he tried ice cream. He embraced all the exotic and sweet tastes she harnessed into her own magical sugar.

"Keep going," Aleeia said, clutching the sheets.

Marcus grinned, feeling her pulsating as he deeply penetrated and edged her with his fingers. "Wait for me," he grunted, shoving his pants off.

Without another word, Aleeia gripped his shaft and kissed him with the universe's thirst for love. As their saliva wrapped around each other, she swung herself on top of his hard cock and sunk down, enjoying every inch he had to offer. "Marcus," she cried, with her feet planted on their bed and her squatted body bouncing up and down on his thighs. "I'm going to come."

Marcus grabbed her butt and jacked his hips up, deepening his penetration. "I want you to come." He quickly flipped Aleeia onto her stomach. "Like this," he said, positioning her butt in the air. "Just like that."

"Oh, Marcus... Right there!" Aleeia panted, feeling his hips slamming against her. "Don't stop!"

Sweat beat down Marcus's chest as he came inside her with one final thrust.

Almost immediately after finishing, his phone rang.

"Don't get it." Aleeia turned onto her back as Marcus looked to see who had called.

"It's Penny," he said, catching his breath.

"Of course it is. Call him back and lay with me."

Marcus put his phone down and rolled into Aleeia's chest, holding her like it was their final hour on Earth.

"You make me crazy. I don't know what I'd do without you," she said, stroking his hair.

"You are my crazy." Marcus reached for her hand. "This trip is just for the weekend." He lifted her wrist to his mouth and gently pressed it against his lips. "And, if you need me to, I can come back, or you can fly out."

Aleeia closed her eyes. "Just hold me."

After a long, silent minute, Marcus pulled himself up and stretched into a cat's pose. "Shower?"

With both her hands resting above her head, Aleeia stared at Marcus tiptoeing backward. "Give me a second. I'll be right there," she said, smiling as he disappeared into the bathroom.

Aleeia tossed their duvet around her body and buried herself into their king-size bed again. *Am I going through with tomorrow? My heart wants something more. I know it. An adventure. The touch of a woman.* As she poked her head out and checked her phone, she heard Marcus singing in the shower. *How am I going to do this again?*

`Let me know if you need help with your little`
`project today. xoxo`

She's driving me crazy. Enough is enough. "Marcus!" Aleeia shouted, ripping the bedsheets from her body. "Don't get out. I'll be right there!"

30

THURSDAY: II

Marcus swung his suitcase into the trunk. *It'll be nice to be away... To be back home and reset.* Although his insecurities about Aleeia were gradually fizzling out, the deep trauma he felt from her past mistakes still haunted him in many ways. Family was his number one priority, but in his gut, he sensed Aleeia falling into another lust-driven escapade. He needed more reassurance.

"Aleeia!" he shouted, staring at the dashboard clock. "Baby, c'mon!" His eyes moved from side to side as he calculated the time to go to the airport. *Why does she always take forever? I can't be late. I don't know about traffic here.* "Let's go!" he barked before honking the horn.

"You have plenty of time." Aleeia's big smirk from their front porch made him roll his eyes. "Besides, if you miss your flight, you'll have to stay with me for the weekend." She stepped toward the car in a baby blue knitted sweater and black sunglasses. "I thought I was driving," she said, sipping a pre-made juice she grabbed from the kitchen.

Marcus quickly put the car in drive. "Don't worry about it."

"Everything okay?"

"I'm fine. I just don't know how long it'll take us to get there." He chuckled to lighten the mood. "What if there's traffic?"

"Marcus, we live in the middle of nowhere. I doubt you'll see another car until we get onto the highway."

"Right." He reached for her hand. "I'm going to miss you. Thanks for this."

"I'll miss you too," Aleeia said, sticking her knees together. "It'll be good for you to see Penny. Don't worry about me. I have plenty to do while you're gone."

Marcus watched her pick at her nails. "You okay? You seem nervous or something."

"It's just this drive, Marcus." She sounded irritated.

With pleading hands, Marcus scoffed. "You could have said no." He reached for the radio and switched on some music to break the silence. "You know I appreciate you doing this," he said, watching her leg move up and down. "You sure you're alright... You know you can tell me anything."

Aleeia rested her head against the window. "I know." She put her hands in her lap and looked over at him. "You know how I get when you leave... worked up. I'm just in my head."

"Is it that? I feel like it's something else. I know this move came with the promise of a family, but the more we've stepped forward in this new life together, the more I feel like that's not what you want."

Aleeia didn't respond.

"And... I don't know. Just the way your energy shifted after meeting Izabelle. Is anything going to happen?" He cleared his throat. "I know you, Aleeia. I'd rather you tell me you want to do something with her than find out the hard way. I mean, either way, it sucks. I'm just trying to tell you what's on my mind. Therapy has been helping."

"What? Why would you think that?" Aleeia stuck her finger at him. "I'm just having dinner with her. Nothing's happening between us, Marcus!"

"I can't just ask a question? Calm down. I told myself I'd be more blunt about it. I mean, you've done something like it before. I just have this gut feeling."

"Fine." Aleeia's tone deepened. "I mean, sure... I think she's attractive... It's not like that. I'm sorry. I mean, if... it's like..." She pressed her fingers to her nose. "I guess I should tell you the real reason I was crying at their house. It wasn't my mom."

Marcus lightly tapped his forehead with his knuckles. "Aleeia, I swear to God!"

"I'm sorry. We didn't do anything. I swear. It was just the feeling. You know my feelings about women will always be a part of me."

"But you didn't do anything? This isn't what your dinner is about, right?"

"No, no. We're literally just cooking."

Marcus looked over at his phone for directions. "I hope you're telling me the truth. I want a family with you, Aleeia. I want it all, but I can't do this back and forth. Please don't do this to me again." He felt Aleeia touch his arm.

"It's nothing more than dinner... I promise. I want a family with you, too, Marcus." Her nails grazed his cheekbones as she brushed his hair behind his ear. "I'm sorry, my head's just been all over the place. Can we talk about this when you get back? I don't want this to stress you more than it has."

"We're well beyond that, Aleeia." He gently moved her hand off his shoulder. "Just promise me you won't do anything I wouldn't do." The way he searched her eyes for an answer left him nervous. "I love you," he said, touching her cold hand to his lips.

"I love you, too."

As they continued their drive, Marcus accepted there was something about Aleeia and their relationship that couldn't be tamed. The ever-changing scenery became a pool of toxic secrecy.

"Besides dinner, do you have any other plans for the weekend?" asked Marcus, pulling off to the airport exit.

"Just dinner and working on the wine cellar. I think you'll like it... I'm starting to get a vision for it."

"I can't wait to see it," Marcus said, gulping. *Was the wine cellar promise a distraction... So I wouldn't think about what happened at dinner?* "Did you get a good start on it yesterday?"

"I guess...." Aleeia cleared her throat. "But if we're not keeping anything from each other, I did find more weird news articles when I was cleaning. It was all about some local people that went missing."

Marcus stomped on the breaks. "What? Why didn't you tell me? Aleeia! Why are you just saying this now?"

"I don't know. A lot was happening when you got home yesterday. I didn't want to add to the fire." She pursed her lips. "I know you're stressed about the move, Penny's mom, and I guess, me." Marcus saw her chest move up and down. "I talked to Izabelle about it because she's also my *friend*, and she said it's nothing to worry about."

"So, you felt more comfortable sharing it with a woman you've met twice than with me?" Marcus bit his index finger to keep his mouth shut. "Look... I'm just going to try to get through the weekend, Aleeia. Then we can talk more when I get back, okay? But if something is worrying you about the house, I want you to feel like you can talk to me about it."

"I know. That's my fault. It's bad communication. It's nice to talk to someone else sometimes." Aleeia squinted her eyebrows. "None of this is malicious, Marcus. You're my person. Some things are just better left unsaid."

"Right," he said, pulling up to departures. "I'm uneasy about leaving you here." His voice cracked. "If anything doesn't feel right, I'm coming home."

"Whatever you want to do." Aleeia's eyes started to water. "I'll make this right. I promise. No more secrets. I swear."

"Alright." Marcus tried swallowing through his choked-up throat. "I believe you."

Aleeia followed him outside the car and hugged him good-bye. "Keep me updated," she said, burying her face into his shoulder.

"Always." He picked up his suitcase and walked away. "Love you."

"Send pictures and give Penny a..." she yelled, watching him fade into a crowd of strangers.

The airport doors felt like a window of lost hope and a place of desperate love.

"This is all fucked," she whispered under her breath.

31

THURSDAY: III

The smell of fresh leather gloves and bubblegum filled the air as the driver clicked a remote control box attached to the car's visor mirror. "When we get there," he mumbled, pointing to the house across the yard. "Grab them and bring them inside." He squeezed his knuckle to his chin. "And don't let them say a fuckin' word. We don't need anyone hearing us. Got it? In and out."

"Yes, boss," said the co-pilot, looking back and signing with his hands at a man in the backseat with two hostages.

"Where are we?" cried a girl, hearing them accelerate down a gravel driveway.

"Get them under control," said the driver. "We've already had them for a day... They shouldn't even be awake right now. Give them more! I want them out cold until the auction."

Waving to the man in the backseat again, the bodyguard in the front seat reached into the glove box and opened a tiny black briefcase with a dozen syringes. He passed two backward. "Boss, are you sure?" The car came to a halt. "It will be better if they can walk, right?" he said in an Eastern European accent.

"Did your mother drop you when you were a kid?" The group leader grabbed him by his shirt collar and growled in his face. "Do what I say. Got it?" He flung open the car door. "And make sure they don't see anything. Keep the pillowcases on them until we get down there."

The two men shrugged and thoughtlessly stuck a needle into each of the girl's arms.

"Sleepy time," the man in the back muttered in an off-pitched voice.

After waiting a few minutes, the two men grabbed the captives from their seats and swung them on the back of their shoulders.

"Let's go!" shouted the leader by the front door. "Hurry! And be careful." His eyes quickly scanned the entrance gate before he gave the door a three-sequenced knock.

"Derek! What the fuck are you doing?!" Izabelle's eyes lit up. "You can't come in this way with them!" She huffed and tightened the strings on her red kimono. "You're fuckin' up left and right these days."

"I know! I know!" he said, pushing his way inside and directing the two men to the hallway. "But we can't hold them at The Lodge anymore. Colleen couldn't do it."

"Donnie's not going to like this."

"But *Donnie's* not going to find out." Derek tapped Izabelle's head.

"You can be so dumb sometimes, hon."

"Don't worry. Everything's fine. I changed the car." Derek pointed to the white SUV in the driveway. "See, white, not black."

As the two bodyguards passed by Izabelle and waited in

the hallway, they started conversing in a mixture of ASL and Ukrainian. "Hey! I can understand you!" shouted Izabelle, motioning her hands at them and tightening her kimono again. The two quickly stopped smiling. "Derek, I don't like this." She turned her around and walked back into her painting room. "You can't just show up with them on my doorsteps, especially in the middle of the day... You know better!"

"Whatever. I'll handle Donnie. The Lodge was busy. There were *way* too many people coming in and out for us to hide there. But trust me... these two are going to be worth it. They're perfect." Derek rubbed his hands together. "And what about your situation? I haven't heard anything about that." He hostilely jabbed her arm.

"As a matter of fact, we're having dinner here tomorrow night. How about that for discretion?"

Derek's jaw dropped. "Well, good for you. Hopefully, she sells. She's older, you know! Who's going to want that?"

"Someone will... Someone always does... She's timeless."

"Well, now you can see how stressful my side of the job is..." Derek yelled, rushing down the hallway. "Fuckin' bitch." He felt a glare from his men as he jabbed the elevator button. "What're you looking at?!" A knot pierced his chest. "Nikola... Next floor!"

"Yes, boss," said his right-hand man, poking the tiny button with his puffy finger.

"Finally." Derek admired his reflection in the glass ceiling. The silence of the room gave him a moment to breathe. "Let's make this quick," he shouted, feeling the hydrologic of the elevator sinking to the next floor. He looked at Nikola, "I'm going to grab it, and then we'll be all set," he said, lunging for Donnie's desk.

"Where are you? Where are you?" Derek mumbled,

cautiously opening each drawer. "There you are... We've got it...." The platinum-colored key card he pulled from the bottom drawer put a twinkle in his eye. As he ran back into the elevator, Derek shoved the key card into his pocket. "Коли ми спустимося, посадіть їх у візки.[1]"

Nikola and the other bodyguard nodded.

"Remember, don't tell anyone," said Derek, clicking the button to the next floor.

As the shiny metal doors gracefully opened to a bright, translucent space the size of a basketball court, the group stepped forward with the girls over their shoulders. Dozens of golf carts were spread across the dirt-covered concrete floors, and a dimly lit tunnel was on the opposite side of the room.

Immediately, Derek snapped his fingers and gave more instructions. "Ключі вже в замку запалювання. Заберіть їх. Я маю подзвонити.[2]"

Nikola quickly directed his counter-partner.

As Derek watched his workers begin their night, he crossed another step off his to-do list. "Nikola!" he said, knocking his chest with his fist. "Ready?"

With a stone-cold face, Nikola gave a thumbs up and adjusted his golf cart mirror to see Derek in the background. "We ready." He looked at his twin and said, "Вікно.[3]"

The other man adjusted their front windshield protector.

"енергія![4]" ordered Nikola, looking down at the cart's electric battery meter. "Пасок безпеки.[5]" The air-tight sounds of a seat belt fastening wished through the air.

---

1. When we get down there, put them in the carts.
2. The keys are in the ignition already. Take them away. I have to make a call.
3. Window.
4. Power!
5. Seatbelt.

Nikola grinned and began revving the engine.

With another reassuring wave, the two drove toward the tunnel and disappeared.

Eventually, their engines faded into the silent noise of their underground kingdom.

"Fuck, now, Donnie." The rapid heartbeat inside Derek's chest was bulging out. He felt his story changing and vanishing from his thoughts quicker than he could think. "Why am I always the one to take the risk?!" he shouted, raising his voice. "And all because of this stupid deal. Business partners, my ass. I could run this ten times better than Donnie or my uncle. We need to be in New York again. We will be in New York." He stomped the ground and pulled out his phone.

"Colleen!" he said with relief. "I need your advice."

"Don't say another word," she said calmly.

"Well, what was I supposed to do? I did it for you. You said we couldn't keep them there anymore." He rolled his eyes and punched the elevator wall. "That meeting point isn't like their house. This is a fuckin' fortress!" He swung his other arm in disbelief. "Izabelle said what? Oh... she's going to have a piece of my mind." He clicked the elevator button." I am calm! I am calm! Bye... I don't care. Why would you tell her?" he rambled. "I had it under control! Bye!"

When the elevator door opened to the main room floor, Derek rushed toward Izabelle's painting room but was confronted by a figure much bigger and stronger than him. "Donnie?" He sheepishly smiled.

"You fuckin' moron!" Donnie's eyes told Derek more than he could comprehend.

"Wait, I can explai–" he squealed before feeling a powerful left hook to the face and a jab to the kidney. He wobbled down and winced in distress.

"Where are your keys?"

"Poc...ket..." he mumbled in pain.

Donnie searched his pants until he found his car keys and the platinum-colored key card.

"Really? The key card? You're done."

Donnie grabbed Derek's hair and slammed his face into the tile floor.

32

THURSDAY: IV

What a day... How long was I down there? Aleeia walked up the basement stairs with her hands full of used cleaning supplies. After arriving home later that afternoon, she needed her project to distract her from her wandering thoughts. *I'm glad that part's done... It gets dark here so fast.* The ticking sound of the kitchen clock made the house's silence feel extra eerie.

Reaching for her phone on the counter, Aleeia huffed, seeing no messages from Marcus and, to her surprise, neither from Izabelle. *Does no one love me anymore?* Her mind and heart were at a crossroads. *He wants kids. Am I ready? Was that my promise?*

As she went to lay on the couch, she imagined tiny, gentle footsteps running around the house while Marcus played the piano in the background. A tear slowly rolled down her dry cheek when she heard a knock at the door. *What was that?* Aleeia perked up and looked around the room. *Who's here? Is there a delivery tonight?* She sat with her hands wrapped around her knees, listening to the deep alto sound vibrating from their oak front door. After another knock, she ran to the hallway and hid behind the dated geometric wallpaper. Her chest raced as she peeked out to get a better view. The distance between her squinting eyes and the door seemed like a mile away.

"Aleeia! Are you home? It's Izabelle and Lindsay!"

The pitch of Izabelle's voice reverberated across the cold floor and sent a chill through Aleeia's spine. A blank space fractured her thoughts as she felt her knees buckle. "One minute," she shouted, rushing to the nearest bathroom to look at her appearance. As she quickly splashed water on her face, washing away her tears, she looked at herself in the mirror. *A promise is a promise, Aleeia. Think about him.* "I'll be right there," she said, walking down the hallway and smoothing ChapStick over her lips.

"What a surprise!" A dry lump caught the back part of Aleeia's throat.

"Sorry to bother you!" Izabelle's pearl-white teeth reflected a new light on Aleeia's face. "We were in the area and..." Izabelle touched Lindsay's shoulder. "I told Lindsay about the little mess you found in the basement. We figured we could help you clean it, hon."

Aleeia felt her face twitch. "Oh, you're too nice. I just finished cleaning it. I think the solutions did something to my eyes." She looked away. "Come in," she said, waving them through the door. *That smell.* Izabelle's scent intoxicated Aleeia as she walked by.

"You should have called me!" Lindsay grazed Aleeia's arm as her eyes drifted into the house. "Well, isn't this lovely? Who helped you style it? I have a guess!"

Aleeia clenched her jaw. "It's mostly stuff we shipped from home. We still have a lot on the way."

"Well, you should have seen this place before." Lindsay

scoffed. "Izabelle was telling me about your project. It's nice to see someone with some home improvement skills. No one in these parts has a clue about anything other than..."

"Where's Marcus?" interjected Izabelle.

Aleeia watched them walk down the hallway and move into the area between the kitchen and the piano room. "Marcus is visiting his friend back home."

Izabelle flipped her head around. "So, you're home all alone?"

An off-beat note rang from the piano. "Do you play?" asked Lindsay.

Aleeia gathered her thoughts, appreciating the distraction from Izabelle's question. "Marcus does. Remember? He's a musician." She walked over and closed the piano lid. "He's very particular about it," she said, watching the black mahogany lid cover the ivory keys. Izabelle's heavy stare pierced her backside. "Did you all want something to drink?"

"A brilliant idea." Lindsay spun around and pressed her hands against the window overlooking the backyard.

Aleeia uncomfortably glanced at her. "I think I have some wine."

"Perfect!" shouted Lindsay. "I just love this view."

As Aleeia moved behind the kitchen island and bent down to their wine rack, she felt Izabelle's nails along her lower back.

"Can I help you with anything?" she whispered.

Aleeia smirked and said, "Just keep her away from the piano." She playfully poked Izabelle on the chest. "Marcus would freak out if anything happened."

"That makes two of us." Izabelle winked.

"This should be perfect," shouted Aleeia, brushing Izabelle's hand from her waist. She flicked her eyes to the piano room and began opening the bottle on the counter.

"I love that sound! It's been so long since I did anything.

Thanks for having us, Aleeia." Lindsay made herself comfortable on a bar stool at the counter and waited for her glass. "What's your plan for the backyard, anyway? It would be perfect for a pool, I'm just saying! I know some great contractors if you ever need anyone."

Aleeia curved her smile and poured three glasses of wine. *Lindsay seems different.* "Cheers!" Izabelle raised her glass to the center.

"To new friends!" chimed Lindsay.

An awkward smile barely met Aleeia's eyes as she studied the women.

"Now, this is delicious! What kind of wine is it?" Lindsay swirled her glass around.

"It's..." Aleeia vacantly stared at Lindsay and passed her the bottle of wine. "It's this. I got it at the store the other day. It's nothing too special."

"Well, it beats my taste." Lindsay laughed, then chugged the rest of her drink. "Could I have a little more?"

"Sure." Aleeia raised her eyebrows at Izabelle and poured more wine.

"So, how about we see this little project of yours?" said Izabelle. "I want to see your vision!" She spread her hands across the room. "You have quite the interior taste. I can only imagine what ideas you have."

Their impromptu visit left Aleeia's brain in a daze. "Right. I haven't gotten very far other than cleaning it." She stood on her tippy toes and pushed her hips into the counter.

"I'm sure it's perfect." Izabelle took a sip and paused, waiting for Aleeia's lead.

When they arrived at the basement door, Aleeia looked down and laughed. "It's funny because I've gotten my shirt stuck on this little doorknob a few times now—that's actually how I found it."

"Hopefully, it didn't rip your shirt off!" Izabelle teased.

Shyly smiling, Aleeia nudged Izabelle on the shoulder and turned on her phone light to guide them down the stairs.

"You know, a lot of these homes were a part of the city's underground system plan. My family..." said Lindsay, watching them from the top step.

"Lindsay!" interrupted Izabelle. "That's enough history for today." She hesitantly chuckled.

"And this is it." Aleeia stepped to the bottom step and looked back. "Lindsay, what did you say?"

"Don't worry about it, hon. The wine makes her chatty." Izabelle grazed her hands against Aleeia's back as she turned on the light switch.

"Aren't you a little touchy today," whispered Aleeia in a flirtatious tone.

Izabelle put her finger over her mouth and walked past her.

"So, I've pretty much got everything out except for this desk." Aleeia felt her flushed face with the back of her knuckle. "And those articles," she pointed, "They were about missing people and..." She watched Izabelle motion her over.

"Oh, I can't go down there. Who knows what's happened in this house," muttered Lindsay. "I'm going to grab more wine, ladies."

"Whatever you need," shouted Aleeia, feeling Izabelle's hands wrap around her body in the dim light. The vanilla and orange scent from her hands sent shivers between her thighs. "We can't," she mumbled with half of Izabelle's lips in her mouth. "I can't."

"Don't be silly." Izabelle kissed her neck and tugged her hair back. "We're just having fun. It's just me and you."

Aleeia gently pushed her away. "Tomorrow."

Izabelle dragged her hand down Aleeia's chin. "Whatever you say, hon. You're all mine then." She stuck her finger to Aleeia's mouth and shouted, "Lindsay, easy on the wine. We should get going."

A loud thumping noise came from the top step. "Already?" Lindsay cried.

"I mean, I could use some help with this desk." Aleeia squinted her face. "It would be super helpful. That way, I can start making it Marcus's dream wine cellar."

Izabelle growled. "Where did you come from? Tomorrow can't come any sooner, can it?"

Aleeia bit her nail.

"Lindsay!" shouted Izabelle. "We need to get this out of here. It's Wally's old desk."

"Wally?" Aleeia chewed her cheek. "I thought his name was Mikal or something."

Izabelle froze. "Yes. He goes by Wally sometimes." She went to one side of the desk and said, "He had a lot of nicknames. Everyone kind of knew him."

"There's no way I'm coming down there," Lindsay said. "Especially in these heels."

"When did he live here?" Aleeia went to the other side of the desk.

"I'm not sure." Izabelle lifted one side of the desk and guided them up the stairs.

"Who?" slurred Lindsay.

"Mikal," replied Aleeia, looking up at her in the doorway.

"Oh, for heaven's sake. He was horrid. A true bandit."

"What?" Aleeia momentarily lost her grip on the desk.

"That's enough, Lindsay." Izabelle held her breath. "Can you help us? Or are you going to control your liquor?"

Lindsay nodded and casually waved them upstairs with a mouthful of wine.

33

THURSDAY: V

"Do I have two hundred and ninety thousand?" said a voice over an intercom system.

"Two hundred and ninety thousand? Once... twice..."

"Three hundred thousand. Three hundred thousand... Do I have any more takers?"

"Three hundred and twenty thousand. Wow! Do we have the best flavors at The Creamery, or what? It's an ice cream party tonight!"

"Three hundred and–"

A patron's suite light lit up.

"Three hundred and fifty thousand. Once... twice... and sold to suite A3. Please claim your prize at The Lodge meeting point."

A young boy in the middle of a platform stage followed

shining lights, guiding him to a tunnel at the other end of the room.

"Next up... we have a two-for-one special... and the flavors... two girls, blonde, sweet, athletic in build, and ready to mingle! Who doesn't love some vanilla with extra sprinkles!?"

"Bidding will start at five hundred thousand, and we're taking bids in increments of fifty thousand. Let's begin!"

Another suite light went off on the far right side of the stage.

"A3 with an early bid. Do I have five hundred thousand and fifty?"

"Six hundred thousand. I see you, A2."

"Wow! A6, seven hundred and fifty thousand."

"Seven hundred and... A3! Wow! A3... You shock us again... Nine hundred thousand..."

"Will anyone beat that? Going once... going twice... sold to suite A3. Please claim your prizes at The Lodge."

The two girls, looking like zombies and dressed in black leggings and vest tops, walked toward a man at the end of the platform, who waved them inside a glowing door.

34

THURSDAY: VI

"So, what did he do?" Aleeia rearranged her grip and started pushing the desk up the stairs.

"Lindsay, we could use your help." Izabelle's voice sounded irritated.

"What didn't he do is the better question." Lindsay's cackle from the top step ran shivers up Aleeia's neck. "I do love this wine, Aleeia. Where did you say you got it?"

"We're almost there," grunted Izabelle, pulling the desk through the doorway. "C'mon!"

Aleeia held her breath. "I feel like I should know something more, right?"

"Hon, I'm telling you. He was the town drunk. Crazy with the girls and a little crazy himself."

Aleeia watched Izabelle roll her head to the side.

"Mikal and... were a thing at some point," Izabelle whispered, quietly shaking her hand under her neck. "I think they hooked up once or something... but it stuck with *her*. She was super young."

Aleeia gulped. "That makes sense... So, all the news articles were..."

"Just him being crazy!" Izabelle grunted. "Watch your step!"

"Fuck!" shouted Aleeia, redirecting her attention to her feet.

"You know you can trust me."

As Izabelle lifted the desk through the doorway, Aleeia noticed Izabelle's eyes fall to the tiny sweat marks on her chest. "I hope I get to see more of that," said Izabelle.

"Just you wait," mumbled Aleeia, taking a sigh of relief. "I can't believe we did it!" Her tiny hand melted into Izabelle's as she reached up to give her a high-five.

"Let's get this into my car so you can enjoy your evening alone. I know we barged in on you."

"Maybe another glass?" suggested Aleeia, feeling Izabelle rushing to leave.

"That sounds wonderful. I'd love another," added Lindsay. "I'll check to see if there's anything else downstairs."

"Whatever you say, hon. Just watch your step." Izabelle rolled her eyes at Aleeia. "I don't know how she survives."

"Everyone's got their ways," said Aleeia, stepping through the front door. "What's that sound."

"The cicadas?" Izabelle guffawed. "They're beautiful until they aren't."

"Everything looks good downstairs," Lindsay yelled from the porch. "Are we ready for that drink?"

Izabelle waved to Lindsay, "You're too sweet! Thanks for all your help, hon," then nudged Aleeia on their way back inside. "I think we can all use another now."

"Agreed. I have no idea how I would have gotten that out on my own."

"I guess you owe me now," Izabelle smirked.

"I guess so." Aleeia felt her face warm.

"How about that wine!" Lindsay gargled.

"I think just a tiny bit more..." Izabelle pushed Lindsay inside, sat her on a bar stool, and went to grab her a glass of water.

"I'm going to open this," Aleeia said, looking at a bottle of Syrah. "It's one of our favorites."

"Sounds yummy." Lindsay sat with her knuckles pressed to her cheeks.

"Here," said Izabelle, sliding a glass of water before her. "Drink this."

"I don't need that!" Lindsay hysterically laughed and fell back in her chair.

"Whatever you say, Linds." Izabelle signaled Aleeia to cut her off. "So, how long is Marcus gone?"

"Just for the weekend." Aleeia pushed her body over the counter again and wet her mouth with some wine. "He needed to get back. His best friend's mom was diagnosed with cancer. It's pretty far along."

"Oh my gosh. Poor thing."

"Yeah." Aleeia paused, feeling the warm wine cuddle her stomach. "Plus, I know the move has been a lot. I think we both need..." A vantage view of her and Izabelle kissing in the basement replayed in her head. "Both need to know that everything doesn't happen overnight. Patience with life, I guess."

"Amen to that." Izabelle raised her glass.

Quickly changing the subject, Aleeia muttered, "Did you hear about what happened yesterday? Marcus got dropped off by a policeman... He said he saw a kidnapping or something... Did Donnie say anything?" She grabbed the cork and squeezed it in her hand.

"A kidnapping?" Lindsay rolled her hand back. "Wouldn't be anything that we haven't seen before."

Aleeia's eyes narrowed. "What? Haven't seen? What do you mean?"

"This town," said Lindsay. "This house. Mikal was..."

"That's enough." Izabelle put her glass down and moved behind Lindsay. "I should get her home. I think she's had a bit too much," she said, pulling Lindsay's arm until she stood up.

Aleeia's shoulders jumped when Lindsay drunkenly banged the counter. "No. What does she mean?" The mood in the house shifted. "You said it was because of a thing they had earlier. I'm confused."

"It's the wine. She's talking out of her ass now." Izabelle aggressively pulled Lindsay up again. "It's been nice, but I should get her home."

"Mikal..." Lindsay blew raspberries. "My sweet boy," she said, stumbling through the hallway.

"See? She's all over the place."

"This feels weird. What is she saying!" Aleeia grabbed Izabelle's arm. "Mikal used to live here. I need to know."

"Like I told you, he just got into a lot of trouble... Him and Lindsay had something... She was young. End of story." Izabelle watched Lindsay clumsily open the car door. "It's nothing to worry about. He's history. These small towns..." She leaned in to hug Aleeia. "Something's never change," she said, pointing to Lindsay. "Just like the people... I'll see you tomorrow night, ya?"

"Yeah." Aleeia pinched her lips, contemplating Lindsay's words. "So, there's nothing I need to worry about?"

"I promise." Izabelle paused. "There's nothing to worry about. You can trust me."

Aleeia looked at the moon's reflection, covering half of Izabelle's face. "Okay," she said with a sigh. "I'll see you tomorrow then."

"Can you wait one more night?!" Izabelle leaned in for a cheek kiss and walked down the porch steps.

Aleeia didn't respond. She thought about where the last few hours went and why she felt more at peace with a woman she barely knew than with someone she promised a lifetime together. After cleaning the kitchen and double-checking every lock and door in the house, Aleeia went upstairs to get ready for bed. The same loneliness she felt when she arrived home trickled into her every pore and dragged a heavy blanket over her chest. In bed, she imagined a full evening alone with Izabelle. *Tomorrow.* Something inside her ignited a deep flame. She reached for her nightstand light and saw her phone with multiple messages.

7:25pm — Hi! Just landed.

8:37pm — Going to Penny's mom's house. I'll tell her you said Hi. What are you doing tonight?

She turned over. Seeing Marcus's name made her happy, but nothing like the adrenaline she got from Izabelle.

Hey! Izabelle and Lindsay stopped by for a few glasses. We moved the desk out of the basement. I miss you, Marcus, and I'm sorry about earlier… I want you to enjoy your time with Penny and his mom, so let's talk tomorrow. Love you! Xx

35

THURSDAY: VII

"I'm taking off." York lightly knocked on Donnie's office door.

"Alrighty. Have a good weekend," mumbled Donnie, hiding his face behind a manila folder.

"Thanks. You too." York waited outside the doorway for their usual dialogue about each other's weekend plans. "Should I lock up?" he asked after a long pause.

"Yeah, if you could," Donnie muttered.

"Okay, sir. I'll see you on Monday then." York waved goodbye and headed out the door to the parking lot. "Just me and you!" he shouted, smiling at his mustard-yellow Mercedes Benz W123. Donnie's short responses left his stomach unsettled, but he tried remembering everything he had on his plate. York threw his belongings into the trunk. "This should set the mood!" he hooted, reaching into his cassette box and grabbing 'The Original Recordings of Charlie Parker 1988.' Immediately, he ran to the driver seat and popped the old, worn cartridge into the car's player. York's worries disappeared within a millisecond of hearing the upbeat saxophone and flirty keys. A glance at the gas meter made him shake his head in satisfaction. "Where are you, Mr. Water Bottle?" he sang, his eyes scanning the car's interior. Eventually, he cut the engine and rushed back inside to find his metal canteen.

Donnie threw a stack of papers across his desk, listening to York's footsteps fading away. After waiting a brief moment, he got up to close the door. "York?" he said, waiting for a response. He shook his head in agreement. As he sat back down at his desk, he pulled out a flip phone from the inside pocket of his undershirt and waited for it to turn on.

"Nope. No report yet. Only the one from the guy that showed up here," heard York, walking past Donnie's office. "I had someone look into it. Don't worry." Interested in the conversation, York crouched down and put his head closer to the door.

"How much?" A loud thumping sound came from the desk. "You're kidding. We already sold the girls? Wally, I don't believe it! We're rich."

Donnie's belly laugh made the tiny wrinkles on York's forehead cave.

"No, no. The kid doesn't have a clue. He's going out of town this weekend to visit family. I planned it that way. Just like always." York recalled the last time he requested time off. "This is too easy, Wally. No one assumes a thing. I am the law!"

"Wally?" said York under his breath, feeling the hair on his neck stand. "Is he talking about me? Who sold?"

"Yep, yep, yep. Izabelle's got the big one tomorrow night, or so we hope. You should have seen her at dinner, Wally. She was smoking! You'll see her before the auction. I promise." York's shoulders shuddered with Donnie's footsteps pacing around the room. "And send the same ice cream party email thread to our group. Tell them we have new **GELATO** flavors. All ages. Crème de la crème."

Donnie's voice was getting closer and louder. "I shouldn't be here," York thought.

"And the password for the night will be **GELATO—435286**. If they want a specific 'flavor,' have them call The Lodge. Colleen knows what to do." York covered his mouth. "Yeah, I trust her. I'll see you soon." Donnie's sporadic movements rang underneath the door and spooked York, causing him to drop his glasses. A cluttering noise rippled on the wooden floor.

"York?!" hollered Donnie, stopping his celebration. "York, is that you?"

Instantly, York hurried across the room and hid behind his desk.

"Matilda?" shouted Donnie.

York poked his head over his cubicle and saw Donnie looking around the room.

"York? Are you here?" Donnie's knuckle crack echoed through the office.

"I'm still here," croaked York, standing by his desk with a guilty feeling stabbing his gut. "I forgot my water bottle."

"What the hell." Donnie slapped his leg. "You scared me!"

"Sorry. I just ran back inside. I hope I didn't interrupt anything." York gulped and met Donnie in the middle of the hallway. "I'll see you, sir," he said, feeling lightheaded.

"You okay, York? You look like you saw a ghost."

"I'm fine. It was just..." His voice sounded shaky. "I wanted to be on the road already. It's a long drive to Tallahassee." In the office light, Donnie's eyes looked like dark black pools.

"Okay, you get out of here and enjoy yourself. Disconnect a little this weekend, York." Donnie rearranged his shirt. "I know how hard you've been working. Enjoy the time with your family."

York felt his face go blank. "Will do," he said, holding his breath.

Donnie gave a thumbs up and watched York disappear out the door again. "Let's get the fuck out of here!" he cheered, stepping behind his desk and pouring a heavier drink than usual. "Time to party!"

As York quickly drove away, his hands shook over the steering wheel. The music that once made him forget his worries became a soundboard filled with fear. He tried remembering all the missing person's reports over the years and frowned. Eventually, he surrendered to gazing into an empty Highway 75, listening to his inner voice, searching for God.

36

THURSDAY: VIII

When Donnie walked into Captain Cooks, his cheekbones hurt from smiling. "Is Izabelle here yet?" he said to the host.

"Donnie! It's good to see you again. Right this way," said the short black-haired woman, pointing to an area in the back where Izabelle, Colleen, Derek, and Wally were sitting at a circular table.

"How about that?!" Donnie said with a chuckle. "My love." He leaned down and kissed Izabelle on the cheek. "Shouldn't we be celebrating? Biggest catch this year!" he boasted before flagging their waitress.

"We were waiting for you, hon," said Izabelle.

"Fuck you, Donnie. Look at my face!" Rage was spewing from Derek's bloodshot eyes.

Donnie timidly shrugged his shoulders. "Can you believe this guy?" He looked at Wally and lightly tapped his arm for approval. "We won. We made a lot of money. On to the next one, right?" Wally didn't respond. "You're taking his side? That's bullshit! He knows what he did." Colleen and Izabelle jumped as Donnie's voice roared. "And it was in the middle of

the fuckin' day, for Christ's sake. Please, if it wasn't for me..."
He huffed under his breath. "This clown almost blew it all!"

"Boys." The sound Wally made by shaking his gold
bracelets silenced the table. "Everything's going to be fine...
Kiss and makeup."

Donnie watched Izabelle shuffle closer to Colleen and grab
her hand underneath the table.

Derek sat with his arms crossed and a stone-cold mugshot.

"Alright..." Donnie looked around the room, searching for
the right words. "I'm sorry about your face." He paused. "But
why the fuck did you bring them to my house without anyone's
permission. You could have fucked everything."

"They needed to leave The Lodge. You don't understand. I
had a bad feeling about it," rumbled Derek, scooting his chair
forward and lowering his voice.

"I had a bad feeling about it, too," Colleen interjected.
"There were just a lot of people there the other day. It's still
just a cafe, Donnie."

"See!" Derek clenched his fists. "It's still a regular business... I don't see you risking hostage situations in public
places."

"Who the fuck do you think pays Bill off? Don't you think
there's a reason you haven't seen him in God knows how long?
You and Colleen run that shop. It's in the fuckin' job descrip-
tion." Donnie impatiently looked over his shoulder for their
waitress.

"I'm sorry, Derek, but he's right. And that's no reason to go
against code. We got lucky," said Wally in a calming tone. "And
even luckier with the price." He held his knuckle to his mouth.
"You've got a talent for finding some incredible..." He cleared
his throat. "That's beside the point. The money's already in
your crypto wallets... but the job's not done. This is *teamwork*.
We have one more job, and then we can lay low for a little."

Wally put his glasses down and leaned toward Izabelle. "Tell me more about tomorrow night, sweetie."

Derek grunted in irritation.

"Everything's set, Wally," said Izabelle. "She's coming over at 6:00pm."

Wally ran his hands through his slick back black hair and rubbed his beard. "I like where this is going. Tell me more."

"And right now, she's fast asleep, resting. Lindsay and I went to hers and moved your old desk out of the basement... Lindsay didn't think to have the house swept before putting it on the market. She's a head case... You really messed her up."

Wally's sniffle broke their conversation as the waitress came to the table.

"How are we tonight, y'all? Can I start ya off with some drinks?"

Everyone looked up with a polite smile.

"I've got some specials if you'd like to hear... It's an oven-fried chicken served with flaky buttermilk biscuits and home-made gravy.

"That sounds divine." Wally licked his lips and looked at Derek, nervously rubbing his forehead. "Give us a moment, would you? I'll have some more coffee when you have a moment."

"I'll be right back with that, sir." The waitress nodded.

"You!" Wally stuck his finger at Derek. "Need to calm the fuck down!" He turned his attention back to Izabelle. "So, how long will it take you to get her down the elevator from when she's supposed to come over? I want to be the first to greet her."

"Don't worry. I have everything set in my head. She'll be over around 6:00pm. So, maybe sometime between 9:00pm and 10:00pm. Are the buyers still on?"

"We're sending our email blast tonight..." Wally's gold tooth shined as he smiled. "If nothing else, we'll have our usual

197

suspects." He looked over at Derek again. "That's it... This isn't a meal type of dinner anymore... You two... Outside, now!" he said to Donnie and Derek. "And I don't want to hear a fuckin' word about it anymore."

"Goddammit," mumbled Donnie, throwing his napkin on the table. "You're always causing something to happen," he said, directed at Derek. "I didn't even get a fuckin' drink."

Before standing up, Wally passed Izabelle a wad of cash. "Can you leave the nice lady a tip? I feel bad for leaving. This'll be quick."

As soon as Derek felt the night sky touch his cheeks, he pushed his face into Donnie. "Why the fuck did you have to hit me? Can't you be a civil human and use words?"

Donnie lightly laughed, doing his best to remain composed. "You fucked up in so many ways."

"C'mon, hit me again and see what happens." Derek's eyes were hot and dry with anger.

"Stop it!" Wally stuck his hand out. "You two fight like fuckin' children. I don't give a fuck what happened. This doesn't work unless we're in it *together*." Wally caught his breath and looked up at the moon. "And Donnie," he grunted, throwing a jab into his stomach. "You didn't need to use force, but a punch is a punch."

"We got it! We got it, Wally." Derek put his hands up in protection. "No more fighting."

"You want to hit him now! Go ahead!" Wally aggressively grabbed the front of Derek's shirt. "Calm the fuck down. The both of you. And remember whose ring you're kissing." He spit on the ground in front of Donnie and walked to his car.

"You okay?" said Derek.

"I'm fine. I can't believe he hit you..."

Derek put his hand on Donnie's hunched back.

"He's still got that fuckin' temper. Even without alcohol... He'll never change."

"That's for sure." Derek reached for a pack of cigarettes in his pocket.

"I'm... sorry about earlier... if something's up, call me before you do anything."

"Yeah," said Derek. "I will."

"Everything alright out here, boys?" said Izabelle. "Where's Wally?"

"He went home," said Donnie.

37

THURSDAY: IX

Marcus's brief visit with Penny's mom left him in good spirits. Her energy always grounded something in him. While her time on earth was running short, she still had a sense of humor that made everyone in the room forget about the severity of her cancer—the hour they spent together in the hospital made Marcus's trip already worth it. After saying their goodbyes, Marcus and Penny found themselves on Fillmore Street, ready to take the night by storm.

Marcus wiggled around in his seat.

"Can I get you two anything else?" asked the waitress.

The slight eye roll and dimple marks on Marcus's cheeks said everything.

"I think we'll have two more espresso martinis?" said Penny.

"Coming right up."

Penny leaned in and whispered, "Me and her used to..."

"No! When was that?" Marcus playfully punched his arm in disbelief.

"You don't need to know." Penny couldn't keep a straight face. "You know, one of those you keep to yourself."

"Look at you!" Marcus slow-clapped his hands. "See, you don't need my help anymore."

Penny let out a sigh of relief.

"Man, I missed this place," said Marcus.

"Fuck, dude! We all miss you... and Aleeia. How long are you two planning on staying out there for?"

Marcus sipped the last of his martini and then washed it down with water. "I don't know. It hasn't even been that long. I think we still gotta give it some time," he gulped. "It's different. That's all I'll say for now."

"You're telling me. You're literally in the middle of nowhere. What were *y'all* thinking?!"

Marcus shook his head with a warm smile. "I mean... you know why we left. It's a change of pace. A different scenery. I love it here... but... we're just trying something new. And besides, we already made some friends."

"Oh, yeah? *You* made friends, or did Aleeia?"

Marcus scoffed.

"Here are those martinis." The waitress placed their drinks down and walked away.

"See what I mean? Like we've never met." Penny opened up his palms and grinned.

Pulling his coffee froth chalice to his lips, Marcus took a moment to look around the room. "Ahh! I missed that. I have to find a place that makes 'em like this!" The sweet, dark liquor sliding down his throat relaxed him.

"Cheers, brother!" Penny raised his glass for a toast and then leaned forward. "So, tell me about these new friends. Do you like them?"

Marcus tilted back in his chair and rubbed something out of

his eye. "I haven't decided if I like them, but Aleeia hit it off with one of them."

"What's that mean?" said Penny.

Marcus cleared his throat. "I mean, before we left, she..." He looked into his martini for the right words. "She said she thinks she's attractive... You know that *twinkle* she gets."

"No! Don't say that!" Penny put his hands on his head. "Dude, I've told you this from the beginning." He sat back down and pulled his shirt out. "You gotta watch her. You've caught her with... what..." He started counting his fingers. "Like two or three other women now? If you did that, she would have already left you."

Marcus buried his palms into his eye sockets. "I don't know. I mean..." He sighed and took a heavy sip of his martini. "You're right, but I want a family with her. I love her so much. I'm thinking more about the future than anything else. I know it's all fucked."

"Dude, it's a never-ending saga." Penny threw his hands down. "I love you, and I'll do whatever for you, but this has to be fixed." Marcus looked at the ground. "I mean... what's she doing this weekend while you're gone... Seeing her?"

A white napkin from Marcus's lap flew across the table. "She's having dinner with her tomorrow night."

"You're kidding?!" Penny nearly spit his drink out. "Not the one you just said she thinks is hot. Motherfucker!" He banged the table. "You know what she's going to do, right?"

Marcus rubbed the back of his shoulder as the dim lights in the room blurred his thoughts.

"You gotta break that up, my friend. We're getting you on a flight first thing tomorrow morning." Penny rolled his eyes around the restaurant. "Dude... Look around... There are so many other women out there, Marcus. I'm just looking out for you." He lightly tapped the table as they sat in silence, looking at the candlelight between them.

"Here's the bill whenever you're ready," said the waitress. "It's nice seeing you, Penny. Maybe I'll see you soon." She winked and walked away.

Marcus rested his hand on his cheek and motioned Penny for the bill. "I got it."

Without hesitation, Penny slid the metal holder across the table. "Thanks, man." He paused. "I love you, dude, and I know I'm not the best to be taking advice from, but man, you gotta not let her walk all over you. Imagine when you have kids. Then what's going to happen?"

Marcus pursed his lips together. "I know... I'm thinking."

"Well, you can do more thinking at the next bar," said Penny, wrapping his arms around Marcus. "We're going to Moana Loa after the waitress comes back."

Marcus checked his phone to see if Aleeia had responded. "Alright, you win." His stomach felt queasy after he saw no response. "You're right. I gotta do something about this." He rubbed his chin.

"That's the spirit. We'll talk about it. Don't worry," said Penny, smiling at the waitress as the waitress picked up their bill to pay the check.

After only a few nightcaps, Marcus was cheesing from cheek to cheek and stumbling over his words. "And get this, get this... you won't believe it." He placed his warm hands on Penny's shoulders and rubbed them in excitement.

"Calm down, Inspector Gadget. I'm right here." Penny waved the bartender over.

"So... I was out for a run the other day and needed some water, so I stopped by this school."

"Oh God. A school?" Penny buried his hand into his forehead. "Where is this story going?"

"Just hang on. I'm getting there." Marcus stood up from his bar seat and started explaining his story with his hands. "I saw these two girls while I was getting water."

"And?" Penny took a sip of his drink.

"Just listen." Marcus closed his eyes. "When I started running again, I saw the same two girls on this random street." He burped. "And then, I mean, they were still far from where I was, but I know it was them. And then BANG!" Penny jumped. "I heard them yelling for help. Like, yelling-yelling! So, I ran as fast as I could down the street, but when I got there, all I saw was two men grabbing the girls and throwing them in the back of a black SUV." Marcus picked up his drink and took a sip. "Out of a movie, right?"

"You saw a... kidnapping? What is this? An episode of SVU? Did you go to the cops?"

"Did I go to the cops?" Marcus scoffed. "I ran there and talked to the sheriff himself."

"What did they do then?" Penny watched Marcus start to hiccup.

"Nothing," slurred Marcus. "Well, one of the cops did. He dropped me off and gave me his number. He seemed like he wanted to help." Penny wiped some spit from his face as Marcus started talking louder. "But the sheriff... I think there's something off with him... Fuck the police!" he shouted with a hoot.

"Alright, alright. Take it easy, now. I think we've had enough."

"No! C'mon, we just got here. Look..." Marcus pulled out his phone. "I'll text him right now and prove it."

Penny quickly waved to the bartender for their check.

Hey York, it's Marcus! Are there any updates
on the missing girls? Has there been a
report yet?

Marcus pushed his phone into Penny's face. "See! A cop!"

Penny shook his head. He hadn't seen Marcus this intoxicated since their trip to Mexico last year when he found Aleeia kissing another girl in the hot tub.

"Thanks for coming in, guys," said the bartender with a smile.

Marcus gawked his head up as Penny helped him out of his chair. "See, I still got it!"

"Thanks," Penny mouthed to the bartender.

As they stepped onto the street, Penny put Marcus's arm across his shoulder and looked around for a hot dog vendor. "Food. We need to get you something to eat."

"I'm not hungry!" Marcus whined, throwing his head back and escaping Penny's grip. "Did I do something wrong, Penny?" He pushed Penny's arm off his shoulder. "Should I call her? Why does she do this to me?"

"What?" Penny scrunched his face. "You're everywhere tonight, man." He tried to grab Marcus's arm. "Don't call her right now. You'll sound..."

"I don't care," muttered Marcus. "If she doesn't pick up. She doesn't..." he burped and put the phone up to his ear. "Nothing... Really?!" he said under his breath.

"Look, man. We need to get you home. It's been a long one. We can talk about this in the morning, but if you think something weird is happening." He rolled his eyes at Marcus, crossing the street. "You need to make that decision."

38

FRIDAY MORNING

As the morning sunlight drifted through the dusty blinds in Donnie's office and touched the rough edges of his thick beard, he dropped his head back and kicked his legs up on his desk. Like a sleeping bear awakening from its winter slumber, he rubbed his chest with both hands and smiled into a place beyond the meadows. He shook his head in disbelief, thinking about everything finally coming together. To calm his excitement, Donnie ran his hands into his thinning hairline and then held them to his face. He tried slowly breathing through the tiny crevasses in his hands, but every time he would start counting to ten, fantasies about Izabelle and him traveling the world canvased his mind. He knew he needed to focus on tonight's auction before thinking about any soon-to-be vacation.

"Good morning, Matilda," he said, entering the break room with a pep in his step.

Matilda politely smiled and pressed her back against the counter. "Good morning, sir! How're you today?"

"Matilda," said Donnie, pulling up his belt buckle. "We couldn't be better... Do you ever feel like things fall into place too perfectly?" He grabbed a recently roasted pot of coffee from the corner and watched it flow into his orange '#1 Husband' mug.

"Sometimes, sir." Matilda put her hands on her waist and looked at the big grin on Donnie's face. "But you're glowing! It seems like you and the missus must be doing something well."

"We're living the dream no more than any other person in this town." He threw his hands back as another officer knocked on the door.

"Sheriff Gallo! There's a Miss Adams on Line 1. She's sayin' she hasn't seen her daughter and niece since Wednesday morning when they went to school." The officer paused. "She wants to see if we've heard anything."

"Tell 'er I'll be right there," said Donnie in a deep, authoritative voice as he blew into his hot coffee.

The other officer nodded and turned the corner to hold the call.

"It's sad, right?" Donnie moved closer to Matilda and waddled his head back and forth.

"I never understand these cases," she sighed. "I have no idea what I would do if I were in the mother's shoes."

"We'll do our best, right?" He raised his mug.

"Yeah," she mumbled, looking down at the floor.

"Don't worry." Donnie patted her on the back and walked out to take the call. "I'll get to the bottom of it."

"Sheriff Donnie Gallo. How may I be of assistance this morning?"

"Hi..." The woman's voice was shaky. "Sheriff Gallo? My name is Elizabeth Adams... and... I haven't seen my daughter or niece in a few days." She cleared her throat. "I figured they were at my sister's house, but when I called her... she thought they were at mine." Donnie pretended to scribble something on his notepad. "It's not unheard of for them to be at either of our houses for days, so we didn't overthink it."

"I'm so sorry to hear that, ma'am. Do you know where they may have been last?"

"We're assumin' school," interrupted another voice. "This is Faith Chatham... Elizabeth's sister."

"Got it." Donnie bit his knuckle. "And so, you said the last place they might have been was their school? Have you reached out to their teachers or classmates?"

"We have. Their teachers hadn't seen them since after Wednesday's break," Faith sighed. "And their good friend, Morgan, said they were skipping class to take a bus to Atlanta to meet two brothers they met online. She said they planned to be back for Thursday's classes."

Donnie swirled his finger into his coffee. "Ahh! I see," he said. "And if you don't mind me asking, has everything been alright at home?"

"Alright at home?" Elizabeth raised her voice. "You don't need to know about our home life! Everything's been..."

"Everything's been fine," Faith grunted between the crackling of the phone connection. "I know Megan, that's my daughter, has been... How do you say it? Just at that age... She uses her phone a lot... wants to go against my word..."

Elizabeth rumbled. "This is all Megan's fault! Cassie would never do anything like this."

"Hold on there, sis! What're you talking about? Don't you remember..."

"Hey, hey, there, ladies." Donnie grinned, feeling their tension. "I'm sure everything's going to be fine. We have cases like this that are always popping up, and the kids usually show up after a quick joy ride... If you know what I mean." He waited for their reply. "But since we have a source that said they might have gone to Atlanta, I can send a note to our folks there."

"Thank you," said Elizabeth. "Thank you."

"Of course, ma'am. And they go to Webster High or...?"

"Yes!" Faith gulped. "Yes, they do." Donnie heard her bang on a table. "Are they going to be okay? Please! We don't know where our babies are." She started to cry. "Please help us!"

"We'll do everything we can. I promise." Donnie, unfazed by their questions, wiggled around in his chair. "Have you two provided us with their last seen descriptions?"

"No, we haven't." The dry lump in Elizabeth's voice fumbled her words.

"We'll do everything we can to find these two," said Donnie in a confident tone as he reached for his stress ball. "I'm going to transfer you back to our case manager, and we'll get a search underway... Hang in there, okay? They'll show up... I know it." He leaned forward and clicked Line 1 on his phone. "Amanda? Hey... So, let's start by taking down the descriptions of the girls." He looked out the window with a devilish grin. "Mhm... Then, let's file a formal report and update ATL once everything is ready... Yup... Alright... Thanks."

39

FRIDAY MORNING: II

Unlike most mornings, Aleeia didn't waste any time getting up. As she quietly stepped toward their bedroom patio, she looked through their glass window and let her mind go blank. After a quick gaze and a moment of serenity, the synapses in her brain began connecting the dots to her evening with Izabelle. *He'll never know. It'll be my last secret.* She pulled her hair up into a messy bun and noticed the moon setting and the sun rising on either side of the sky. The picture-perfect scene reminded her of Marcus's favorite saying, "Watching the sunrise and moonset in the same morning is like watching two souls destined to cross paths. It's beautiful." The thought of his warm hands around her waist made her feel at home but empty inside.

On the patio, Aleeia pressed her body against the wooden wall. In an instant, she remembered Marcus pounding his hips against her. She reached for her neck and squeezed it tight. A fiery sensation burrowed between her thighs. The fear of him finding out about her plans and feelings about Izabelle put knots in the center of her chest. *Her lips.* She fell back onto their patio furniture, imagining Izabelle between her thighs.

"No," she shouted into the sky. *What am I doing?* She dug her nails into her hair and hung her head into her lap. *He won't find out, right?* She yearned for something she could only have once in a blue moon.

Back inside, Aleeia checked her phone and saw Marcus had called her twice. *What am I supposed to say? He needs to enjoy this time apart, right?* She sighed. *But I don't want him to think I'm going to hurt him again.* She grabbed her phone and sent him a message.

Good morning!
How are you feeling this morning? Xx

I need to clear my head before tonight. Aleeia threw her phone on the counter. *Just be calm. He won't find out. He's on the other side of the country.*

40

FRIDAY MORNING: III

Hanging over the side of his hotel bed in his silk boxers, York stared at his phone with a frown. His head ached after looking at the five unanswered text messages from the woman he planned to meet this weekend. The story about him seeing his family for a baptism was the only lie York had told in years, and today's lunch was the only date he'd planned since his wife's accident. After opening the blinds and hoping that sunlight would turn his day around, he looked down at the pink, neon 'No Vacancy' sign and scoffed. Dating wasn't high on his life agenda, but he knew he needed to put himself out there again. The more times he tried calling his date, the more he doubted everything about himself. Eventually, his calls went straight to voicemail. With every step around the stained motel floors, York felt his chest tighten. The pictures of his date that once made his heart race now made his body itch. To distract himself from going down a darker hole, York picked up his phone and called his only friend at the police station, Matilda. After his wife's passing, she became his closest companion. Something inside him told him to pursue Matilda as more than a friend, but because they worked together, he closed that door.

"Matilda?" York bit his thumb. "Hello?"

"York! How's Tallahassee? Did you meet up with your friend? I want to hear about it!"

The vibration of her voice made York's empty stomach turn warm. "It's great," he cleared his throat. "We're grabbing lunch today."

"That's wonderful news, York." She sighed. "I'm so proud of you. This is a big step."

York walked over to his hotel window again and rested his forehead against the glass. "Yeah," he said, pinching his nose. "It should be a fun afternoon."

"Are you feeling okay? A little nervous?" Matilda laughed to lighten the mood. "You're a real catch, York. Any woman would be lucky to have you. You know that, right?"

A blanket of euphoria showered York's back. "You think that?" He cleared his throat again. "I mean, you're right." He felt the bits of his fingers warming up with pins and needles. "But, yeah... just a lot on my mind at the same time. Can I ask you a question?" York heard the metal door of the police station open in the background.

"Sure. I'm just getting back to the office from a quick walk."

York pulled his shirt collar. "It's nothing big." The faint sound of Donnie's belly laugh echoed in his mind. "Did anything ever come up about those girls that guy reported the other day? It's just been on my mind."

As Matilda sat at her desk, the sounds of her organizing her space interrupted the conversation. "You know, I was with Donnie earlier this morning, and their mothers' called about it... They said something about meeting people in Atlanta. I didn't really ask too many questions, though."

York fell back onto the bed. "That's some news," he said as his voice cracked. "Can you let me know if you hear anything else? I just promised that guy... Marcus... that I'd let him know if anything came up."

"Is that it York? You're funny. This date has you feelin' some type of way, huh?" She laughed. "Maybe, one day... you'll know why..."

"Matilda, I gotta go." He scratched his forehead, remembering the last time Matilda said those words. "I'm sorry... My friend's calling."

"Do your thing!" she said.

York could feel Matilda's smile through the phone.

"Call me if you need anything. I'm here for you."

"Thanks." York hung up and stared at his reflection on the TV.

```
             Marcus, it's York.
      Give me a call when you have a second.
      I have an update on the missing girls.
```

41

FRIDAY MORNING: IV

"How're you feeling this morning, big guy?" Penny found Marcus passed out on his couch. "I bet." He threw a pillow at him. "You were feeling yourself at the end of the night... Do you remember calling Aleeia?"

Marcus looked up with one eye open and pillow marks on his cheek. "What did I say?" He grunted and pulled a blanket over his head.

"I mean, there's a lot to unpack, buddy." Penny went into the kitchen and grabbed him a cup of water. "There's Aleeia with her new friend." He rolled his eyes. "And then you were going off about seeing these two girls on your run... And you texted a cop or something." He waved his hands in confusion.

"No. No. No." Marcus pushed his legs into a fetal position. "Why did we drink so much?"

"I think that question pertains to you. I stopped drinking near the end of the night. I just got back from a run to the bridge." Penny pulled off his shirt and looked at his view of the Palace of Fine Arts.

"You fuckin' overachiever." Marcus sat up and recalibrated his senses.

"Are you sure you're okay to be here?" Penny asked, falling back onto the windowsill. "Last night was..." He pushed his hands into his black, curly hair. "A lot... I haven't seen you like that since..."

"Mexico." Marcus shoved his hands into his face. "I know." A quiet whimper fell through the cracks in his hands and spewed throughout the room. "I don't know what the fuck I'm doing, Penny." Marcus unleashed a violent sigh. "I mean, one minute, everything's fine... and then... I moved across the country for her. I give her all the sex I can, and it's still not enough. I want a family with her." Tears poured from his brown eyes.

"Hey, hey, hey." Penny jumped to the couch and wrapped his arm around his best friend's shoulder. "I'm right here." Marcus's body was shaking. "We can work through this." Penny looked around the room. "Have you checked your phone this morning? Maybe we can call Aleeia and figure something out." He placed the water cup in Marcus's hands.

"I hate this." Marcus's emotions were more scattered than roaches seeing daylight.

Penny could see thick teardrops falling into Marcus's dry mouth. "It's okay. I know it's tough right now. A lot is going on. It's okay to be stressed."

"Yeah!" Marcus yelled. "But I feel like it's never-ending." He stood up and stomped around the living room. "I have to figure this out. We can do it together. You were right last night... I can't let her do whatever she wants," he shouted.

Before giving Marcus a moment to break down on the floor, Penny quickly hugged him. "I got you. I got you." He watched his spine move up and down. "Should we call her?"

Marcus buried his face into Penny's chest and unleashed another thunderous sigh. "I just want to fix it right now."

Penny caressed the back of his head. "I know you came out here for my mom, and I love you for that... But the doctors said she's got at least six to seven months." Penny paused, feeling Marcus catch his breath. "She loved seeing you yesterday."

"I know." Marcus's hand was trembling. "I loved it, too. You know how much she means to me."

Penny nodded. "But we have more time," he said. "I want you to save your..."

"I know," shrieked Marcus again, reaching for his phone. "I need to call Aleeia!" His home screen was full of notifications. "I called him, too?!" The tears from his eyes blocked his vision.

"Let's get you some coffee," said Penny. "It'll do you good."

Marcus sniffled his nose clean. "What do you think I should say to her?"

In the kitchen, Penny turned on a pot of coffee. "I mean... Like I said, I haven't seen you like this..." Penny bit his lip. "I know I can say this to you, and you won't hate me, but your emotions are a mess." The sound of the coffee maker cut the silence in the room. "I love you, Marcus, but after you told me Aleeia said she thinks her new friend is 'hot'... and that they're having dinner tonight." He shook his head. "The answers are there. Go home. We'll all be waiting for you... and *Aleeia*. I want to see you happy, man."

Marcus scratched his chest. "Yeah," he whispered, holding more tears back.

"You've done more irrational things before." Penny laughed. "Flying across the country to see my mom and have dinner with me for a night is not even that crazy. Go home and get this under control... I want to see you like yourself again." Penny passed him a cup of coffee.

The weight on Marcus's chest poured onto the floor.

"You're right... And I called a cop?" He moaned in embar-rassment.

"You sure did. It was a whole thing."

Marcus sunk himself into the corduroy cushions on the couch. "Well, he says something was reported," he said, looking at his phone. "I'm going to text him."

"Inspector Marcus!" joked Penny.

"Get outta here," said Marcus, walking over to the window overlooking the park. "I gotta look at flights still." He took a big sip of coffee and looked at a couple sitting on a bench, enjoying the overcast morning. "I need to save my marriage."

42

FRIDAY MORNING: V

Before slipping into her black yoga pants, Aleeia admired her naked body. *I knew I still had it.* She dragged her hands down her waist. *Why can't I have them both?* She sighed. *I need to get out of the house and do something.* Aleeia reached for her phone and searched for parks nearby. *This looks interesting. A.H. Stephan State Historical Park.*

The brief moment she had on their bedroom porch made life feel effortless. *What a beautiful day. Let's focus on you, Aleeia, and take today hour by hour.*

When Aleeia got into their car, she opened the sunroof and felt the warm sun kiss her chest. She listened to the wind in the background. *Stop thinking about her. Don't think about him. Just be in the moment.*

Before leaving their driveway, Aleeia fixed her messy bun and reached for the pack of cigarettes she put in her black crossbody bag. As she counted the hours until 6:00pm, she let the nicotine shoot through her veins. Each drag she took felt like a game of 20 questions. The little voice in her head kept telling her that Marcus didn't have to know, but even with that, her emotions slowly ate at the different layers of her heart. *This is the last time. I promised him a dream life. I have to keep that for him.* Her decision process was like scattered paint in an artist's workshop.

While she continued pondering her life, staring out into the marshlands next to the highway, she choked on her smoke when she saw Marcus was calling.

43

FRIDAY MORNING: VI

"Aleeia!" Marcus gasped, clenching his phone with a dreaded look on his face.

"Hi, baby." Aleeia's voice sounded horse. "How are you? Is everything okay?"

Feeling his words loading at a snail's pace, Marcus blanked and felt his body float to the ceiling. "Everything's been great. We saw Penny's mom after the airport, and she's in high spirits." He rubbed his temple and paced around Penny's apartment. "And then Penny and I were out for a bit in the Marina last night. I just wanted to call you," he said with a lump in his throat. He felt his eyes slowly start to water.

"That's great news! I'm glad you're having fun," Aleeia said, holding her breath.

"Where are you?" asked Marcus, studying her muffled voice. "I'm having trouble hearing you." He felt his blood shoot from his head to his feet, sensing she wasn't home.

"I'm going for a hike at a park near the house. It's a beautiful day, Marcus! I wanted to get outside and clear my head."

Marcus put the conversation on mute and yelled across the room. "She said she wants to clear her head."

Penny calmly raised his hands and mouthed, "It's going to be fine."

"Right," said Marcus under his breath, unmuting his phone. "That's great." He could feel his body warming, thinking about how he wanted to express his emotions. "I... Uh," A dark space ran through his train of thought as he saw Penny using his hands to rock an imaginary baby. "I've been thinking about our conversations, Aleeia." He leaned up against the wall. "The move, those articles you almost forgot to tell me about." He waved his hands around. "But more importantly, I'm hurt about what you said in the car before I left." He gulped. "I feel like I should be home with you. We have a lot going on... and a lot to work through. I feel like we've been distant since we've moved and..." Marcus looked at Penny, rolling his hands forward and mouthing, "The girl." Marcus nodded and said, "I'm worried you're going to do something like Mexico again."

"Marcus!" Aleeia shouted. "I wouldn't ever want to put you through that again. That whole situation ate me alive for months, and even to this day, I could never." Marcus heard her pull off the side of the road. "I'm sorry about what happened, and I don't want you to be insecure about anything. There's nothing to worry about... You have to trust me."

Marcus grinded his teeth. "Aleeia, I hear what you're saying, and we've obviously worked on and been through a lot, but right now, I feel like we should be together and start working on this family thing." He felt the back of his throat tighten. "I was thinking irrationally. I should have stayed with you. I have too much on my mind and need to do better."

Aleeia blew her lips together. "Okay," she said, taking a second to respond. "Look, if you're worried about this dinner with Izabelle, I promise you, nothing is going to happen... And with the articles... Izabelle and Colleen said it was nothing to worry about... I'm starting this little project for you. It's going to be something for the both of us." Marcus heard her shuffle around. "And with us, yes, it's been rough with the move. I thought seeing Penny for the weekend would be good for the both of us, but that's obviously not the case."

Marcus put his hand on his forehead and internally waved a white flag. "I get it, Aleeia." He looked at Penny for confidence. "The articles are one thing. The dinner is another. The list keeps going, and right now, I'm making the decision to come home. We have to work on this together, and it's going to take time, but I want to make it work. I want to make it work because you're worth it. You'll always be worth it."

"What is this the Notebook, Marcus?" Aleeia grunted. "You can do whatever you want to do, baby. I'm going to go for this hike and clear my head. I obviously love you and always want to be with you, but I thought this time apart would be good... I guess... just let me know about your flight. I'm still going to dinner. I'm not canceling plans with my only friend in town."

Marcus scratched underneath his eyes. "Okay, well... Okay... I'll keep you updated on my plans and when I'll be home. Don't worry about me. And..." He felt his mouth go dry. "And I trust you about tonight. I just want to be there for you when you get home and all of that."

"I love you, Marcus. I'm sorry you are feeling this way. Maybe we can do therapy together again. We'll work this out."

"Promise?" said Marcus.

"Promise."

44

FRIDAY MORNING: VII

"What are the news articles?" said Penny, sitting beside Marcus.

"I don't know. She found something in our basement and then lied about it to me. I'm trying to get past that, too." Marcus slumped back onto the couch.

"I got it," said Penny. "I'm here for you. If anything is ever on your mind, you know, you can always talk to me."

"I know," said Marcus with a loud sigh.

Penny gave him a moment before asking, "So, how do you think that went?"

Marcus pressed his hands into his face. "With her, I'll never know. I'm just glad I said something. I feel better." He looked up at Penny with watery eyes.

Penny patted him on the back. "I think you're making the right call. I know you love her and want to make it work. You two will get through this." He comforted Marcus more. "I know she loves you two. I've seen your relationship since day one. You're both going to fight for each other no matter what."

"Yeah, you're right." Marcus yawned and rubbed his eyes. "I guess I need a flight now."

"I'm way ahead of you, brother," Penny said, showing his phone to Marcus. "Flights at 9:17am. It'll be close, but I think you can make it."

"I'm glad I didn't have to unpack my bag." Marcus laughed. "Let me change and brush my teeth," he shouted, getting up from the couch and running to the bathroom.

Penny smiled. "That's my guy!" he shouted, wandering to the window where he saw a couple arguing on a park bench.

45

FRIDAY MORNING: VIII

I can't believe him. Aleeia slapped the steering wheel. "Ugh!" *Why the fuck does he have to come back?* For a moment, her tempers flared. Nothing but the adrenaline of her speeding down the highway could soothe her chest. "Calm down," she whispered. Memories of Marcus and her moving into their first home together flooded her mind.

"Turn left onto Cunningham Lane," stated the car's GPS.

Aleeia froze as the smell of warm fall leaves drifted through the sunroof. The empty dirt road and white cottages felt like an oasis for a confused mind.

"You've arrived at your destination."

Aleeia rubbed her temples. *I can't do anything about it now. Be in the moment.*

Immediately, her eyes gravitated toward a sign that said, 'Box Office.' Intrusive thoughts and questions were a thing of the past as she slowly touched every tree branch in her way. The ruffling wind in the background was white noise from heaven. Finally, a new spark ignited inside her. She smiled at the dark green building and quietly opened the door.

"Hello?" she whispered to the ticket clerk, asleep behind the counter. "Hello? I'd like a ticket, please." His groomed beard and classic features gave him a rustic look. "I'd like to go into the park." The lullaby-like snoring from his nose made her feel like she was in another time period. "Hello?" she said again, looking at the ticket board price as $10. She slid a $20 bill across the counter. "Oh well, this should cover it."

The silence of nature made Aleeia feel alone, but for the oddest reason, she liked it. Not another person or wild animal could be heard for miles. Her mind was free to escape. Old horse stables caught her eye, and in the distance, she noticed a dock that overlooked a marsh.

"And hello to you... and you..." she mimicked in an English accent.

"Such a lovely day, isn't it?" Aleeia fell into her imagination.

"Oh, your husband doesn't let you do what you want? Me neither!" Her different voices began bouncing ideas off each other.

"But he's the sweetest," she said in a deeper tone.

And what's this? Aleeia reached down and picked a yellow flower. It reminded her of The Sound of Music, a movie she would watch with her mother. A hum from her favorite song fell out of her mouth as she glued the flower to her chest and wandered to the edge of the dock. Creaking sounds from the flimsy, worn wood sent ripples into the water. Eventually, she sat down and swung her legs over the mossy lagoon. The bright, overcast sky made her squint her eyes as she laid back. Even amidst the gray clouds, the sun made her cheeks warm. Loud sounds from critters in the background reminded her of the deep bass keys Marcus plays on the piano. It was romantic to feel the stillness of the park caressing her soul.

After dozing off, Aleeia felt tiny splitters poking her back. The sunny sky that once hugged her face turned into dark, wet cotton candy. *Rain?* A drizzle fell onto her hand as she felt her pant pocket vibrate. *Marcus?* There was a moment of irritation before picking up. She knew he was likely calling to tell her every detail about his travel plan. She lifted her phone, looked at the screen, and then gulped, seeing Izabelle's name.

"Izabelle! How are you?" Aleeia held her breath.

"Hey, you! I was just calling to see if you wanted a ride to dinner tonight. With this storm coming in and us drinking, I figured you wouldn't want to drive."

Aleeia turned her mouth in circles. "Storm?"

"Have you not heard?" Izabelle laughed. "You'll learn soon enough. This weather can be deceiving, hon."

Heavier raindrops began to hit Aleeia's neck. "I haven't heard anything. But I'd love a ride. That's so generous of you." A warmness grew between her thighs as cool raindrops began showering her whole body. "Is there anything I should bring?"

"Nope! If you want to bring a bottle of wine, that works. Otherwise, just yourself." Izabelle hummed and kissed into the phone. "6:oopm still good?"

Thunder cracked in the background. "Did you say 6:oopm?" Aleeia stood up and plugged her other ear with her finger. "Izabelle?" She looked at her phone's reception. "Hello?"

"Sorry, it must be the connection. Are you outside, hon? This storm's about to come down at any moment."

The shifting clouds in the sky dimmed the scenery. "I'm at some park right now. I was just about to head home." Aleeia paused. "6:oopm sounds great. I should get going."

"Okay! I'll see you then. Be safe!"

As Aleeia stood, a howling wind began pushing against her

back. The raindrops that once relaxed her turbulent mind began falling thicker and thicker. Without warning, her next step on the dock went through the rotten wood and sunk half her leg in the water. "Help!" she cried, struggling to see through the dry wind pelting her eyes. The more she twisted and turned her leg, the harder it became. She realized that it was latched onto something beneath the water.

"Hold on!" shouted a faint voice along the horizon. The ticket clerk in a tan poncho and ranger hat ran toward her. "Are you okay? This dock is old. It's off-limits. I should have told you that." He inched his way down and reached his hand out for Aleeia. "Grab my hand!"

"I can't! My shoe's caught on something."

The man looked at Aleeia's frantic face and knelt next to her. "I'm going to try and pull it off. Ready?"

Aleeia nodded and watched the ranger reach his muscular arm down her leg. "It's right there. I can feel it!" she shouted.

"I got it." Her soon-to-be hero quickly stood and pulled Aleeia up. "Look at that!"

"Thank you," she said with tears running down her cheeks. "I can't... I can't." Aleeia's knees buckled on the grass alongside the marshland. "Thank you," she gulped.

"C'mon!" he shouted, putting his hand out. "We need to get you home."

"Right," she said, grabbing his hand and following him back to the parking lot.

"You get home safe now." He wiped the rain from his face. "Do you know where you're goin'?"

"I think so. I have my phone, so I'll be okay." Aleeia started the car and rolled down the window. "Thank you so much again." She paused and looked him up and down. "I owe you, sir."

The man smiled and politely tipped his hat.

My phone. "Wait," she yelled.

The man turned around.

"I think I dropped my phone in the water. Can you help me?"

Raising his hands, the ticket clerk hurried back to the dock.

After ten minutes of watching the rain crash against the front windshield, Aleeia saw him running back with a sour grin.

"It was in the water," he said, passing it to her. "I would try putting it in some rice."

Aleeia shook her head and placed her phone in the drive-side cup holder. "I'm not sure how to get back now. I take this left, right?" Her face furrowed.

"Yes, that takes you to the main road." He directed his hands toward the entrance. "Then, once you get there and hit a stop sign, take another left. That'll get you back to town, at least."

Aleeia caught her breath and pulled her hair behind her ear. "Thank you... I really do owe you now." She stared into his eyes and felt something inside her arouse. "I should get going."

The man tipped his hat again and watched her drive away. "Any time, ma'am."

46

FRIDAY MORNING: IX

"You're slick... I'll give you that... I didn't even think to pick her up." Donnie poured himself a scotch and walked back to his desk.

"You underestimate me. You and Wally both," said Izabelle, wrapped up in a blanket on Donnie's man cave couch.

"So, you'll pick her up, have a drink, and lure her downstairs?"

Izabelle huffed.

"Wow... I thought that was all for show." He leaned back in his desk chair and put his hands above his head. "Promise me, I get to watch."

Izabelle eyed Donnie from across the room. "I think I could make that work," she said, dropping her blanket to the floor. "You know, we don't have to do anything with her. She can be my little toy. You know how much I've wanted one."

Donnie slowly caught his breath. "Right. What did you have in mind?" He unbuckled his belt.

"Hmm, maybe me and her *just* have dinner." Izabelle seductively ran her nails across every inch of furniture on her way to his desk. "Besides, what's Marcus going to think when she goes missing? I've been texting her off my other phone, but still."

"That chump!?" Donnie hesitantly laughed. "I'll make something up. I'm the boss and have been for years." He paused. "We'll forage a trip... that's what we'll do." An idea brightened his face. "We'll make it look like you two ran away with each other... After all, this is the last one for a while."

"Seems fishy." Izabelle began crawling across Donnie's desk. "You'd let me run away with her?"

The bulge in Donnie's pants was growing. "Anything... for you," he mumbled, feeling Izabelle's warm hands slip into his pants.

"You'd do that for me? Let me run away with her and have a moment?" She swung her legs toward his face and slipped off her white sweats. "I'd like that," she said, watching Donnie push his face between her thighs. "How long would I have to be gone for?" She dug her nails into his scalp.

"I don't know." Donnie's voice sounded intoxicated. "What's the best cover-up?"

"You tell me, mister sheriff. We've been doing this for years." Izabelle felt his big tongue licking her clit. "We'll have to be away from each other so we can sell it." Her breathing sped. "I can come back after a few months and say we went to Mexico or somewhere and got in a fight."

"Maybe," mumbled Donnie, gently sticking his finger inside Izabelle. "Sounds foolproof. I'll handle everything here."

"Will you?" Izabelle pushed her legs up higher.

"Anything for you, Bella." Donnie pulled his head back and dropped his pants to the floor.

47

FRIDAY MORNING: X

"Can I have a pack of Parliaments?"

"ID, please," gargled the store clerk. The smell of tuna flew into York's nostrils.

"Sure. I haven't had that in a while," he said, pulling out his wallet.

The older woman nodded. "Cash or card, hon?"

"Card, please." York stuck his ID back into his wallet and tapped his card. "Thanks."

Back in the car, he unraveled the plastic around his cigarette box and paused. The smell of tobacco always reminded him of his late wife and the years they spent partying together. He pouted his face. As he flicked his Zippo lighter down, he saw his phone light up with a message from Marcus.

What have you heard? I'm in San Francisco but heading back to Atlanta now. Can I give you a call when I'm checked in?

A voice in York's head made him doubt everything that

happened in the last twenty-four hours. He knew what he heard, but still couldn't believe it. He needed an outside opinion. "Fuck it," he mumbled, reversing his car out of the parking lot. "I got a hunch... It's God's message... and I follow him." He began thinking about how to best tell Marcus about what he heard.

48

FRIDAY MORNING: XI

"We should get going," Penny said, shutting the window in the living room. "I made you a Bloody Mary and toast." He slid a plate across the counter.

"Just like old times." The spicy Worcestershire sauce tickled Marcus's nose. "Cheers."

"You know." Penny walked down the hallway. "I think you're making the right decision. If your gut is telling you something, listen to it."

"Oof! This is strong!" Marcus shook his head from side to side. "It feels good to have said what I said on the phone. I could tell something was off with her... I don't know. I'll be happier knowing we're sleeping in the same bed tonight." The fresh celery stock sticking out of the glass invited Marcus for a bite. "After her dinner, of course," he said with sarcasm.

"Keep me posted on it. I'm always here for you." Penny jingled his car keys. "I'm going to get in the car... Come out when you're ready." He looked at his watch. "You might even have time to grab a drink at the airport if you hurry."

Marcus hooted and pounded his chest. "Give me a second. I'll meet you downstairs."

Twenty minutes later, Penny turned onto Highway 101. "How're you getting home from the airport?"

Marcus's burst of euphoria was slowly evaporating from his bloodstream. "I'll take a taxi or something." The window was a nice resting place for his throbbing head.

"You okay?" Penny looked at him, dozing off and tapping his leg. "Anxiety?"

"You know how I get when I drink too much. Add flying into the equation, and it's quite the combo. I just need another drink, and I'll be fine." The faint jazz radio in the background momentarily relaxed him.

"Alright. Let's talk about something else." Penny tapped the steering wheel. "What about that cop?" The cop!" He playfully laughed and punched Marcus's arm.

Marcus felt a heavy weight crack in his chest as he reached for his phone. "I forgot. I need to text him," he said.

"What do you think he's going to say?" Penny couldn't hold back a laugh.

"I'm telling you. I saw something that day." Marcus scratched the back of his neck and sent York a message. "If he's updating me on a police report, that means I saw something."

"Marcus Bynes. American Musician and Crypto Enthusiast by day. World-class detective by night." Penny gestured his hands to present the new Marcus to the world.

Marcus shook his head. "Just watch. Trust me."

49

FRIDAY MORNING: XII

York barged into his hotel room and quickly threw all his clothes into his dark leather travel bag. He rubbed his eyes and scanned the room. A sharp knot stabbed into his stomach. His worries were causing him physical pain.

"I'd like to check out of room 102, please. I'm checking out early." York placed his credit card down.

A heavier-set person at the front desk wearing a headset reached over and grabbed a cheese puff from a wholesale-sized bag sitting next to them. "Mhm... Was everything okay with your stay, sir?" they mumbled, clicking their long nails against the computer's keyboard.

"Yes," responded York, pushing up his glasses. "Everything was fine. I have to leave to go somewhere."

"It happens!" The receptionist smiled and clicked the next track on their cassette tape. "You're all set!"

"Can I get a refund for the nights I'm not here?"

They looked at York with a bizarre expression. "It says here you already pre-paid in full for a discounted rate. I can't refund you, sir."

York pushed his lips together. "Oh. That's right. Thanks for your help, anyway."

50

FRIDAY MORNING: XIII

Marcus leaned over his knees. "I don't feel good, Penny. My anxiety is..." He took a sharp inhale.

"You'll be fine. Just get another drink. Everything's going to work out." Penny patted him on the shoulder. "Think about tonight. You and Aleeia together under the same roof."

"Keep it moving!" shouted airport security. "You can't park here!"

Penny waved his hand. "It'll just be a minute."

"I know," mumbled Marcus, trying to smile. "It's breaking me inside... and so is leaving you so quickly. I know it's not the trip we expected." He opened the car door. "I'll be back soon."

"Of course, you'll be back!" Penny ran around the car to hug Marcus. "Don't worry about it. You gotta do what you gotta do... Give Aleeia a hug for me." A cool breeze came by the terminal. "I'm here if anything comes up... And solve that case, Detective Bynes."

Marcus chuckled and stepped inside the airport doors. As he stood in the security line, the loud, sporadic announcements from every direction didn't help his worries. He pulled out his phone and scrolled through his messages with Aleeia. Her name made his stomach drop.

I made it to the airport.
I'll let you know when I land.

Marcus looked around. The room felt like it was shrinking. *Count back from a hundred.*

"Next," said the TSA clerk, looking at Marcus's ID and squinting his eyes. "To the left!"

Marcus ripped his bag from his shoulder and flung it into the bin. "Forty-four," he whispered, following the directions of the TSA officer behind the body scanner. His heart felt like it was hung on a ball and chains. "Sixteen," he mumbled, walking away from the security area.

"Can I have a double Bloody Mary? Extra spicy, please." Marcus slapped his hand on the bar and sat with an uncomfortable grin. He bounced his legs on the footrest almost immediately.

"Here you go." The bartender quickly placed his drink down and moved on to the next person.

"Thanks," he said.

Even after feeling the thick tomato juice plunder his bloodstream, Marcus couldn't calm his suspicions about Aleeia. He tried remembering their first fight and what they promised each other. As he retraced their years of love, he was hit by a brick wall when he thought about her yelling at him the first time he found her with another woman. His throat choked up, and he waved at the bartender again. "Can I have another, please?" He knew his trip down memory lane wasn't healthy, so he distracted himself by texting Aleeia again.

Thinking of you.
Let me know when you make it home.

Why'd my message go through as a text? Marcus moved his lips around. *Whatever. Don't worry about it. You're going home.* "York!" he blurted, knocking back the last of his horseradish concoction. Marcus waved the bartender over for the check.

"Hello?" York answered with a dry, stern voice.

"York! It's Marcus. How're you?" He shouted. "Is now an okay time to talk? I saw your message."

"Yes. Right. Thanks for calling me back, sir." Marcus heard a car's engine start in the background. "I wanted to inform you that the girls' mothers called yesterday and asked if we've heard anything. I think it was regarding the same case. I don't think too many kids would go missing in a week."

"That's great news! Well, not great, but..." Marcus looked up at the gate board. "I guess it's better than nothing." He could hear York heavily breathing in the background. "Is that it?"

"Well." York cleared his throat. "I don't want this to be on the record, but I wasn't sure who else to tell since all my other friends are cops."

Marcus's eyebrows narrowed. "You can tell me anything!"

"Okay," said York, taking a deep breath. "When I was at the station last night, I overheard a conversation from Donnie's office." He loudly gulped. "He was talking to someone named Wally. And then Donnie asked if the girls had already sold..." There was a pause. "And they did."

"Sold?" Marcus hesitantly laughed, signing his check. "What does that mean?"

"I haven't gotten that far, but my gut tells me something's off... And he mentioned something about Izabelle having a big one tomorrow, which would be tonight, I guess."

Marcus gasped. "What? What did he say about Izabelle? Aleeia and her are having dinner tonight."

"I'm not exactly sure. I needed to tell someone that isn't also a cop. He also mentioned something about an email thread for an ice cream party. The password is **GELATO**."

"Ice cream?" whispered Marcus, taking a seat at his gate. "Let's back up. What is Izabelle doing tonight?" He started squeezing and flexing his hands into a fist.

"I don't know. That's all I heard."

"Alright, let me try and call Aleeia... Stay on the line." Marcus's temperature and anxiety rose as he clicked her contact number.

Hey, it's Aleeia. Leave me a message, and
    I'll get back to you as soon as I can.

"The fuck..." he mumbled, feeling faint. Marcus tried calling her three more times but only received her voicemail.

"York, are you still there?"

"Yep, still here."

"I called her, and it went straight to voicemail. What should I do?" Marcus pulled out his Xanax prescription and asked, "Are you in town? Can you go by my house and check on her?" He funneled the tiny pills into his palm and tossed a few in his mouth. "I knew those people were fuckin' weirdos!"

York cleared his throat again. "I'm driving back from Tallahassee right now, but I can when I'm back in town. I've also got a friend who could stop by. No promises, though."

Marcus heard his plane's announcement for boarding. "And you said the guy's name was Wally, huh?"

"Yeah. I don't know anyone in town named Wally," said York. "You said you're flying back to Atlanta right now?"

"Mhm." Marcus was trying to catch his breath.

"If you want, I can pick you up from the airport and take you back to town. It should be about the same travel times."

"My mind's all over the place." Marcus picked up his bags and got in line to board the plane. "I guess that works... I don't know why... I talked to her this morning, and everything was fine."

Now boarding at F22.

"Marcus, are you alright? Are you there?"

"Hmm," Marcus said, remembering what his therapist recommended in emergencies. *Lean over and hug yourself.* Marcus crouched down and hugged his knees, feeling his world spiraling out of control. He massaged his hands to relieve the stress tightening in his chest. "York," he mumbled. "I don't have a ride home. So yeah, can you pick me up?" He pinched the top part of his nose and closed his eyes.

"Just text me your flight information... and I'll be there." York paused. "And don't worry too much. We'll get in touch with Aleeia. I'll check with my friend."

Marcus hummed in agreement. "That sounds good. I just texted you my address and flight info." He felt his Xanax kicking in. "I'll have Wi-Fi on the plane, so text me with any updates."

"You got it, sir," said York.

"And York..." Marcus closed his eyes. "Do you truthfully think there's some connection between the missing girls and Donnie?"

"I... I don't know yet."

"Fuck," mumbled Marcus. "If Donnie's connected to the missing girls, what's Izabelle to Aleeia then."

"I don't know yet. I can only assume, sir," said York. "I'm just connecting dots and following my gut."

"Alright," Marcus grunted. "I'm about to scan my boarding pass. I'll text you."

"I'll be waiting to hear from you," he said as they ended their call.

51

FRIDAY AFTERNOON

An awkward tingle wrapped around Aleeia's left ankle as she looked at the scratches on her thigh. *Is this my karma?* She hobbled up the stairs and turned on the shower. The boiling droplets burned her skin in all the right ways—the hotter the water, the better the cleanse. She slowly drew a heart on the misty glass door. *Is this my karma?* There was a razor blade sitting on the edge of the bathroom counter. Temptation lurked as she thought about her past. *I can't. I've grown from that.* The feeling of watching blood fall to the shower floor played with her heart. *I don't want Izabelle to see something like that.*

52

FRIDAY AFTERNOON: II

York pulled down the skin below his eyes. The mess he found himself in was gross. He knew he shouldn't have heard what Donnie said, but the longer he sat, thinking in the car, rubbing his mustache, the stronger urge he had to call Matilda. It worried him to send her to check on Aleeia, especially if his gut feelings about Donnie and Izabelle were true. York couldn't help but run through all the different narratives in his head, but after a while, he couldn't focus, so he lit another cigarette. "Oh, fuck it!" he shouted, pulling out his phone. "Matilda?"

"York! I didn't think I'd hear from you until you were back. How was lunch?" Her voice inflection had a vibrating interest in York's love life.

"She didn't end up coming to lunch." York took a heavy drag. "I'm on my way home now."

There was a deep pause of relief and confusion.

"Oh, York. I'm so sorry to hear that. We can go to dinner or get a drink when you're back... I'm so sorry." Matilda waited for his reply.

"I'd like that. Another day, though." York sighed. "Could

you help me with something before I get home? It's kind of urgent... and sensitive. I need you to keep it to yourself for now."

"Anything for you, York." Paper filing sounds cluttered the background. "What's going on?"

"Can you promise me that you'll keep it to yourself?"

"Whatever it is, York. You can count on me. You know that."

"Alright... good." York nodded. "So, here's what I need you to do... Do you remember Marcus, the guy I told you about? He came into the office to report the missing girls he saw near the high school."

"Yes, what about him?"

"Well, he's on a flight back to Atlanta right now from San Francisco, and he's a bit worried about his wife, Aleeia. He can't get a hold of her... It's a long story. Could you drive by their house and see if she's home?"

"I can do that, York, but I don't understand. Why is he nervous about her being home alone?"

"I promise when I see you, I'll explain everything as best I can, but in the meantime, can you go there when you're free?"

"Yeah. I can do that."

"It would mean a lot to me, Matilda."

"Well, send me the address. I can't go until later."

"Later will work... I think... It's the best we're going to get." York tapped the center console. "And please, Matilda, don't tell anyone about this."

"Should I be scared?" She chuckled.

"No, there's no need to worry... I just sent you the address... Call me when you get there." He hung up and lit another cigarette.

53

FRIDAY AFTERNOON: III

Matilda slowly pulled her phone away from her ear and stared blankly at her computer. She wondered if Marcus was just paranoid about his wife being home alone or if there might be something else. With her mind repeating York's vague instructions like a late-night infomercial, she stepped into the breakroom for a coffee.

"Hey, Rebecca. You're just who I was looking for."

"Girl," shouted her work-wife, hiding her face. "That's never a good thing."

"It means I was thinking of you." Matilda sat across the table.

"You've got that look." Rebecca playfully laughed. "What do you need from me now?"

"Nothing." The coffee maker on the counter made a loud noise. "It's just... Donnie told me about those missing girls this morning."

Rebecca stopped chewing her burger. "Yeah, their moms called. They were a wreck."

"And?" Matilda questioned, scooting her chair forward.

"And... I don't know. Donnie talked to them. It sounded like a wild goose chase, in my opinion. We sent a report to ATL with their last seen descriptions... Some of their classmates said they were going to the city to meet some boys."

"Gotcha," Matilda said, clearing her throat. "I hope they show up. I don't know what I would do if I were their parents."

"Me neither." Blank thoughts passed between them for a moment.

"See?" interjected Matilda. "I didn't need anything from you this time." She got up to pour herself a coffee. "I hope we get some good news on them soon."

"Me too. Me too."

For the rest of the afternoon, Matilda waited on the edge of her seat. She knew York wouldn't hide information from her unless it were something big. It killed her inside to imagine him driving back from Tallahassee with a broken heart.

"Where are you going? It's not even 5:30pm yet." Rebecca leaned down into Matilda's cubicle.

"I have somewhere to go." Matilda rolled her eyes, trying to maintain her goofy character.

"It's Friday night, girl, and York's out of town. You got a hot date or what?"

"Hot date?" Matilda scoffed. "I'll pass."

"That's my girl." The zipping sounds from Matilda's backpack cut their conversation. "Everything alright? You got something on your mind?"

Matilda watched Rebecca step behind her. "It's nothing."

"You're sad he's on that date, huh?"

Finding the right words to say, Matilda agreed. "Yes." She paused. "I haven't heard from him. I'm trying to..."

"Keep playing the long game!" Rebecca guffawed. "You

know, you two are just one handhold away from an HR violation," she joked.

Matilda pressed her index fingers into her nose and faked a laugh. "You're right. You're right," she said, throwing her hands up. "And trust me, you'll be the first to know when that happens." Matilda winked and walked toward the exit.

54

FRIDAY EVENING: PART 1

Aleeia held up another dress in front of the mirror. *Will she like this?* Half her wardrobe was scattered across the floor. The more she looked at the digital clock on Marcus's bedside table, the more her stomach fluttered thinking about Izabelle's arrival. *This one?* Finally, Aleeia found a winner. The short, black V-neck dress said sexy but classy. *But will this be easy?* Aleeia mimicked, pulling her shoulder straps below her waist. The feeling of watching her dress slide off her body made her clit tingle. *I can't wait.* She took a deep breath and went to the bathroom. A tiny purple bottle sitting on the white countertops drew her attention. It was her favorite vanilla and lavender fragrance, a scent that drove Marcus crazy without any foreplay. She admired her waistline as she patted it across her arms and neck. *Is this enough?* She scooped her hands under her breasts.

"I am enough," Aleeia whispered, feeling the inviting scent from her lotion relaxing her body. Her mind felt confused. The daydream that lurked in the back of her mind was finally here. *Just a quick one. It's to clear my head.* Aleeia pressed her hands against her hot chest and rushed across the room. Contradicting images of Marcus and Izabelle shot through her mind. *What am I doing?* A blank stare kept her in a trace, and after a long second of temptation, Aleeia stuck her hand into her bedside table and pulled out a yellow vibrator. Before lying down, she flexed her hips and cat-crawled across their bed until her butt was arched in the air. She imagined Izabelle's face behind her, licking her like a Tootsie Pop. Wet splashing noises blocked her vision.

As she flipped onto her back and opened her legs, Aleeia grabbed her toy and smirked. She watched her little trinket twist and pulsate until her legs quivered in agreement.

55

FRIDAY EVENING: PART 1: II

Donnie stood at the bottom of the stairs, cracking his knuckles. "Izabelle! When're you picking her up?" He looked at his watch. "We're on a timer!"

"Hold on!" Izabelle puckered her lips and took a long look in her mirror. "I'll be right down," she shouted, leaning down and grabbing a small vial from the bottom drawer. The tiny cork she pressed up with her nail effortlessly flew off. She sprinkled a white, powdery substance on her hand. Instantly, a numbing vibration pinched her nose and dripped into her throat. "I'm coming!" Izabelle cleared her nose and hit another bump. "Let's have some fun," she whispered, rubbing her nail into her gums.

"Donnie!" she said, still catching her breath. "Donnie, baby!" A new rush was bubbling through her body. "I'm so excited!" Izabelle stood atop their stairs, posing with her hands. "What do you think?" she said, carefully stepping down the steps in her stilettos. Her dark green blazer dress danced across the line between sophistication and intimacy. "Do you think she'll like it?" Izabelle spun around and quickly wrapped her arms around Donnie's neck, smiling as she felt his body responding to her touch.

"Okay? Okay, would be an understatement. You look... You're hot." Donnie lifted her down from the bottom step and kissed her forehead.

"Don't try anything, baby! You already had your time." Izabelle pulled away, feeling his hand fall below her lower back. "I'm saving all of myself for tonight. A promise is a promise, right?"

"Save a little for me later?" he said, reaching his hand under her dress. "Are you even wearing underwear?"

"Wouldn't you like to know?" Izabelle winked. The naked feeling between her thighs made her feel liberated. "I'm going to show her your man cave. I think it might be the perfect hand-off. So clean it up a bit, would you?" She grabbed the keys off the hook by the front door and looked back at Donnie, biting his knuckle.

56

FRIDAY EVENING: PART 1: III

The aggressive white noise from her blow dryer distracted Aleeia just enough to help her lose track of time. As she slowed the speed and parted her hair, she turned around and looked at her black dress from behind. It enhanced her voluptuous backside and gave her a feeling of confidence. "She'll want that," she muttered, picking up her Dior nude velvet lipstick on the counter. As she carefully applied it to her naturally plump lips, Aleeia stared at her dilated eyes and accepted her whole self. *I'm ready. He can't stop me.* She exhaled and walked downstairs.

FRIDAY EVENING: PART 1: IV

"York?" Matilda parked her car a safe distance away from Marcus and Aleeia's house. "I just got here. What am I looking for?" The buzzing sounds from cicadas blocked her thoughts.

"Anyone leaving or arriving... I think." York's voice crashed against the howling highway winds.

"And if I see anyone, what should I do?" Matilda listened to a chopping, helicopter-like sound piercing the background.

"Follow them, I guess. But don't let them see you." York cleared his throat. "If you see Aleeia, Marcus's wife, leaving for any reason, follow her."

"I can do that for you, York, but I need you to tell me what's going on." Matilda pressed her forehead against the driver-side window. "I mean, you still haven't told me a lot. What's this all about? I mean, why am I at *this* house? It doesn't make sense." Matilda saw a car approaching from the driver's side mirror. "There's a car, York! There's a car!" she whispered, sinking lower into her seat.

"Who is it? Who is it?" shouted York.

"I can't tell."

"What kind of car is it?!"

"A black SUV."

"A black SUV," repeated York. "It's gotta be Izabelle. Stay hidden! Just..."

"Izabelle?" Matilda didn't like his sporadic tone. "What's going on, York? Girls are getting together to have dinner. Why is this a big deal?"

"I'm going to tell you... just not right now." He gulped. "I need you to follow them if they leave, but please, don't get too close. Don't let them see you."

"Fine." Matilda kept her eyes glued to the car. "But you need to tell me..."

"I'll tell you when I'm with Marcus! I promise. I'm just pulling up to the airport."

"Are you serious? York, you need..." The sound of the call dropping beat into her ear.

58

FRIDAY EVENING: PART 1: V

While sipping wine to calm her nerves, Aleeia impatiently paced around the house. Every few minutes, she'd peek through the front window. With no phone, she didn't want to miss her opportunity. She had no way to get a hold of Izabelle. *She's coming, don't worry.*

The knots in her stomach grew worse by the second, but when she heard a knock at the door, her pain immediately faded. *Stay calm. You've done this before.* Aleeia ran to the bathroom to flatten her dress and make sure everything was as perfect as can be. "You got this," she mumbled, taking a deep breath behind the front door.

"Aleeia! It's me." Izabelle knocked again. "I hope you're ready!"

"Izabelle!" Aleeia felt her chest melt as time stood still. "Hi! I... I love your outfit," she said, opening the door.

"Thanks! I got it a while ago. I just haven't found the right time to wear it." Izabelle grinned and looked at Aleeia from head to toe. "But this," she touched Aleeia's waistline and ran her fingers up her body, "Is so sexy."

Aleeia blushed. "Thank you." Her mind went blank as they stood in the doorway, admiring each other's gentle gaze.

"Should we get going?" Izabelle motioned her hand to the car.

"Yes! Just let me grab a jacket and that bottle I promised."

Izabelle smiled. "I'll be waiting in the car. Take your time."

59

FRIDAY EVENING: PART 1: VI

The stewardess looked at Marcus, scrunched up in his seat. "Sir?" she nudged his shoulder and passed him a water bottle. "We've landed in Atlanta."

"Huh?" Marcus rubbed his sleepy eyes awake. *Oh, man.* He yawned and stretched his body. *That was quick.* Looking around, he realized he was one of the few left on the plane. "Thanks for everything," he said, grabbing his bags and walking into the sky bridge. As his foggy mind regained consciousness in the congested airport terminal, he felt his benzo wearing off. The hair on his neck stood up when he realized why he was back in Atlanta. Pulling out his phone, he called Aleeia again, but it went straight to voicemail. He pressed his eyes in and took a small sip of water. He called her again and then looked at his reflection in the airport train window until he saw a text from York.

Outside arrivals.
I'm in an old, yellow Mercedes Benz.

The more he awakened from his short-lived escape, the deeper he drowned in Aleeia's whereabouts.

`I'll be right there. Just got off the plane.`

60

FRIDAY EVENING: PART 1: VII

"So..." Izabelle rolled her eyes at Aleeia, sitting in the passenger seat. "How was the park? Tell me about your day?"

Izabelle's words flew through Aleeia's ears. "It was... It was relaxing, but..." She turned to the window, fighting the urge not to let her wandering eyes hyper-focus on Izabelle's body. "You wouldn't believe what happened!"

"Oh, yeah? Try me."

Aleeia squirmed around in her seat. Izabelle's large, green eyes widened as she turned down the car's volume. "Well..." Aleeia cleared her throat. "The ticket person was asleep when I got to the park." She remembered the rush she felt as he pulled her out of the dock. "It was weird, so I just left some money on the counter."

"A little rule follower! I see."

"Only some days." Aleeia felt her cheeks warm. "But after walking around a bit, I ended up sitting on an old wooden dock. It was so peaceful until it started raining."

"You'll learn soon enough!" Izabelle said, lightly tapping Aleeia's thigh. "This town is full of surprises."

Aleeia pushed her legs together, feeling a warm tingle beneath her waist. "I like surprises."

"You'll have one tonight." Izabelle brushed her hand across Aleeia's arm.

"Oh, really?" Aleeia pressed the skin in the middle of her V-neck dress.

"So, what happened? That doesn't sound so bad."

"Right?" Aleeia shook her head. "After we got off the phone, everything took a turn for the worse." Aleeia watched Izabelle flick on the front windshield wipers. "It was crazy! When I started walking off the dock toward my car, my leg fell through the boards!" She pulled up her dress and pointed at her scratched thigh.

"What!?" Izabelle slammed on the brakes and immediately reached for Aleeia's cuts. "You poor thing! What can I do to make it feel better?"

The soft touch of Izabelle's hand on Aleeia's inner thigh made her clit rumble. Her thirst for physical touch grew stronger. "Really! It's fine." She brushed her hand away, trying to build more foreplay. "But when I fell, my phone dropped in the water." She shook her head and sighed. "It was a whole fiasco. It's water-logged or something. It won't turn on."

"Wait, what? You lost your phone?" Izabelle narrowed her eyes.

"No, I didn't lose it, per-say, but it was in the water long enough to damage it." Aleeia paused. "Do you think I could message Marcus from your phone? I haven't been able to get a hold of him."

"Oh, my God, of course, hon." Izabelle unplugged her phone and passed it over. "Please text him."

"Thanks." Aleeia looked down at the screen but couldn't type a message. Izabelle's scent was driving her crazy.

"How did you get off the dock then?" Izabelle glanced down at her leg again. "I mean, those are some good cuts."

Aleeia quietly inhaled. "I think the ticket person heard me because he ran to help me up and got me back to my car in a matter of minutes. Of course, when I fell through the wood, my foot got caught underneath the dock," she joked.

"Well, I'm glad you're okay. That's so scary," said Izabelle, pulling the car to her gate entrance and watching the doors swing open. "No problem with the sensors tonight."

Aleeia smirked. "I love your house. It reminds me of back home."

"Really? It took a team of designers and architects to help us decide. I know Donnie only cared about the man cave and that damn elevator, but I wanted the house to be different than all the others around here."

"It's definitely different from everything we looked at."

"Well, you know, mi casa es su casa!" said Izabelle, parking the car and cutting the engine.

There was a feeling of tension as they sat with the car off.

"Dinner should be fun. I have everything ready... for the most part." The twinkle in Izabelle's eye sent an inviting message.

"I'm looking forward to it," whispered Aleeia, unclicking her seat belt and turning toward Izabelle. She felt her pussy growing wetter as each second of tension passed between them. "I love this." Aleeia took a chance and reached for Izabelle's necklace. "Is it Citrine?" Her voice cracked.

"It sure is. How'd you know." Izabelle watched Aleeia softly rub the amber stone.

"I had a friend whose birthday was in November. She was my favorite," said Aleeia, looking into the yellow fire inside the gem.

"I'm sure she was amazing."

Aleeia's short breaths pushed into Izabelle's chest. "She was... She was my first girlfriend."

"Girlfriend?!"

"Yeah," whispered Aleeia, dropping the necklace and slowly dragging her middle finger into Izabelle's cleavage. "She was... How do I say this." Izabelle let out a faint moan and hesitantly approached Aleeia's lips. "A perfect teacher."

Aleeia felt Izabelle's hand on her cheek, pulling them closer.

"Maybe I can show you something," mumbled Izabelle, locking their lips. The heavy sounds of raindrops knocking on the sunroof left them in a spell.

Finally, Aleeia's fire met Izabelle's water, completing each other's desires and sending them both into a high. As their hands explored each other's bodies, Izabelle stuck her face into Aleeia's neck and kissed her cheek.

"We should go inside." Izabelle's slow words and peppermint breath tickled the inside of Aleeia's eardrum and ruptured her thought process.

All her worries washed away by being in Izabelle's presence. "Yeah, we should," said Aleeia, leaning in for another kiss.

Izabelle flirtatiously pulled back, leaving Aleeia wanting more. "It's a long trip to the door. Are you going to make it?"

Aleeia's eyes dilated. "I think I'll be okay. I'll follow the woman in the racy green blazer." She pulled up her dress shoulder strap. "I heard she's quite the entertainer."

As they ran up the front doorsteps, Aleeia felt Izabelle grab her butt as she ran past her.

"Hurry up! You're going to get all wet!" Izabelle looked back and winked.

"I'm already wet." Aleeia grinned and watched Izabelle twist open the front door.

61

FRIDAY EVENING: PART 1: VIII

Matilda slowly pulled over and parked near Donnie and Izabelle's gate entrance. She pressed her left hand into her cheek. "York, you better have a good explanation for this," she said. The bright, full moon shone across the wide street, illuminating the night. After pondering the sky and wondering why she was outside Donnie's house, she felt her phone vibrating.

62

FRIDAY EVENING: PART 1: IX

"York?" Marcus put his phone to his ear and stood outside arrivals. "I don't see you anywhere. I'm out front."

"I'll be right there. I had to go around again."

Still disoriented from the flight and the lingering effects of his Xanax, Marcus paced around the cement sidewalks. "Let me know. I'm wearing a white corduroy jacket."

"I see you. I see you." York honked and slowly parked his car.

A gigantic grin shot up from Marcus's uneasy stomach when he saw York's car in full detail. It reminded him of his grandfather's Mercedes he learned to drive in. "Wow." He opened the door and admired the refurbished leather seats and wooden dashboard. "I love the whip! I haven't ridden in one of these in a while." Marcus threw his leather duffle bag in the back seat and strapped on his seat belt.

"An oldie, right? I've had her all my life." York rubbed his hands up and down on the steering wheel and moved his chair forward. "She's still going after all these years... How was the flight?"

"I slept the whole time, thankfully... My head is spinning, though." Marcus buried his hands into his face. "I tried calling Aleeia again, but she didn't pick up. What's the latest with your friend?"

"The last time I spoke with Matilda, she was outside your house." York clicked the radio on. "She said she saw Izabelle pulling into your driveway."

Marcus banged his leg. "Well, I know they're having dinner. That's not out of the ordinary yet, but she could have driven herself," he grunted. "But I don't understand why she'd turn her phone off. Something's not making sense."

"I know, but I've got a hunch. Something seems off with everything Donnie mentioned in his conversation last night. I think there's more to this dinner than you think... But that's just me."

"Yeah," said Marcus, blowing raspberries.

"I told Matilda to follow them if they left." York waved his hand out the window, thanking another driver as he merged onto the road.

"Let's get Matilda on the phone," said Marcus impatiently. "I mean, even if Donnie is doing something with these missing girls, I don't know how it would involve Izabelle or even Aleeia. What do you think is going to happen?"

"I'm not saying anything is going to happen *yet*. I'm just following my gut based on what I've heard... I've had enough of Donnie's wishy-washy commands over the years. I think he's doing something shady now."

"And Izabelle?" Marcus huffed. "You think she's involved with the missing girls? You think they're selling people?" Marcus uncomfortably swallowed. "I'm back because I think Aleeia's going to cheat on me again, not because she's in the middle of some conversation you heard from Donnie."

York hit the brakes and held his breath. "Oh, right."

"It's not like that. I mean... I'm worried about Aleeia and am listening to what you're saying, but... " The more Marcus felt like unraveling his story, the sicker he felt. "We've had our problems... Can we call Matilda? I want to make sure my wife is having dinner and nothing more."

"Yes, yes! Let's call her when we get on the highway." Marcus looked over at York, frantically looking for his phone. "Give me one second. I don't want to be distracted by this traffic." Marcus heard him gulp. "Trust me, Matilda is a good friend. I know she's looking out for everyone."

"Right," said Marcus, pulling out his phone again and calling Aleeia. "Look." He showed York the voicemail message. They both paused. "Fuck! Alright... Tell me everything about this fuckin' conversation you overheard from Donnie again. What do you actually think of it?" he said, turning this body toward York.

"Honestly, I've been thinking a lot on my drive, and I know something doesn't add up." York pulled a tissue from his pants pocket and wiped his nose. "I heard him asking about the girls and how much they sold for... I mean, what do you think of that?" He adjusted his glasses and flicked on the car's headlights. "And then the password thing. I don't think he's doing anything undercover. I could feel his excitement through the door when he heard how much they sold for. And he never works late." York shook his head. "I wouldn't put anything past him. I've always had my suspicions. I mean, have you seen their house, for God's sake."

Marcus pushed his knuckle into his nose. "And what happened with the missing person's report?"

"I haven't heard much about it besides what Matilda told me. She said the girls planned a trip to see some friends in ATL for the day."

"Of course." Marcus sighed.

"And Donnie also said something like, 'He's going out of town this weekend to visit family. I planned it that way. Just like always.'" York squeezed his knuckles. "I think he's talking about me! Like I told you, I'm always out of town when something like this happens," he said frantically.

"I gotta digest this." Marcus rubbed his eyes, listening to the hum of the highway.

"Do you smoke?" York offered his packet of cigarettes.

"I only smoke when Aleeia does but fuck it. I need to calm down." He shrugged and glimpsed his silhouette in the window's reflection.

Light, hazy smoke covered their vision as they each sparked a cigarette. "Doing my due diligence as a cop, Marcus, has everything been alright with you and Aleeia at home? I mean, besides this whole cheating thing you're worried about?" York cracked their windows and pointed to his makeshift ashtray in the center cup holder.

The heaviness in Marcus's chest subsided as he inhaled and felt his head lightening. "I would say so. But, you know, moving can be a lot... I thought everything was okay." He paused and collected his words. "But, honestly, I knew something was off since she met Izabelle. She gets this twinkle in her eye whenever she sees an attractive woman." Marcus tapped his cigarette ash over the gas station paper cup. "This wouldn't be the first time she did something behind my back. She's had a thing for women, or does I guess."

York scratched his chin. "I see. I see." He kept his eyes on the road and waited for Marcus to continue explaining.

"I don't know. It's confusing." Marcus rubbed his fingers together. "And she didn't even fight it when I mentioned visiting my friend in San Francisco whose mom has cancer. I was supposed to be there for the whole weekend." He turned his body toward York again and dropped his cigarette into the cup. "She and Izabelle have this planned dinner. It seemed too synchronistic with her cheating on me again, so I came back early." Marcus closed his eyes. "But then, with whatever you overheard at the police station about Izabelle having a big one tonight. What the fuck does that mean?! My stomach and heart are all over the place, man." Marcus slammed the center console. "Are they planning on doing something with Aleeia? Why the fuck do they have such a nice house and an elevator. We're in bum-fuck nowhere of Georgia!"

York jumped in his seat when Marcus raised his voice. "Everything's going to be alright. We'll get to the bottom of this." He pulled out his phone. "It's a straight shot from here. Let's give Matilda a call. Maybe she can give us some good news."

"Hey, Matilda?" said York, holding his breath. "Are you okay? I'm with Marcus. Where are you now?"

"You're going to have to tell me more about whatever's going on, York. I'm your friend, and I'm fine helping you, but you need to tell me if it puts my job and safety at risk."

"Where's Aleeia?" interjected Marcus, pushing his face towards York's phone.

"Calm down! I followed them to Donnie's house, and they went inside a few minutes ago," said Matilda.

"What did you see? What else was going on? She's not picking up her phone!" exclaimed Marcus.

York saw his eyes watering. "Matilda, stay put. We'll be there in the next forty-five minutes or so."

"No, York. I'm going to leave unless you tell me what's going on... I'll do anything to help you. You should know that. But I'm getting nervous, especially with how Marcus talks about Aleeia and why I'm following them."

York rolled his eyes and scratched his chin again.

"York! Are you there?" said Matilda.

"Yeah. Yeah. We're here. I'm trying to find the right words." He sniffled. "There's no easy way to say this, and it's going to come off crazy and wild, but keep this just between us."

"York! Tell me, already!"

"Well, late last night, when I was leaving the station, I overheard a conversation from Donnie's office about the missing girls."

"And... what did he say?" said Matilda.

"Not what I was expecting. Originally, I thought he was doing some undercover work, but when I heard him ask how much the girls sold for with a deep belly laugh, I was stunned."

"What? What does that even mean? He sold the girls?" asked Matilda.

"I mean, I'm not saying yes, and I'm not saying no, but then he said Izabelle's got a big one tomorrow, which would be tonight, and her and Aleeia are having dinner." Matilda gasped. "And then he said something about a password for the evening and an email thread. He was talking to someone named Wally."

"The fuck. Wally? Like that guy who used to live in town? What was his first name? Ah! Fuck, I can't remember it," said Matilda. "He became a ghost at a certain point. I remember hearing stories about him growing up."

"I have no idea, Matilda. I'm not from here," said York.

"Well, what the fuck are we going to do about it?" Marcus pulled his hair back and shook his head. "Aleeia's not picking up my phone calls, and I'm not about to call Izabelle and ask her about Aleeia. We need to do something!"

"Matilda, can you hang tight until we get there? I wanna make sure we aren't missing anything," said York. "You can leave right after. I promise. It would mean so much to me. I'll take you to that restaurant you want to try."

"Fine. So that's it? You want me to stay and watch the house until you get here?" she said.

York scratched his head and looked at Marcus.

"I still find it hard to believe Donnie could do something like this. It all sounds like a joke. Don't you think he's maybe undercover? You don't know for certain," said Matilda.

Marcus watched York roll his eyes.

"If you don't believe me, call him and see what you think about the situation. Don't you two get drinks sometimes after work?"

"Yeah, we do." Matilda paused. "I guess I can. I want to figure out what's going on... I'll call him and see what he's doing tonight."

"Wait, wait, wait," shouted York. "Do you know what you are going to say? I mean, don't ask him about what I just told you."

"Of course not. I'm not that dumb. You should know me better, York!" Matilda awkwardly scoffed. "I find it hard to believe that the town sheriff is selling people and kidnapping them in broad daylight."

York waited. "Yeah, I don't know. Let me know what you can figure out. We'll be there as soon as possible."

"I fuckin' hate this, York. But now I'm invested," said Matilda. "If I find out anything, I'll fill you in, but there's no way I'm going into that house myself if anything happens."

"I know. Just stay put and stay hidden. I don't want you in the middle of anything by yourself," said York.

63

FRIDAY EVENING: PART 2

Donnie smashed his fist onto the table. "And you wouldn't believe what Izabelle was wearing before she picked up Aleeia." Rippling sounds echoed off his scotch glass.

Derek turned back. "I'm sure nothing out of the ordinary."

Wally inhaled another drag from his cigar and said, "You two fight like a married couple, you know that, right?"

"You better watch what you say about my wife." The veins in Donnie's neck poked through his white collared shirt.

"Whatever you say." Derek continued polishing his handgun with a soft cloth. "I just hope she delivers tonight."

"That's enough. Do you want me to remind you why we're all here again?" Wally pushed himself up from the couch and walked towards an auspicious bookcase near the corner of the room. "Drop it for the evening." He shook his head. "It's every hour with you two. One minute, it's laughter, and the next, it's slaughter. Remember, we're in this together."

Donnie aired his shirt out and snatched a glass decanter from across his desk.

Scanning a key card over the leftmost middle book, Wally

watched the bookcase push in and unveil a hidden wall with one gigantic monitor and six smaller television screens. "Home sweet home," he muttered. "This view. Our operation. Are we really taking a break after tonight?" Wally animatedly gestured his hands up in excitement, pointing at the television screens that recorded the outside of Donnie's house, his living room, the basement floor, a check-in entrance, two hallways, and The Lodge. "We're on top of the fuckin' world!" he shouted with a mischievous look in his eye.

Derek scoffed, "Whatever you say," and continued staring at the aquarium.

"Look at this! We've built so much over the years, and for what? To get out while we can?" Wally turned his attention to Donnie. "You're the fuckin' goddamn sheriff of this shitty little city. We're untouchable, guys! Let's live a little." He exhaled. "We can become the *elite*, keep building an empire, and one day soon..."

"And what about my fuckin' uncle? He showed you everything." Derek raised his voice.

"You little shit." Wally pressed his fists together and walked across the room. "What about your uncle? We haven't heard from him in a while. This is my territory, anyway. He's got everything from New York to fucking Ukraine." A darkness inside Wally's chest unraveled into his tone. "Your uncle..." He stepped back. "Your uncle fucked me over enough times for one lifetime. It's my turn to give him a taste of his own charity."

"Do we have a problem over there, Wally?" Donnie edged up from his seat and cocked his gun underneath his desk.

"No problem," said Derek, putting his hands up. The heavy silence in the room sped his heart rate.

"You're lucky to even be here, Derek." Donnie jabbed Derek's shoulder with his gun as he moved towards the monitors. "Don't bring your uncle into this now... Wally, what's goin' on over there? Any movement yet?"

Wally pointed to the middle screen. "We got ourselves a fuckin' show tonight!" He inhaled the faint caramel scents floating from Donnie's mouth.

Cracking his knuckles, Donnie stepped closer and watched their SUV pull into their driveway. "Just in time. Just like that, Izabelle." He turned back to Derek. "Look at what she can do."

Derek threw a pillow over his lap and rested his chin on the couch's armrest. "And what's the plan when Marcus asks about his wife."

Both Wally and Donnie turned their backs.

"What is the plan with that?" said Wally.

"Don't worry! We've got it covered. After tonight, Izabelle's going to go into hiding. We'll pretend like they ran off together. I have Boris looking into the best cover-up." He nudged Wally's shoulder. "We knew she was the one from the first time we saw her. It's all about the cash flow tonight!"

"As long as you're okay with it, sheriff." Wally directed their attention back to the screen. "Oh, baby. Do we have a show tonight? A lil' party for us boys!"

"What're they doing? C'mon, Bella. Get out of the car now." Donnie pounded his chest and looked around for his scotch glass.

"Come to Papa," shouted Wally.

"Oh, fuck no, Bella," said Donnie. "Already?"

Wally glared at the screen. "Looks like they're getting a little *frisky*." He cupped his hand and shouted towards Derek.

Donnie curled his eyebrows.

"What're they doing?" Derek popped up from his seat and ran up behind Wally and Donnie.

Silence stirred the room as they watched Aleeia and Izabelle moving around in the car's front seats. Derek scratched his forehead with a big grin. "I hope she delivers, alright." He sarcastically laughed, trying to agitate Donnie.

"Would you look at that? Real kinky stuff, Donnie." Wally looked back and patted Donnie on the shoulder. "We all knew this was going to happen... The good news is I have front-row tickets for us."

"Will you two fuck off?!" Donnie ran back to his desk and quickly poured another glass of scotch. "I'm turning it off. This is her time, not ours."

Brushing his hair out of his face, Derek stepped back and said, "Whatever you say, boss."

"What'd you say, you little shit?" Donnie lunged toward Derek. "You say one more word, and you're done. You hear me?"

Derek put his hands up again.

"Ahwoo," howled Wally, grabbing the remote and changing the main channel as he watched Aleeia and Izabelle running towards the front door. "Pay-per-view event tonight, boys!"

Before snatching the remote from Wally's hands, Donnie heard his phone ringing across the room. "You better turn that off right now," he shouted, stepping back to his desk. "Why the fuck is *she* calling me this late?" He agitatedly shook his head. "One second, this could be work."

"Whatever you say. I'm not leaving this spot anytime soon... They're beautiful," whispered Wally, pressing his face closer and closer to the screen.

64

FRIDAY EVENING: PART 2: II

As Izabelle opened the front door, Aleeia couldn't take her eyes off her silky hair cascading down her back. She felt her pussy pulsating through her black dress.

"Should we put that bottle on ice?" Izabelle turned around.

I'm hooked. Whatever you say, Izabelle. Literally, whatever you say. Aleeia shrugged. "I think that's what we're supposed to do," she joked, sitting at a barstool behind the kitchen counter and handing over the bottle.

Before grabbing an ice bucket from a bottom cabinet, Izabelle leaned across the counter and grazed Aleeia's cheek with her thumb.

"I guess things got..." muttered Aleeia, looking into Izabelle's chest.

"Steamy?" said Izabelle. "I'm just glad we're on the same page, hon."

Aleeia blushed, smelling Izabelle's scent lingering by her nose. "Me too. I didn't know what was going to happen, but ever since that first night, you've—"

"Can I get you anything to drink?" interjected Izabelle.

A glow in her eyes told Aleeia to relax. "What're you having?" Aleeia straightened her back and looked around the room to distract herself.

"I wouldn't mind a shot of tequila," Izabelle suggested with a shimmy. "Doesn't that sound yummy?"

Aleeia anxiously circled her right ankle. "Tequila always makes for a good night... A fair warning: it turns me on. Who knows what we'll get into." She hesitantly smiled and placed her hands in her lap.

"Isn't that a good thing?" Izabelle poked Aleeia's hip. "Tequila makes me want to have all of you. Is that good enough?"

Fighting the urge to jump across the counter and strip Izabelle of her blazer, Aleeia raised her eyebrows. "I think that would be alright with me."

Izabelle twirled her necklace around her neck. "Good," she said, walking to the wet bar and grabbing a bottle of Clase Azul. "Will this do?"

Aleeia smiled. "That's one of my favorites."

"Of course it is." Izabelle brought over the tall blue and white bottle and poured two shot glasses to the brim. "Salude!" She waited for Aleeia to toast her.

"To new friends," whispered Aleeia, effortlessly gulping the warm agave down her throat.

"Well, that's a good sign." Izabelle grabbed the shot glasses and placed them in the sink.

"Me and tequila have a love-hate relationship." Aleeia leaned back in her chair.

"Oh, don't we all." Izabelle threw her hands up. "I usually end up around the toilet or with my clothes off. There's no in-between."

Aleeia's warm chest made her arch her back forward. "I wouldn't mind that." She bit her lip, hoping to get more of

Izabelle's attention. "I'm the same way. At least, I hope I don't end up around the toilet tonight."

"I know something better you can wrap your arms around."

Confidence ignited inside Aleeia. "Can I help you with anything? I still want to see how the magic happens. I mean, your last dinner was a delight," she said, stepping behind Izabelle and running her hands down her waist.

"Straight to the point, I see?"

"You just have me." Aleeia blushed.

Izabelle reached for the refrigerator handle. "Do I?"

With a nod, Aleeia tugged Izabelle's blazer down. "You do."

"Well, give me a second," said Izabelle, placing eggs, flour, and olive oil on the counter. "Why don't you make us some drinks?" She flicked her eyes towards the wet bar.

"I can do that!" Aleeia stepped closer, embracing the vanilla and jasmine fragrance slithering up her thighs. "Vodka, right?" she asked, walking across the room.

"You remembered. Vodka works with me, hon."

A tingling sensation froze Aleeia's forehead. "How dirty do you like your martinis?" She knew that the right amount of sweet brine could make any grown adult feel the warmth of their inner soul.

Izabelle looked Aleeia up and down. "Dirty. Just like me."

"I like dirty." Aleeia bit her bottom lip.

"Then we have ourselves a winner." Izabelle pulled a stepping stool from below the sink and looked up at the top cabinet.

This is everything and more. Aleeia poured a generous serving of olive brine into a shaker and closed it with security. It was like corking a wine bottle to her marriage for the evening. "Everything okay over there?" she shouted, staring at Izabelle, struggling to reach the top cabinet. *Now, that's a view.*

"Ahh!" shrieked Izabelle, losing her balance. Her pouty

face was asking for help. "I'm always so nervous about grabbing these bowls from the top. Can you make sure I don't fall?"

"Of course." Aleeia quickly placed the shaker down. "What do you want me to do?"

Izabelle stepped onto her tippy toes. "Just keep your hands up and hold my butt." She grabbed Aleeia's hands and stuck them underneath her dress. "Mmm!" she moaned. "Your hands are so cold."

"Are they?" Aleeia pursed her lips, staring at Izabelle's hairless pussy from beneath her blazer. "Does that work?" She swallowed, watching her thumbs gently spread Izabelle's butt cheeks. "Like that?"

"Yeah," said Izabelle, lengthening her body.

The warmth Aleeia felt from Izabelle's pussy made her wet. "Did you get it?" she said, out of breath.

"Almost!" With a final thrust, Izabelle stuck her body out and guided Aleeia's fingers inside her warm slit. "Ahh," she sighed. "I've been waiting for this."

Aleeia looked up at Izabelle's arched back and gently stroked her fingers up. "Me too. You're so wet." Every detail of Izabelle's vagina ingrained a new memory inside Aleeia's dreams.

"Keep going," whispered Izabelle, syncing her body motions to Aleeia's finger movements. Splashing sounds filled Aleeia's ears as wetness from Izabelle's pussy covered her hand. Their souls connected. "I'm so close." Izabelle panted.

Aleeia could see her thighs quivering. "Are you?" she said, removing her hand and slowly running her tongue in a circle. She kept them in a space between euphoria and liberation.

"Oh, my God. I'm going to come."

The high-pitched moan Izabelle cried left Aleeia in a daze.

"I got the bowl," sighed Izabelle. "That was..." She stepped down with shaking legs.

"Hot?!" Aleeia wiped her mouth. "I think the rest of tonight will be magical."

Izabelle leaned in for a kiss. "And for you, we'll have a little special surprise."

Aleeia held her breath. "I can't wait." Her eyes wandered to Izabelle's chest. "And these are nice too."

"Well, tonight, they're all yours." Izabelle moved closer and caressed Aleeia's neck. Her breathing ran chills down Aleeia's spine. "I like you next to me."

Aleeia leaned in for a kiss. "I agree."

"Does Marcus know you're here? Is he okay with this?"

Marcus? Aleeia's stomach dropped. "I'm not sure what he thinks. I tend to hide these experiences from him. He's caught me more than once." *Where is he right now?* "But with you, everything feels different. I feel at home." Her chest felt tight as she stepped back. "I should text him, right? I forgot to do that in the car." Aleeia walked to the wet bar to grab the martinis. *What is he going to think?* "Can we just keep this our little secret?" She placed the drinks down. "I want these experiences, but..."

"I get it. I'm the same way." Izabelle sipped her drink, feeling the hardy olive brine trickling down her throat. "Oh, those are dirty, hon." She winced. "But in all the right ways."

The thought of Marcus coming home haunted Aleeia for a split second. Her sixth sense came for a visit, and guilt began to buckle her knees. "Can I text him? I should keep him in the loop. He hasn't heard from me since before the park."

"You didn't text him in the car?"

Aleeia frowned. "I got distracted."

"Maybe I can continue to distract you."

The energy in the room shifted. "No, really. I think I should text him," said Aleeia.

"Do whatever you need to do, hon." Izabelle opened a

293

drawer and slid a phone across the counter. "Use this one. It's our 'home phone.' I left my phone in the car... I guess I got distracted, too."

"Thanks." Aleeia thought about her lies and dormant desires. *What do I even say?* She was dancing with fire and slowly burning their relationship again. "Maybe I'll just see him at home? We won't be too late, will we?" She bit her nails. "I feel guilty."

"Don't overthink it, hon. We're just having dinner, remember?"

Aleeia sighed. "You're right. I should still text him something." She watched Izabelle raise her eyebrows.

```
          Marcus! It's Aleeia.
 I dropped my phone in the water at the park
         today, and it's not working. I'm at
 Izabelle's for dinner now. This is her phone,
  so text me if you need anything. Love you,
          and I can't wait to see you.
```

"Thank you." Aleeia touched her chest again.

"No problem. Anything for you. Should we get to cooking?"

Aleeia took a heavy breath. "Please!"

65

FRIDAY EVENING: PART 2: III

"Donnie?" Matilda's voice sounded timid. "How are you?"

"Matilda, how's your Friday evening?" Donnie sunk into his black leather chair and dipped his head back.

"Everything's going great." There was a pause.

"You there?"

"Yes, sorry. I think I have a bad connection."

"I can hear you now. What's going on? Did something happen at work?" Donnie put his hand up and tried to shush Wally and Derek.

"No, not that. I just wanted to see if you wanted to grab a drink. I know we haven't in a while."

Across the room, Wally and Derek started snickering at the television screens.

"Well, Matilda," said Donnie, slowly getting up. "Tonight isn't going to work. I've got some plans with friends already, but maybe next weekend, or better yet, how about sometime after work this week? How's that sound?"

"That would be wonderful." Her voice sounded deflated.

"Everything okay? I know it's late," said Donnie, creeping up behind Wally and Derek.

"Everything's fine. I just wanted to get together tonight, you know, since York is out of town."

Donnie furrowed his forehead. "Right. He is out of town," he said, pushing his way to the front of the television screens.

"Mhm." Matilda sighed.

"No way," shouted Derek, pointing to the screen.

Donnie's jaw dropped. "Hey Matilda, I gotta run, but let's plan on getting together this week. The first round is on me," he said, quickly hanging up and pushing Derek out of his way. Izabelle was stepping onto her stepping stool. "You gotta be kiddin' me!" Donnie shouted, knowing what comes next.

"This is a real show!" Derek punched Donnie's shoulder and watched Izabelle move her butt onto Aleeia's hand.

A wavering electric shock gravitated through Donnie's body. The fantasies he shared with Izabelle weren't private anymore. For a short moment, he was mesmerized, but as he placed his whereabouts, his jealousy and alpha-ness plundered his mind. "Alright! The show's fuckin' over!" he said, grabbing the remote from Wally's hand.

"Quite a nympho, Donnie! I always knew there was something about her!" Wally attempted to bear-hug Donnie.

"But, my God, Aleeia? She's a keeper," said Derek, smirking to himself. "I mean, the way she just stuck her face in there. What a lucky woman! How you feelin', Donnie?" Derek clapped his hands as he went to sit on the couch.

"I think that's enough for tonight. I can't watch anymore." Donnie clutched his palms.

"Well, the good news is that it's just for a night. Aleeia will be out of the picture in a few hours." Wally lit his cigar again. "Think about it like a fantasy come true for Izabelle. You love her, right?"

Donnie nodded his head.

"Well, think of this as an act of kindness. It's something she wanted. I mean, c'mon, did you see how hot that was? I can't imagine what they're going to do next." Wally went to sit with Derek on the couch. "And besides, now Aleeia will have a glow about her for the rest of the evening. What kind of buyers wouldn't want that? The price will be high tonight, gentleman." Wally slapped Derek's thigh.

66

FRIDAY EVENING: PART 2: IV

Marcus impatiently gazed into the dark, empty county roads. "How much longer?"

York watched Marcus wiggle his legs back and forth. "I'd say we've got another 20 minutes before we're there." The highway dividers started distracting York. "I promise, I don't normally smoke this much," he said, sticking another cigarette in his mouth and offering another to Marcus.

"It's fine." Marcus cracked his window and watched the cigarette's ember burn like his heart.

"A big reason I stopped smoking for a while was this cough. My late wife was a chain smoker, so naturally, I was too. I still keep a pack for stressful times, but I know it's a bad habit." Marcus saw York's eyes float to a car's headlights in the distance.

"I'm sorry about your wife. I know she was probably amazing."

"She was great. The best, actually." York coughed. "I'm sure, just like Aleeia."

"Aleeia... Yeah. She's great, but even better when we figure out what's happening with her." An invisible bullet shot Marcus's chest. "Speaking of, do you think Matilda ended up calling Donnie?"

York flicked his cigarette out the window. "Let's give her another call," he said, passing Marcus his phone.

Marcus looked at his screensaver. It was a photo of a woman. "Was this your wife?" He flipped York his phone.

"Yep, that's Daisy. My Daisy," he faintly whispered.

"She's beautiful," said Marcus, holding his breathing. *I hope you're okay, Aleeia.*

"She was a special one. She could party like a man and love like the best of any woman."

"Yeah," said Marcus, putting the phone on speaker.

"York! Are you guys close?" said Matilda.

"Hey, hey, yes," York said, looking at Marcus. Matilda's voice sounded restless. "We'll be there in 20 minutes. What happened? Did you call Donnie?"

"Yeah. I called him. He seemed normal but then rushed off the phone."

"What did he say he was doing? Can you see any cars in the driveway?" interjected Marcus.

"I mean... I haven't looked. I can only see the front entrance." Matilda hummed. "I don't like waiting outside my boss's house because I think they are trafficking someone. This sounds like a huge misunderstanding, York. Is this going to put my job at risk?"

"I've got more than a hunch, Matilda."

Marcus could feel York pressing harder on the gas pedal.

"Just hurry. You understand how big of an allegation this is, right? I hope you have a plan before you get here."

"What is the plan?" Marcus muttered.

"I'm working on it. Just hang tight." York pushed up his

glasses. "I'll owe you big time for this, Matilda," he said, quickly hearing her hang up.

"All of this is...," mumbled Marcus.

"We'll get there and figure out what's going on."

"I hope so... What do you think we should do? Let's try and talk through it." Marcus clutched the sides of his chair and pulled out his phone to see if Aleeia had returned any of his messages. "What?!" he saw a text from an unknown number. "Aleeia texted me off Izabelle's phone?"

York jerked the brakes. "Are you going to respond?"

"I don't know. I guess." Marcus put his hand on his head. "It says she lost her phone."

"And?"

"That's it... and that she's at Izabelle's." Marcus gulped. "I'm torn... Where is this evening going? All I wanted to do was confront her about cheating on me, and now I'm thinking she's in the middle of something bigger."

York grabbed another cigarette. "I have a gut feeling, man," he mumbled, flicking his lighter open. "Respond if you want to, but we'll be there soon enough."

67

FRIDAY EVENING: PART 2: V

"Have you made pasta before?" Izabelle cracked an egg into a pile of flour on the counter.

"When I was younger, I remember making it at a friend's house, but since then, I don't think so," said Aleeia, looking at Izabelle's delicate fingers kneading the dough.

"Making pasta has always been a tradition for Donnie's family." Izabelle placed her hands over her heart. "His grandmother was from Italy... I miss her... She was a sweetheart."

What will those fingers feel like inside me? "I love that," said Aleeia, sipping her drink. "What kind are we making?" The metal machine Izabelle slammed on the counter made her jump.

"Cacio e Pepe... It's too bad this wasn't on the top shelf." Izabelle winked and wiped her floury hands across her apron.

Pull my dress off already. "Mhm, agreed," said Aleeia.

"Well, I enjoyed every bit of your assistance." Izabelle playfully poked Aleeia's arm. "Now, after we roll out the dough... and the texture is to our liking, we'll use the pasta machine to make my favorite part."

Aleeia watched her blow a strand out of her face.

"Gosh, aren't you just the cutest?" Izabelle growled. "If you keep staring at me like that, I'm not sure I'll be able to finish cooking for us."

Aleeia blushed.

"I like my pasta thicker than most. I think I got that from Donnie's grandmother."

"This is incredible," Aleeia said, watching the strips of dough come out the other end of the machine. "Marcus and I aren't exactly chefs."

"Here, hon." Izabelle slowly put her hand on Aleeia's waist and scooted her closer. "Come give it a try," she said, undressing her apron from behind.

"Okay, what do I do?" Aleeia felt Izabelle tug her dress straps to the floor. *Did she just take my dress off that quickly?*

"Like this." Izabelle admired Aleeia's naked body from behind, then placed her apron over her head and loosely tied the strings together.

Your touch. Aleeia pulled her hair into a ponytail. "I guess I'm ready now?"

"I would say so," whispered Izabelle in Aleeia's ear.

Her soft, gentle voice gave Aleeia goosebumps.

"Just let me lead."

Aleeia watched Izabelle's hands run up her waist and into her torso. *Keep going.* The soft touch of her fingers across the backside of her lower back made her push her knees together. "Like that?" asked Aleeia, feeling Izabelle softly pull her hair.

"Just like that."

The more Izabelle used her breath to paint warmth and desire across Aleeia's skin, the more Aleeia pushed her butt into Izabelle's waist. "Mmm," Aleeia moaned, feeling Izabelle's fingers wander between her thighs. "I want you." Switching positions, Aleeia quickly turned around and grabbed Izabelle's cheeks. "I want you!" she repeated, closing her eyes and devouring her with wet, slow kisses.

"Do you?"

Aleeia watched Izabelle creep down her body and put her head between her thighs. Nothing but her heels and apron laid on her body. "Oh my God." Izabelle's nails crept into Aleeia's underwear seam and pulled them to her ankles. Aleeia couldn't help but tilt her head back. The warm feeling of Izabelle's tongue on her clit felt like honey. "Fuck, that feels so good," whined Aleeia.

"Does it?"

Izabelle looked up at her from a squatting position. "Are you ready?"

Aleeia held her breath and watched Izabelle slowly stand and sensually start to unhook her blazer buttons. "Oops," she said, staring at Aleeia with fierce eyes. "Come get me." Izabelle purred and dropped her blazer to the floor.

Aleeia froze. Izabelle's lush skin and natural curves unlocked the box she'd been hiding for years. In the blink of an eye, Aleeia thrust herself at Izabelle and caressed her body.

"You like those, don't you?"

Aleeia twirled circles with her tongue across Izabelle's hard nipples. "Is that too much?" She pinched them with her teeth.

"It's perfect. Let's move to the couch," Izabelle said, reaching for Aleeia's hand and guiding them to the conversation pit. As they walked through the kitchen, Izabelle wore nothing but her black stilettos. Her noisy heels echoed into Aleeia's body like a vibrator awakening her on an overcast Sunday.

Aleeia exhaled and climbed down into the conversation pit.

68

FRIDAY EVENING: PART 2: VI

"Hey! Hey! Hey!" shouted Derek. "The show keeps getting better."

"Jesus, fuck!" muttered Donnie, rushing toward the screens. "I told you to turn those off." Derek's grin made Donnie's neck veins stick out. "Bella, what is this?" Violent knives jabbed the inside of Donnie's stomach as he watched Izabelle drop her blazer to the floor.

"She's really into it tonight," said Derek slyly, stepping back to Donnie's desk. "What a show!" he hollered, reaching for a key card from the bottom drawer.

"Alright, that's enough!" Donnie punched the air between him and the screens. "I can't do this anymore."

"This is a once-in-a-lifetime opportunity." Wally walked behind Donnie. "You gotta let her do what she wants to do."

Donnie felt Wally's hand squeeze the back of his shoulder. "Once in a lifetime opportunity for her and me," he grunted, "Not you!" Blood rushed around his forehead. "You two," he said, catching his breath, "You two need to go to The Lodge and prepare everything for tonight." His hand started to tremble. "I'll get them down there as soon as I can. This party is about to be over."

"Are you for fuckin' real, Donnie!?" shouted Derek from across the room. "So, you get to watch these two go at it while we twiddle our thumbs in your underground city." He stuck the key card into his pocket. "My uncle wouldn't have any of this. You know it!"

Donnie turned around with bloodshot eyes. "What'd you say?"

"You and your fuckin' uncle again." A heavy sigh fell from his mouth. "I'll handle this."

Donnie shook his head and watched Wally push himself into Derek.

"You just don't stop, do you? You think your uncle's still some hot shot?" Wally shoved Derek into the elevator. "I'll handle you and your fuckin' uncle," he said, smirking back at Donnie. "Let's leave this guy."

Donnie waved his fist and slouched onto the chair near the couch for support.

"You're lucky we don't have a TV set down there." Wally winked. "Don't have too much fun without us!" he said, humming into the elevator. "And make sure she's lookin'..."

As the elevator doors closed, Donnie clutched the remote and watched the screens, listening to Izabelle and Aleeia's faint moaning. With each sound, he found himself more aroused, and in a rush, he quickly dragged a chair in front of the screens and unbuckled his pants.

69

FRIDAY EVENING: PART 2: VII

Hearing a loud engine in the distance, Matilda peeked from the window. "Finally," she mumbled, seeing York and Marcus pull in front of her. Immediately, she jumped out of the car and crept towards York's backseat. "Open the door!"

York fiddled with the unlock button, but it didn't budge. Matilda shuffled the door handle like an impatient child waiting to get into the car before their parents.

"Fuckin' A," said Marcus, reaching back and opening the door from the inside.

"Turn your car off. Turn it off!" Matilda hit York's shoulder and then hid in the back seat below the window. "How are you two just so... Ah!"

York and Marcus side-eyed each other.

"It's okay, Matilda. Breath. We're here now," said York.

Marcus watched her anxiety melt away as York touched her hand. "So, what are we going to do? Did you see anything else, Matilda?" His heart ached to hold Aleeia.

Tightening her grip around York's hand, Matilda flipped

her hair back. "Nothing's changed. They went inside a while ago, but no cars or anything since I spoke to you guys."

"Well." Marcus cleared his throat. "I'm no Sherlock Holmes, but we need to get inside and see what's happening."

York closed his eyes, thinking about trespassing onto Donnie's property. "I know," he muttered." The steering wheel became a pew for prayer. "Don't you think he's got cameras?"

"The man probably has a security system for everything," said Matilda.

"Look." Marcus raised his voice. "I don't know about you all, but I need to get inside. Aleeia's probably..." He paused and used a calm, convincing tone. "After everything we've talked about and what York overheard... I mean, a *big one* and their *password* for the evening. That tells me there's something else." Marcus reached for the cigarette box and put one in his mouth. "And Aleeia's inside, for God's sake!"

York pinched his nose. "What're you thinking?" He looked back at Matilda and then at Marcus.

Matilda exhaled. "Promise me, York, that you'll take the blame for this. I can't afford to lose my job right now. If we get caught..."

"We're not going to get caught."

Marcus saw York move his legs together.

"I promise, Matilda. But we are solving something bigger than our jobs. God's guiding me." York kissed his cross necklace.

Marcus tried not to scoff. "So!" he said, looking at the house. "What's the plan?"

"We have to get inside." York flicked his eyes across the center console.

"Fuck it! If you two are worried about your jobs, I'll go in and see what's happening. If they catch me, I'll plead I'm a weirdo and was worried about my wife," said Marcus.

"What do you remember from dinner?" I've never been inside," said York, agreeing with the plan.

"Me neither," chimed Matilda.

Closing his eyes, Marcus pushed his palms into his eyes and said, "There were big windows by the conversation pit and their backyard..." The smoke from his cigarette prickled his nose. "Maybe we can try getting in from the backside." He looked at the moon through the sunroof. "I remember their living room backing up to a big backyard—you could see it through these glass windows." He gulped. "If they're cooking dinner, they'll be in the kitchen, and we'll be able to see."

York shifted his car into drive.

"Keep your lights off! You can see, right?" said Matilda. "It's bright with the full moon." The fear in her voice dissipated, and the woman who graduated from the police academy with honors came to the plate. York followed her instructions, turned off his lights, and parked on a side street near their house.

"What should we do now?" York cut the engine.

"I can look over that wall." Marcus pointed. "And see where we are on their property."

"Wait!" Matilda grabbed Marcus's arm as he quickly lunged out of the car. "What if they have those automatic lights that turn on with motion?"

"That's what we're worried about?" said Marcus, sticking his head back in the door. "It's Aleeia..." He looked at York, thinking over the steering wheel again.

Matilda pushed her lips together. "This guy is fuckin' crazy!"

"He's doing the right thing. He's in a weird position." York looked at Marcus, stepping up to the ivy wall surrounding the side of the house. "To think your wife is cheating on you and then find out she might be a part of something bigger. He's got more balls than me."

"Come here!" whispered Marcus, waving York over. "We need to get up there. C'mon!"

"York," said Matilda, swallowing a lump in her throat as he opened his door. "Be careful!"

"I will," York replied, feeling Matilda tug his arm back and pull his lips to hers.

Marcus rolled his eyes. "C'mon!"

York happily sighed, glancing at Matilda's juicy lips before quickly running to meet Marcus.

"How did that happen?" said Marcus as York got out of the car. "I thought you two were just friends."

York wiped his mouth and placed his body against the wall. "Get onto my hands, and I'll boost you up," he said, positioning his foot and hands on his knees as a footrest.

Marcus smiled. "Clearly, you like each other!"

York looked back at the car. "Just hurry up," he said, waving Marcus onto his knee.

Hauling himself up and over the wall, Marcus hung at the top and looked at the glowing lights coming from the side of the house.

"What do you see?" said York in a tighter voice.

Marcus scanned the yard. "I can see through the window into the dining room, but there's no one there." He grunted. "Can you hear that?" Marcus looked down. "I can hear something."

"I can't hear anything down here," said York. "Just tell me what you see."

"Wait, there they are," exclaimed Marcus. "Izabelle's..."

York felt his grip slipping on Marcus's feet. "Izabelle's what?"

"Oh, God." Marcus watched Aleeia and Izabelle kiss. "You have to be kidding me!"

"What is it?" said York. "I don't know how much longer I can hold you."

"They're kissing... Why does she do this to me?" Marcus yanked himself over the wall.

"Where are you going?" shouted York, watching Marcus disappear.

"What are you doing?" York saw Matilda step out of the car and rush to his side.

"Is he serious? He can't just do that," she said.

York looked up at the night sky. "I can't let him go by himself."

"Absolutely, not York! This isn't worth your job. Stay out of his relationship and whatever Donnie's doing. This goose chase already makes no sense. Let's get out of here while we can." Matilda reached for his hand.

"I need to do what's right." York wrapped his arms around her body. "Help me get over there, and I promise I'll make it up to you."

"York!" Matilda raised her voice. "How are you choosing to break the law and potentially lose your job for a guy you just met?"

"It's not just Marcus and whatever is happening with him and Aleeia. It's what I heard Donnie say. I got him in this mess. I know something's going on inside that house. Something is going on in this city."

Matilda took a deep breath. "Fine, but I'm staying on the outside. If anything comes back to me, you'll be to blame; remember that."

"York!" shouted Marcus from across the wall. "Are you coming?"

York stared at Matilda's lips again. "I'm sorry," he said, grabbing her cheeks and passionately kissing her. Matilda dropped her hands to her waist and fell into York's arms.

"York!" shouted Marcus again. "I know she's cheating, but I can't let anything else happen to her. I need you. You heard everything from Donnie's convo."

Matilda pushed York away. "Let's do this. I can't think about it anymore." She shoved him aside and ran to the wall. "Get in and out as fast as possible. And don't be seen," she said, resting her back on the wall and making a footrest for York. "If you see anything, let me know."

He nodded and stepped back for a running start.

"One, two, three," Matilda said, bracing for York's impact.

As York's body swung past her eyes, she couldn't help but fantasize about them together. "Almost there," grunted York.

"C'mon! This way." Marcus pointed to the right and waited for York to follow.

70

FRIDAY EVENING: PART 2: VIII

Aleeia closed her eyes and let Izabelle take control. "Like this?" she said, feeling Izabelle lay her back on the couch. Aleeia's eye caught the sparkle of Izabelle's necklace dangling off her chest.

"Mhm," said Izabelle, repositioning a pillow behind Aleeia. "You just relax."

The dim lights over Izabelle's face made her look like a goddess. Aleeia watched her drag her mouth down her stomach and between her legs. She flinched her hips as Izabelle's tongue circled her clit. "That feels so good."

"Faster or slower?" asked Izabelle, stretching Aleeia's legs further to the ceiling.

"Faster," she said, giving into the moment.

"Just tell me what feels best." Izabelle dropped her saliva onto Aleeia's vagina.

Lost in a haze of pleasure, Aleeia moaned. "Don't stop." Her heart raced with excitement like running from a burning firework—she knew there would be sparks and a grand finale. "Right there," she sighed again. Izabelle's tongue began to unlock their hearts' hidden desires.

"Is that what you like?"

Aleeia felt her legs starting to shake. Her rosy face lit up. "Don't stop," she said again, losing her breath. Izabelle's tongue movements became a living canvas, a masterpiece of pleasure and liberation. Then, without warning, Aleeia squirted. No words were spoken.

71

FRIDAY EVENING: PART 2: IX

Aleeia's soft-pitched moaning was like music to Donnie's ears. Her half-naked body lying on his living room couch sent signals down his chest and tightened his pants. While watching Izabelle play with Aleeia between her thighs, he played with himself and quickly released his frustrations. His guilty pleasure was no match for the rush of diabolic emotions he felt after clearing his head.

"She's fucking done," he said, running toward his desk and pulling out a small safe from the bottom drawer. After punching in a code with his knuckles, he cautiously placed a nylon doctor's bag on the desk. Donnie pulled a medical-grade needle injection from the bottom and laid it on the desk. Like the small juices overflowing from the top of the needle, Donnie's darkness and irrational thinking plundered his mind as he walked to the elevator, feeling a mixture of emotions and holding a strong sedative.

72

FRIDAY EVENING: PART 2: X

"Look!" York pointed. "There they are."

With a sinking feeling in his gut, Marcus's heart grew heavy. Watching Izabelle bend Aleeia's body like an origami sent shivers down his spine. "No," he whispered, "No, no, no!"

When Aleeia's legs rolled back to the ceiling, he knew what would happen next. "Here she goes," he mumbled, watching Aleeia's body quivering.

York refocused their attention. "Hey, we know she's inside. Should we go back?" He looked at Marcus, staring at Aleeia through the window. "I know it's not my business to tell you anything about your relationship, but we know she's here. Matilda got me worried about what we're doing. Who knows where Donnie is." He crouched closer to him. "We can still go back now without them finding out we were here."

Caught in a storm of conflicting emotions, Marcus found himself at a crossroads. "I don't know. I don't know what I want right now," he admitted. "You might be right, but what about the whole Donnie thing? Isn't that why you're here?" Marcus glanced at York for an answer, but out of the corner of his eye, he saw Donnie tiptoeing towards the conversation pit, holding something in his hand. "What the fuck?!" he shouted, feeling York's hand tighten on his shoulder as he tried to lunge forward.

73

FRIDAY EVENING: PART 2: XI

"Where are you going?" said Aleeia, trying to grab another kiss.

"Shh." Izabelle placed her fingers over Aleeia's mouth and slithered down her stomach again.

Aleeia looked up at the ceiling. "Oh my God," she moaned, feeling Izabelle sliding her fingers in and out of her vagina. "You're really good at that." Izabelle's face beneath her waist made her flushed.

"I want you to come again." Izabelle gently kissed her clit and rubbed it with her fingers.

"Just keep going like that."

Sensing Aleeia tightening, Izabelle moved her body up and slowly pinched Aleeia's nipples with her other hand.

"Fuck, fuck, fuck," whined Aleeia, scooting her hands to her clit. "Keep using your fingers."

"I love watching you like this." Izabelle quickly stroked deeper. "You're so close."

"Keep going, keep going." Aleeia flexed her body. "I'm coming," she shouted, and as she rolled her head off to the side, she immediately felt something stab her neck.

"Donnie!?" shouted Izabelle. "What're you doing?"

Aleeia's eyes slowly faded. "Donnie?" she mumbled. The last image she saw was Izabelle flailing her arms at Donnie.

"What the fuck! What're you doing?" Izabelle banged on Donnie's chest like someone trying to escape a locked room. "Are you insane?"

Donnie cleaned his teeth with his tongue.

"Why?" Izabelle said, looking up at Donnie's emotionless face. She knew he was on a devil's high. "You broke the rules?" she whimpered. "How could you? I hate you! You crazy son of a bitch!" Her puffy eyes became pools of fire as she dropped to her knees.

"How could I? How could you?" Donnie viciously threw his left hand at Izabelle's face, smashing her cheekbone with his gold wedding ring. "Just a night, my ass." He pushed Izabelle to the floor. "Really? Her over me?" he said, waving his hands over Aleeia and stomping his foot. "I mean, goddamn." Donnie collected his saliva and spit on Izabelle. "That's what you get, you stupid bitch." He stood above Aleeia with a grin from cheek to cheek. "This will do."

"Why?" cried Izabelle.

"You were so close, Bella. So close," he said, picking up Aleeia's dead-weight body and throwing her over his shoulders.

"You pussy," whispered Izabelle, pushing herself to her knees. "You coward!"

Donnie stopped his walk to the elevator and looked back. "What did you say?"

"You're a fuckin' coward, Donnie. You're worse than the devil. Go to hell!" she said, hearing lightning strike in the background.

Donnie's nostrils flared. "You're nothing without me!" He rushed to Izabelle's side and winded his foot up. "You're nothing!" he roared, stomping her face into the ground and spitting on her body again. "And that'll be the last of it," he mumbled, jabbing the elevator button and waiting for the doors to open.

74

FRIDAY EVENING: PART 2: XII

"Aleeia!" screamed Marcus, watching Donnie puncture her neck. "What did he do to her?" Aleeia slumped back on the couch.

York watched him lunge forward. "Wait," he said, tugging on his jacket again.

"C'mon!" grunted Marcus. "We have to do something! What're we waiting for!?" Marcus looked at York, scratching his chin. "Please!" he begged, feeling York's grip tighten on his elbow.

"Wait. We'll get in there. Just give it a second."

Marcus threw his head back and wailed. "What is he going to do with her? I can't fuckin' take this." He pushed York's arm off and crouched down, moving towards the kitchen side door.

York shook his head and followed him. "Just stay low," he mumbled, watching Izabelle and Donnie arguing by the conversation pit.

"I don't give a fuck if he sees me." Marcus quickly moved across the grass.

"Did you see that?!" York jumped back.

"See what?" said Marcus, barely taking his eyes off the door.

"No!" York pointed at Izabelle's warped body on the ground. "He hit her."

"Aleeia?" Marcus turned his head and glanced up through the window.

"No, Izabelle!" said York.

Marcus furrowed his eyebrows. Izabelle was begging from her knees.

"Go! Go! Go!" said York, pushing him forward.

Seconds later, they watched Donnie curb-stomp Izabelle to the ground. They could see Donnie's veins popping from his neck as he shouted from the top of his lungs. Izabelle's bruised, bloody face and Donnie's heavy combat boots and flowy pants ingrained an unforgettable image in their minds.

"Jesus." York's hands began to tremble. "I don't believe it," he muttered, making the sign of the cross. "Marcus! I'm calling Matilda for backup."

"Fuck backup! We need the goddamn Army," said Marcus, looking back at York's ghostly white face. "Pull it together! We have to get inside."

"I can't believe it!" York grabbed Marcus's shirt. "Donnie's doing this?!"

Marcus pushed York's grip from his shirt and shoved him back. "Fuckin' focus, York! You're the cop. Forget about him being your boss. Aleeia's inside, and he's taking her to God knows where." Marcus exhaled. "Get Matilda on the phone now and tell her what's going on."

"You're right. You're right. There's something bigger to worry about... By God's grace, please protect us tonight."

"Matilda?! Can you hear me?" whispered York, plugging one of his ears.

"York! What's going on? I'm still parked where you left me."

"You gotta get out of here and get back up as soon as possible." York swallowed and looked at Marcus, moving his hands forward to hurry him up. "Donnie injected Aleeia's neck with something, and she passed out."

"What? York, are you joking?" Matilda gasped.

"No." He paused. "And then he hit Izabelle. She's bleeding all over their kitchen floor. She needs attention as soon as possible. The amount of blood is a worry."

"I don't believe it." York heard her gasp. "Get evidence. Send me pictures and videos of what's going on, and I'll do what I can."

"Matilda, this is all fucked. Donnie's not the guy we all think he is."

"We don't have time for this, York. Send me the pictures and get inside."

"Let's go!" said Marcus, motioning for York to hang up.

York tried calming himself down. "Okay. Okay. I'll send it as soon as I can." For his whole life, York wanted to solve a real crime, not in the office and with paperwork, but in-person—in real life, a real story. Matilda's voice gave him a burst of self-reliance. "Hold on." He moved in front of Marcus and snapped photos and videos of Izabelle's body through the glass windows.

"Did you get it?" Marcus took a deep breath. "We gotta keep going, York."

"I got it," he said. "Let's go."

As they scurried to the sliding door near the living room, York and Marcus could see a bloody puddle painting the floor near Izabelle. Her body looked paralyzed.

"What do we do?" Marcus tried opening the door, but it was locked.

York flicked his eyes toward the open kitchen window. "The window," he whispered, tugging on Marcus's shirt.

Marcus's eyebrows rose. "I'll lift you," he said, positioning his body at the foot of the window while he watched York back up for a running start. "One, two, three!" Marcus felt his adrenaline overtake his anxiety. As York pushed himself inside the window, Marcus watched him wiggle his body through the tight space. Immediately, he ran to the sliding door after York's legs dropped to the other side.

"Good job." York quietly opened the sliding door and put his pointer finger over his mouth. Using his eyes, he directed Marcus to the hallway and pulled out his gun. He gave Marcus a 'calm down' signal as they passed by Izabelle. Her eye socket looked like a smashed pumpkin. "Dear God." One of her eyes twitched open as York crouched down and picked up her head.

"York! She's the reason we're in this mess. Leave her!" Marcus stood over York's shoulder. "C'mon. C'mon. They're getting away."

"Hold on." York put his hand up. "Grab me a pillow from the couch."

Marcus looked down at Izabelle. "You think she's a part of this." York didn't respond. "Here," said Marcus, throwing him a pillow. Flashbacks of Aleeia's pleasure and misery started haunting his soul. "Hurry!" he shouted, pacing around the room.

York pushed the pillow under Izabelle's head and watched her eyes flinch open again. "Where did they go?" he said.

Marcus watched her lips start to shake.

"Where?" York leaned closer. "I can't tell what she's trying to say."

Marcus put his hands on his head and walked into the kitchen. "Get her to say something, York," he said, pulling a large cleaver knife from a cutting block. He looked at York, lightly tapping her cheek. "Move!" Marcus pushed York out of the way. "Where did they go?" Izabelle's eyes barely flinch open. "Izabelle! Please! Help!"

"Down," she mumbled.

"Down?!" shouted Marcus with tears and sweat in his eyes.

"Downstairs." York placed her hands on her chest and stood up. "What's down there?"

"His man cave." Marcus paused. "And then I remember seeing another button... Is it the unmarked floor?" he shouted at Izabelle. "Please!"

She nodded and dozed her head off.

"C'mon!" York led them to the hallway. "We'll check them both." He clicked the elevator button and cocked his gun.

75

THE UNMARKED FLOOR: PART 1

Dropping his cards to the table, Derek mumbled, "Three Jacks."

"Fuck!" Wally made a sour face. "You've been waiting for that, huh?"

"Can I get you two anything?" asked Colleen, standing behind Derek.

Wally looked up. "I'll have a–"

The back door flung open. Donnie barged in, holding Aleeia around his shoulder. His face was pale white. "Move!" he shouted, dropping her to the table.

The room stayed quiet as everyone looked at her, nodding in and out of sleep.

"Donnie! We were playing a game! I was about to win!" Derek threw his cards over Aleeia. "Is this your first time? She's supposed to–" He felt Colleen grab his shoulder.

"Shut the fuck up!" yelled Donnie, squeezing his knuckles by his side. "I'm done!"

Derek scoffed and watched Wally brush Aleeia's hair out of her face.

"Shush, shush, shush," whispered Wally, dragging the backside of his hand down her body. "It'll all be over soon." There was a shimmer in his eye that made his pupils black.

Colleen winced. "I mean, why her? We just had dinner with them."

"Because." Wally held his breath. "She's perfect... I've known since I first saw her at the gas station." His grimy fingers crawled across Aleeia's stomach. "Anyone have a problem with that?" He closed his eyes and listened to the silence. "And that's what I thought."

"Wally, we have to finish our game. I was finally going to win."

"I'll give you the win, Derek. There's two times in Zimbabwe: now and not now."

Derek pushed his lips together, "Fine," and listened to Wally's sinister laugh.

"And now..." Wally rolled his hand out like an actor beginning their First Act, "For my favorite part." He reached into his black coat pocket and cracked a smelling salt packet. "Ah!" he shouted, feeling the alcohol and ammonia shooting through his nose. "Your turn."

Aleeia gasped.

"I fuckin' hate this part." Colleen rubbed her forehead.

Wally continued waving the smelling salt near Aleeia's nose.

"Let me get that!" said Donnie.

"No." Wally tilted his head back. "Not yet."

Aleeia's body jolted up. "Where am I?" she grunted.

"She's perfect." Wally covered his mouth in awe.

"Where am I?!" Aleeia turned on her side and coughed. "Where am I?!" She looked around the room with half-open eyes. The bright lights made everyone look blurry.

"Alright, she's awake." Donnie clapped his hands together

and put a blindfold over Aleeia's eyes. "Derek." He flicked his eyes across the room. "This is all you."

"Why is that?" Derek raised his voice. "How did I get such a fun job?" He walked up to Donnie and stood his ground. "I guess I'm the only one with the balls to deliver." He poked Donnie's chest. "Where's Izabelle, huh?"

"Calm down, Derek," said Colleen in the corner.

Donnie clenched his jaw. "I'm just following our rules."

"I am calm. I'm fine." Derek grinned at Donnie. "I'll take care of this. Don't you worry."

"Are you supposed to be threatening?" Donnie crossed his arms. "I mean, what do you think you're going to do? Do you want me to ship you back to Ukraine? Is that what you want?"

Derek continued shaking his head. "You think you're funny now, huh?" He paused. "Colleen, can you call Nikola in? We're ready for him." Derek gave his best poker face.

"That's enough." Wally stuck his hand up. "Just calm down, for God's sake, Derek, and listen to your wife."

"I am listening." Derek waved Nikola over as he entered the room. "Візьміть дівчину. Підготуйте її до шоу. Переконайтеся, що вона прокинулася через тридцять хвилин.[1]"

Nikola addressed the room with a bow and then gracefully picked up Aleeia and carried her away.

"I'll make sure she's ready," said Derek, standing in the doorway of the next room. His light shined underneath the ceiling light.

"Okay, thank you for doing your job."

Wally jabbed Donnie. "Stop it."

---

[1]. Take the girl. Prepare her for the show. Make sure she is awake in thirty minutes.

"You'll learn soon enough..." Derek shook his head. "I want the price of the boy tonight."

Donnie watched Derek slither into the darkness behind the door. "What's up with him?"

"You two fight like a..." Wally sat down at the table. "He's getting what he wants tonight."

"What?" shouted Donnie from the bar cart in the corner of the room. "No way!"

"He's got a hot head and keeps bringing up his uncle." Wally gulped. "We gotta do something about it. We gave up a lot of connections in New York."

As Donnie poured himself a drink, he listened to Wally's fingertips taping the wooden table. "You know what I'm going to say." He took a heavy sip. "But..." The room-temperature liquor funneling down his throat began to ease his mind. "We need him. I know this isn't the end of what we're building. We just need to take a break after tonight and clear our heads."

"Should we really give him the price of the boy?" Wally lit a cigar and waited for his reaction. "A quarter million at a minimum."

The smoke from Wally's cigar filled the room and dried Donnie's eyes. "You think that'll make him stay and be less crazy."

"I think Colleen would tell him to sit his ass down and do whatever we want him to do for a quarter-million in fifteen minutes," said Wally.

Donnie listened to the ice clinging around his glass. "Fine, but you're on the hook for this one."

"Whatever." Wally waved his hands. "We're all already on the hook for everything we're doing. What's the difference of one sale if we continue to do this?" Donnie saw his gold tooth twinkle in the light. "That is what we're going to do, right?"

Wally knuckle-punched Donnie's arm. "I want to do this until we can't anymore. What's one more year? Sure, we can take a break... but..." He leaned back and puffed his cigar. "C'mon? You can do it, mister sheriff."

Donnie frowned. "Let me think," he cleared his throat. "I think that can work. I mean, the plan is for Izabelle to go into hiding after tonight, so it looks like Aleeia and her ran off." He sipped his scotch and said, "Boris is taking the car to Texas and dropping it."

"Atta, boy!" Wally spanked Donnie's knee. "I knew you were perfect for this job."

Donnie watched Wally slowly walk toward the exit door and open a closet with shelves of animal-face masks.

"Well, time's a tickin'. We better get going," said Wally. "Who do you want to be tonight?"

An image of Izabelle lying on the floor punctured Donnie's mind. "Surprise me," he mumbled, drinking his sorrows away.

"Is Izabelle joining us tonight?" Wally threw Donnie a duck mask.

"I think she's going to hang back tonight," said Donnie. "She's tired."

Wally gripped his green fish mask. "Did anything good happen after we left?"

"They had fun alright." Donnie looked down at his drink.

"I bet we missed out, but it'll be good for business. These guys are going to smell her pheromones from a mile away." Wally walked towards the door that led them to the suites and auction room.

"I guess you could say so." Donnie pulled his mask over his head. "Ready?"

Wally opened the door and guided Donnie through. "You bet!" he said, making a cash register sound.

76

THE UNMARKED FLOOR: PART 1: II

"Click the second button." Marcus pulled his shirt out to wipe his forehead. "That's where I went the night we had dinner." The knife he held by his waist made him feel secure. "Are you ready?" York's chest was moving up and down.

"Yeah," whispered York. "I'll cover you no matter what."

Marcus's neck burned. "Here we go." The elevator pulley quickly dropped them.

"We'll find her. I promise," said York.

We're going to get you out of here, Aleeia. Marcus looked at his reflection in the elevator. *I just want to get you home safe. I don't care about anything else.* The cranking sound of the elevator doors opening scrapped his temples.

Immediately, York and Marcus sprang to opposite corners and waited.

York's eyes moved from side to side. Their ears magnified to water trickling in the background. "Hey!" York drew Marcus's attention to his leg with his hand. "One, two, three," he mouthed before shooting into the open. As he moved forward and flushed his gun around the room, Marcus heard a heavy sigh. "What the heck?" York put down his guard and admired the illuminating aquarium on the other side of the room. "An aquarium?"

Marcus felt his anxiety playing ping-pong with his adrenaline. "I know. It was a shock when I first saw it," he said, watching York press his hands against the glass window.

"I don't believe it." York's eyes followed two fish around the bottom. "Where did he get the money for this?" He looked back at Marcus creeping towards the corner of the room. "What is that?" said York.

Moving closer to a multi-screen set-up, they watched Derek and another man playing cards at a table. York adjusted his glasses. "Who are these guys? She kinda looks familiar."

Marcus pointed his finger and whispered, "That's Derek. He's a friend of Donnie's. And ...and that's Colleen. She works at The Lodge." Marcus pinched his upper lip. "I don't know who the other guy is." The smell of cigars and scotch was glued to Marcus's nose. "What're..." he said, watching York circle the room with his phone.

"I'm recording everything and sending it to Matilda." York stopped the video.

"Let's keep going down," said Marcus. "They have to be below us then."

"Wait, wait, wait!" shouted York, pointing at the screen. "It's them."

A flushed, zombie-like state took over Marcus when he saw Donnie barge in with Aleeia on his shoulder. "Noooo!" he shouted, feeling his legs buckle. York caught him from the back as he tipped over. "Cover her up!" he cried. "We have to keep going, York! They're on the unmarked floor. I know it! They have to be!"

"What is this place?" whispered York, looking at the white porcelain walls and red carpets. "I don't believe this." Ropes, handcuffs, blindfolds, wiping tools, and various sensual outfits hung on the walls surrounding Aleeia. She was in the middle of a sex dungeon entrance, someone's twisted mind, and a business operation that never saw the light of day.

"York! C'mon, we have to leave now. We can't wait any longer." Marcus stared at York, frozen by the discomfort that lurked beneath them. "I'm going!" Marcus ran toward the elevator. "York!" he said again, catching his breath.

A muscular man with a detailed neck tattoo of a baby devil praying to an angelic figure picked up Aleeia and left the room. "Did you see that?" York looked back at Marcus.

"York! I need you. I can't do this without you!"

"Hold on." York stepped closer. "I don't get it," he said, watching Donnie and the other man put on animal masks.

"Hurry!" Marcus rolled his neck around. "And send the video to Matilda... We can't take them down by ourselves."

"Right."

Marcus could feel the lump in his throat growing. "C'mon!" he said, watching York press his phone to his ear.

"York! Is everything okay? I'm waiting for backup."

"Hey," said York, feeling the reassurance in Matilda's voice. "We made it to the second floor, and you wouldn't believe it." Marcus was waving him to the elevator. "I'm going to send you another video. Please get in here as soon as possible! We're going to the bottom. It's the unmarked floor on the elevator. It's where we think they have Aleeia."

"Hurry."

York put his hands on his head. "I gotta..."

"Let's go!" Marcus clicked the elevator button and waited for the doors to open.

77

THE UNMARKED FLOOR: PART 1: III

After putting Aleeia into a black shirt and sweats, Nikola wrapped his plump, veiny hands around her waist and dropped her on a metal chair in a spine-tingling cold, dark room. Without hesitation, he strapped her arms and legs to the chair with zip ties.

"Who are you?" said Aleeia, half-conscious.

"All better," mumbled Nikola, cracking and inhaling a smelling salt from his pocket. He waved it near Aleeia's nose until her eyes jolted open.

"Where am I?" she shouted again. Nikola's enormous body towered over her frail soul. "Please! Where am I?"

Nikola laughed and put on black latex gloves. "Prepare. I prepare for boss. I am Nikola," he said in a rustic European accent.

Aleeia looked at his bulky chest. "Help! Somebody help!" she yelled, attempting to break free.

"Shh." Nikola covered her mouth with his thick fingers. "Calm. I am nice." Aleeia's eyes began to water as he stared at her with an innocent grin. "No tears." He slowly patted her teardrops with his other hand. "I make you pretty. Do not worry." Pushing Aleeia's body upright, Nikola clapped his hands and pulled up a chair. "Number 1 is clean." He reached for a small box on the table.

"Who are you? Where is Izabelle? Where's Donnie?" Aleeia gulped and scanned the room. "Please, sir." She shook her head and looked at his feet. "What is your name again? Nick? Nikola?" she said, fighting the urge to close her eyes.

Nikola knocked on his chest.

"Yes, Nikola. Look, I have no idea what's going on. If you get me outta here, I'll give you any amount of money. I promise. My husband is a musician and..."

Nikola quickly snatched Aleeia's jaw and held her mouth shut. "Shh!" Before releasing his hand from her mouth, he opened the small box and pulled out a hairbrush. "I do hair. No talk. No trouble for me." He pounded his chest again and swept his bloated fingers underneath her hair.

"No! No! Help! Somebody fuckin' help!" screamed Aleeia, convulsing her body.

"Calm, calm, calm."

Aleeia felt his tight grip on the top of her head. "Please," she pleaded. Tears dropped down her cheeks. "Please! I'll do anything," she shouted, feeling Nikola combing the last knots in her hair.

"Now we do lipstick." Nikola gracefully smeared cherry lipstick over her mouth.

"Stop!" squealed Aleeia, kicking her legs up.

"All ready," he said with a grin that showed his crooked teeth. "I'll be back."

Aleeia wiggled around in the chair as Nikola stood and walked out the door without another word. As he closed the metal door behind him, the silence swallowed Aleeia from the ground up. "Help! Anyone?!" she screamed from the top of her lungs. The veins on her forehead bulged. "Get me outta her!" Feeling hopelessly immobile, Aleeia's irrational decisions about Izabelle haunted her. "Izabelle! I hope this is a joke! Get me the fuck outta here! Donnie?"

After fifteen long minutes of shouting to herself and hearing her voice echo off the metal walls, Aleeia gave up. She dropped her head into her chest and started to cry. *Marcus. Marcus. Where are you? I'm sorry. I deserve this.* A knock at the door interrupted her nightmare. Aleeia's eyes shot open from the screeching sound of the door unlocking. Nikola submissively entered the room. Aleeia could see someone hiding behind him. "Please, Nikola. Please help me! I'll give you anything you want!"

"Anything you want?" said the person behind him. "That's a large promise for a minimal return."

Aleeia squinted her eyes. "What the fuck is this? I cheated on my partner. Is this what I get? Is this the new fuckin' treatment? I've learned my lesson. I won't do it anymore. Please. Please," begged Aleeia.

"Isn't that the story?" Derek popped out behind Nikola and winked. "Sounds like you've got yourself in a big, big mess, Aleeia."

"Derek?" she said. "What the fuck is this?" Aleeia's energy shot through the roof. "This is fuckin' bullshit. Let me go."

Derek slowly walked toward her. "We'll let you go." He paused. "In due time!" His fresh leather gloves overpowered the room's aroma. "Apple? That's your favorite flavor, right? That's what he saw." Derek knelt and placed his hands on Aleeia's thighs. "Mine too," he said, licking his lips and pulling out an apple-flavored lollipop.

"What?"

"Right here, Aleeia." Derek used two fingers to bring her

attention back to him. "That'll be $1.99, ma'am." Derek laughed and stuck the lollipop in his mouth.

"What? How do you know that?" Aleeia felt dizzy. "Help! Please! Somebody! Marcus!" She gulped and closed her knees together. "You fuckin' piece of shit. Let me go! Please! We'll give you anything. Please!"

Shaking his head, Derek pulled the lollipop out of his mouth and leaned closer to Aleeia. "I'm not the decision maker *yet*. Just the errand boy." He glided his hands up Aleeia's thighs and smelled her cheek. "You see, Aleeia." He waved the lollipop around her face. "This is only the beginning. I've got a plan for us. A big plan!" She could hear him sucking his teeth. "And the best part..." He pulled a white powdery bag from his jacket and emptied it on the table. "The best part is no one can stop it."

"Please!" The dim lights in the room shone into her broken heart. "I fucked up. Please! If this is some joke, let me go! Where is Izabelle?"

Derek dunked the lollipop into the powder like it was Fun Dip. "Hold her," he said to Nikola, waving him across the room.

"No! No! No!" Aleeia shut her mouth and aggressively shook her head.

"Don't make this harder than it has to be, Aleeia." Derek tried lightly pushing the lollipop toward her, but Aleeia kept her mouth pried shut. "Choo, choo! Here it comes!" sang Derek, pretending to feed her like a child. Aleeia could see his hands and eyes twitching every other second. "Alright, you win." Derek pushed his chair back. "I'll tell you what." Aleeia slightly opened her eyes to Derek, cracking his neck and chewing on his tongue. "I'll make you a deal to get you outta here. All you have to do is take half." He threw his hands in the air and dramatically licked half the lollipop. Aleeia was stunned, watching his sour-faced reaction. "See? That wasn't so bad. Your turn."

Aleeia tucked her chin into her neck. "I'm not taking that. Give me the phone, and I'll call Marcus. We'll give you anything you want. We have all the money you'll ever need."

Derek cleared his throat and moved closer to her ears. She could hear him swallowing. "That's not going to work," he whispered, pushing her head back and prying her mouth open. "C'mon! You little shit!" he shouted. Aleeia screamed for her life.

"Take it!" Derek's strength finally won out. "Just like that," he said, swirling the lollipop around her clenched mouth. "You'll be perfect. Trust me." He watched the sour and sweet effects of the drugs numb her tongue and shower her mind with a blanket of euphoria. Aleeia felt her puffy eyes dry out. "In five minutes, bring her out." Derek brushed Aleeia's hair out of her face and walked out the door.

Nikola crossed his hands and sat across from Aleeia. "Good stuff?" He asked, smiling at her changing facial expressions.

78

THE UNMARKED FLOOR: PART 1: IV

"Hello! Hello!" Wally's muffled voice echoed in the hallway leading to the suites. "It'll be quite an evening, friends! Oh, do we have something special for you?!" Donnie watched him start to clap.

"Not a busy night?" Donnie counted the green and red lights above each suite. "Only seven suites filled so far. They better keep coming, or we'll have some empty ones! Did we get the RSVP list?" Donnie turned to Wally, eyeing someone walking towards them in an owl mask. "Did you send the usuals the ice cream party thread?" The shadowy hallway was a continuous circle foyer with twelve suites reserved for the first dozen buyers to enter the underground auction house with the evening's password.

Wally patted a patron on the back. "I left it to Derek." He sighed. "I wanted to see what he could do. It was my normal list."

Donnie punched the wall. "Fuckin' A, Wally. Why would you leave that up to him?" He grunted. "We were supposed to pull some big buckets tonight, and now our chances are much lower with empty suites. Think about those odds!"

Wally dismissed Donnie. "You have a lovely night," he said to the person passing by. "We've got some specials. We appreciate your business." The patron nodded and continued down the hallway.

"God dammit! Would you calm down? We don't need any negative thinking. Positive visualizations, Donnie. That's eight suites now. Let's go!" Wally threw his hands up and marched into the door behind Donnie. "Besides, the boy's first and juveniles always sell for a good price. We'll give Derek the minimum on that. Nothing more."

"Right." Donnie watched Wally fling his mask off and walk toward the big glass window overlooking the auction platform.

"And Derek bribed a stripper from Florida to come back with him last night," said Wally. "She has no idea what she's in for. She thinks it's a one-night-stand type of deal."

"Where does he find these people?" Donnie put his knuckle up to his mouth.

"I don't ask too many questions. He's good at what he does." Wally admired the carved stone walls. "Can you believe we built all of this?" He turned to Donnie and grinned. "Who woulda thought the old underground permits would have built all of this?" He laughed. "At least everyone's vote is going to good use now!"

Donnie nodded his head. "Yeah."

"What's up with you, tough guy?" Wally scratched his chin. "Do you need a drink? We should be celebrating! I mean, look at this. Think about what Izabelle brought in tonight, too! We're winning." He sat next to him on the couch and nudged his shoulder. "Smile, would ya?"

Donnie slouched over. "It's just..."

"I know. I know. You want to take a break from this

madhouse." Wally turned to him. "Trust me. I do, too, but we're so close." He slapped him on the thigh and walked to a desk in the corner. "It's not every day we get to be in the same room as these important people, Donnie. The work we do is needed. Think about the secrets and leverage we'll have moving forward." He flicked on the intercom system and stretched a mic to his mouth. "This place runs itself with our password system and crypto payment or whatever Derek set up. As a matter of fact, he should be the worried one. He has to make the handoff with the buyer. We don't even have to do that! No one knows it's us!"

Donnie straightened his back and grabbed a scotch decanter on the glass table. "I know, Wally. What I'm trying to say is that I'm nervous about tonight." He poured himself a drink. "Izabelle was upset when they finished and..."

"Oh, c'mon! That's all part of the game!" shouted Wally, waving his hands up and clicking buttons on his audio pad. "Don't stress about it! She'll find another." He raised his eyebrows. "And then maybe you can join!" Donnie rolled his eyes around the room. "We're living the dream!" shouted Wally, hooking a laptop to the intercom system.

Donnie looked down at his drink and thought about Izabelle lying on their kitchen floor upstairs again. As his mind raced to the unthinkable, his shoulders jumped up when he heard a knock at the door.

Wally snapped his fingers and popped up from his seat. "Yes?"

"It's Chújú, sir," said a high-pitched voice behind the door.

Covering his chest, Wally rushed to the door with a grin. "Come in, sweetheart."

As the door opened, a petite woman with straight black hair and a bunny mask walked up to Wally and bowed. "Hello, Chújú. How are you tonight?" Wally kissed the top of her head and affectionately wrapped his arms around her tiny body.

Donnie blew out a deep breath.

"I'm fine, sir. And you?" Chújú pushed her body into Wally's waist when she felt him squeeze her butt. "Don't you wish you had one of these?" he cheered, looking at Donnie sitting idle on the couch. "I mean, she's so tiny. And the outfits, c'mon! Donnie, take a look." Wally bit his bottom lip. "Hmm. Chújú, why don't you go show Mr. Donnie your flowers."

"Yes, sir. Of course." Chúju untied her lace top and dropped it to the floor. "Like this?" she said, turning around and bending over in front of Donnie.

"You see that!" shouted Wally, running behind Chúju and hitting her butt. "Have a feel, Donnie! Live a little." The scent of Bulgarian roses and cinnamon drifted into Donnie's nose.

"Look at this!" Wally pulled Chúju's thong tie ribbon down her leg.

"Enough, Wally. Let's focus." Donnie covered his face and turned. "We have a big night."

Wally stuck his chin out. "Fine. Chúju, that's enough," he said, snapping his fingers and pointing her to the door.

Chúju bowed again and put her outfit back on. "Sir, before I go, as always, I came to update you on our current suites. Everyone's virtual wallets are connected and linked to our crypto wallet for payment. Nine out of the twelve suites are ready now. I double-checked our payment system at The Lodge, too. Derek watched me."

"You see that?" Wally looked at Donnie. "You can go now, Chúju." Wally waved her out the door and sat beside Donnie on the couch. "Everything's going to work out. Relax," he said, pounding Donnie's chest.

"Whatever you say." Donnie chewed the inside of his cheek.

Wally shook his gold bracelet and slapped Donnie's back. "You'll be okay. You'll thank me later," he said, walking across the room and sitting at the intercom system. "Let's get this party started!" His eyes lit up as he switched a power lever near the side of the desk. "And my favorite song to get things going," he howled, playing Tangerine Speedo by Caviar. "Cha, Cha, Cha, Cha!" he sang. "Cha, Cha, Cha, Cha!"

"Welcome, friends, to another night to remember... and tonight... Do we have something to celebrate!"

Wally pressed the on-button to the speaker and smiled into the mic.

"We have three lovely prizes for you: one young, one experienced, and one arguably the most beautiful you've ever seen!"

"Our first round auction will begin in twenty minutes. So, please settle yourself, get comfortable, and buckle in for another night at The Creamery. Best of luck to all our bidders."

As his distorted voice echoed through the speaker system, Wally's cheekbones pressed into his eyes from smiling so hard. "If that doesn't get you excited, I don't know what will!" He stretched back into his chair. "What's going on with you? We're so close. Don't overthink it now!"

Donnie uncrossed his arms. "I think... I think the whole Izabelle thing is getting to my head."

"Ya know." Wally cleared his throat. "I need you to buckle

the fuck up and forget about that for two seconds. I need you here now!"

The drink in Donnie's hand began to wobble. "I'm here, but I also want her here. After all, she did bring in Aleeia. She did well." Donnie watched Wally walk up to the auction window.

"Yes, she did well. We're all doing well. I know you want out of this as much as anyone else, but I need you here tonight when this thing starts. It's good luck." He swallowed and looked down at Donnie's pasty white face. "I've been thinking about taking Chúju and me on our own little vacation. You and Izabelle should do the same."

"I know she'd like that." Donnie could feel sweat sliding down his forehead like the blood dripping from Izabelle's face. "Can I go get her?" he interjected with an off-pitched tone.

Wally turned his neck around and lightly jabbed his knuckle into his forehead. "Fuck," he whispered. "If you're not back by the time the first auction starts, you're dead to me." Wally shook his hands out. "Go! She should have been here to start."

The boom in Wally's voice sent shivers down Donnie's spine. "I'll be back," he mumbled, pressing his mask onto his face and walking toward the door.

"And Donnie?" Wally paused. "If you see Derek, tell him about our little gift. You can confirm with him. It's just the minimum."

The thought of Derek walking away with more than his average share of the cut made Donnie's stomach turn. "You got it," he said, playing with his neck skin. "I'll make it back in time. I promise." Images of Izabelle's gashed face fluttered through his mind as he turned the door handle and ran to save her.

79

THE UNMARKED FLOOR: PART 1: V

The hydraulic sounds of the elevator doors prickled the back part of Marcus's mind. "Let's go!" he said, staring at York. "We need to move faster!"

"She's going to be down there." York held his gun at the door. "The real question is going to be what we'll find." Marcus watched him pull out his cross necklace and kiss it.

"I should have known there was something wrong." Marcus jabbed the button to the next floor. "It's unmarked," he mumbled, listening to York pray under his breath. *Aleeia, I'm coming for you.* Marcus's throat choked as the elevator doors closed. With each second of silence he felt in the tiny metal room, his subconscious was playing the devil.

"Promise me." York paused and tucked in his shirt. "If anything happens to me, you'll tell Matilda that..."

"Stop!" shouted Marcus, raising his hand. "Nothing's going to happen to either of us. C'mon! We're in this together." His voice cracked. "I promise. We'll walk outta here alive and with Aleeia."

York nodded and crouched down. "Get behind me," he whispered.

Marcus felt him tug at his jacket.

"Stay down." York's fingers shot up.

"I'm right here if anything happens," said Marcus, peeking over York's shoulder. The doors finally pulled apart and opened to a dark, silent room. Marcus's eyes moved side-to-side with York's gun. "Huh?"

"I don't understand."

Marcus stepped forward. "There's a tunnel." He watched York's head look at the excavated rock structures. "There are so many golf carts. Should we take one?"

York spun around. "What is this place? How did they do this?"

"York, let's get back to it." Marcus ran to the nearest golf cart. "I don't give a fuck about this underground madhouse. The keys are in the ignition. Let's go!" He started the car and turned on the headlights. "They have to be through that tunnel."

York brushed his hand on the wall. "When did they have all the time to build this?"

Marcus grunted and eyed the dark, black hole on the other side of the room. "Come on!"

York looked at his phone. "No reception. Matilda will have to figure out a plan." He jumped next to Marcus. "This fuckin' elevator!"

80

THE UNMARKED FLOOR: PART 1: VI

Donnie turned his head from side to side. The dark ambiance of The Creamery hallways made him sick. Bloody visuals of Izabelle's broken body painted a vivid picture in his mind. Each step felt like a midnight walk in hell.

"Hey!" shouted a voice behind him.

Donnie felt his knees buckle. "Yes?" he said, turning around and seeing Derek in his regular serpentine mask.

"Where are you going? The show's about to start."

He sensed the excitement in Derek's voice. "I'm going to get Izabelle. I'm checking to see if she wants to watch." Donnie scratched the back of his head. "After all, she did bring in Aleeia."

Derek chuckled. "Sure. Whatever you say, Donnie." The lights in the hallways began flickering. "Why didn't she come in the first place?"

"You know what, Derek," Donnie said, gently raising his hands. "I don't have time for your games right now." A draft blew through the hallway, rumbling in the background. "We're giving you and Colleen the minimum price of the boy tonight. Are you happy now?" Donnie watched his face shoot back.

"What? You've gotta be kidding." Derek put his hands on his hand. "I don't want any jokes right now. Are you telling me the truth?"

Donnie felt him lightly punch his arm. "Seriously. It was Wally's idea," he said, biting his lips. "Can you let me go now?"

"That's like..." Derek started counting his fingers. "I can't believe it." He paused, then let out a howl. "You two are great. I... I don't know what to say."

"You don't have to say anything. Can I go now?" Donnie sarcastically bowed and continued walking towards the exit. "And Derek," he said, turning back around. "Don't spend it all in one place."

81

THE UNMARKED FLOOR: PART 1: VII

After watching Donnie walk away, Wally sat alone in their control room. The only sound he heard was the slow ticking of the clock near the door. Each click agitated his mind like a fly he couldn't catch. "Stay calm!" he shouted, jerking from the couch to the platform stage. He pressed his hands against the window and watched them stretch down the glass. The pulsating beat from the clock grew louder. Wally flicked his wrist and listened to the jingle of his gold bracelets. "Who doesn't like that song?" he grinned and ran toward the intercom system. "Cha, cha, cha, cha," he sang the beginning of Tangerine Speedo by Caviar again. "Cha, cha, cha, cha," he hummed, scooting closer to the mic and clicking an on button.

"FRIENDS, MY FRIENDS. IT SEEMS WE'RE HAVING TECH-NICAL DIFFICULTIES AND ARE BEHIND SCHEDULE. PLEASE ENJOY A BOTTLE OF REFRESHMENTS ON THE HOUSE."

Reaching underneath his desk, Wally pressed a button.

"Cha-ching!" he said, hearing the clicking sounds of bottles pumping through the walls.

"IF YOU LOOK TO THE LEFT-HAND SIDE OF THE ROOM, YOU'LL FIND A CHAMPAGNE BOTTLE AND FLUTES FOR YOUR ENJOYMENT. SO PLEASE, SIT BACK, RELAX, AND BE READY FOR AN UNFORGETTABLE NIGHT AT THE CREAMERY."

He smiled at the green lights on his keypad, confirming the delivery. "Enjoy, enjoy we shall," he said, laughing and queuing his song intro again as he went to sit on the couch.

82

THE UNMARKED FLOOR: PART 1: VIII

"Colleen! You're not going to believe it!" shouted Derek, bursting through the back door. The big grin on his face said it all. "Colleen! Where are you?" A knock at the door startled him as he looked around the waiting area beneath The Lodge.

"Boss," said Nikola.

Derek looked up at his big, bald head covering the doorway. "Where's Colleen?" He bear-hugged Nikola and kissed his forehead. "We're going to be more than set."

Nikola shrugged and pointed across the room.

"You're the man! Don't let anyone tell you otherwise." He nudged his burly body.

"Hey!" Derek frowned. "What're you doing?" he said, staring at Colleen, holding Aleeia in her arms.

"What did you give her?" shrieked Colleen. "Why her? She can barely move." Derek felt her hit his chest. "You gave her too much!"

"Shh, shh," he whispered in Colleen's ear.

"I don't get it!" Derek watched Colleen dry her tears into

his jacket. "I liked her, and so did Izabelle... I told you, enough is enough. This is the end."

"It's going to be fine, my love," said Derek, combing her hair to the side. "Everything's all set."

Colleen squinted her face. "I tried giving her water, but she's on one. Where the fuck did you get this batch?"

Derek took a calming breath and walked to Aleeia, sitting hunched over in her chair. "She'll be fine." He pulled her chin up. "I gave her no more than I'd give a child."

"You're fuckin' crazy!" Colleen lunged at Derek again. "I want this to all be over. I'm done."

"Trust me. It'll all be over soon." Derek watched her yell at the roof.

"Oh, yeah!" Colleen raised her eyebrows.

"Nikola!" Derek snapped his fingers. "Give her more water," he said, pointing to Aleeia.

Colleen walked away. "This is no way to live, Derek. We're better than this."

"I know," he muttered, stepping behind Colleen. "It will be over soon." He smelt her neck and tried feeling her waist. "But... I have good news."

"Don't touch me!" Colleen brushed Derek off and grunted.

"Okay! Well, I guess I shouldn't tell you that Wally and Donnie are giving us the minimum price of the boy tonight." Derek waited for Colleen to turn around.

"What!?" she said.

"And they have no idea about our little plan." Derek watched Colleen fly into his arms. "I didn't believe it either, but Donnie told me." He kissed the top of her head. "He said it was Wally's idea."

"You're a fuckin' genius, Derek. I love you," mumbled Colleen, smearing her wet lips across his face. "Your uncle is going to be so proud of you."

"You think?" he said with an awkward laugh. "We still have a lot to do."

"Whatever you say. You're the boss. You've always been the boss, baby," she said happily.

Derek pinched Colleen's lips together and pulled them closer. "And..." he took a breath between kisses, "Chúju changed the wallet addresses... so... I need you to go back into the office and change it ours." Derek pushed her away and handed her the key card he took from Donnie's desk. "I'll send you my wallet's address. You just have to copy and paste it into the system."

"It's that easy?" Colleen threw her hands up. "And then back to New York?"

"It's that easy." Derek smiled. "We'll go anywhere you want, but I want to give a portion of tonight as a gift to my uncle and his operation."

"You two are fuckin' insane," mumbled Aleeia, spitting on the floor. "You'll never get away with this. You're both pieces of shit."

"Put a sock in it, honey. You're in the system now. Good luck getting out!" shouted Colleen.

Derek put up his hand. "You think what we do is a joke, Aleeia? This is just the start. You have no idea what comes next." He walked across the room. "But trust me, I do."

"I'm never fuckin' doing anything for you. No matter what you do." Aleeia kicked her feet.

"Right... We're going to have fun," said Derek.

The licking sound he made with his lips made Aleeia's stomach growl. "Fuck you! Marcus will find me. And all of you will rot in jail."

"That's cute, Aleeia, but you're one of us now." Derek patted her head like a dog. "This is where it all ends, and your new life begins." Derek turned Aleeia's cheek to Colleen. "She'll be perfect, right?"

"Yeah." Colleen gulped.

"You fuckin' bitch! You don't even want me here!" screamed Aleeia to Colleen, feeling Derek's fingers digging into her cheek.

"Derek, let her be!" Colleen tried loosening his grip. "Please, just let the night go as planned. What do I do after I change the address?"

Aleeia could see the rage in Derek's eyes. "You'll never get away with this," she mumbled.

"Colleen..." Aleeia could see Derek breathing heavily. "You just need to..."

"Go fuck yourself!" Aleeia laughed. "Both of you go fuck yourself."

Derek lit a cigarette and waved it in front of Aleeia. "You just need to get the car ready with Nikola..." He looked into Aleeia's eyes and pressed the cigarette to her lips. "And then us four will leave after the last auction. I'll bring her up through The Lodge, and this place will be history."

Colleen moved Derek out of the way and took his cigarette.

"So long to this goddamn city!" Derek screamed. "Nikola, bring her to me when the time's right. I need to get the boy and woman ready for the auction," he said, walking out of the room.

83

THE UNMARKED FLOOR: PART 1: IX

"There!" Marcus looked at York, perched up in his seat. After ten minutes of driving through dark tunnels, they finally saw a shining light. Marcus slowed down and cut the engine.

"This is fuckin' incredible. I still can't..." York hung onto the top of the golf cart as he looked around.

"How do you think we get in?" Marcus gulped, running to the door. A cold breeze ran through the tunnel as they heard their voices echo. "C'mon! This can't be it." He threw his hands up. "We need to get in there!"

York quickly scanned the room. "Hold on," he said with patience in his voice. "We'll get in! Let me think." He ran his hands over every inch of the thick metal door.

"What're you doing?"

"Looking for a switch or something. If they've built something like this, there's got to be some security, right?" York looked back at Marcus. "Come feel this?"

Marcus rubbed his hands over the wall. "Plastic?"

York pulled it off.

"A keypad!" said Marcus.

"This has got to be where we use the password for the evening," muttered York, still analyzing the giant wall. "What was it again?" He put his knuckle on his forehead. "Fuck. Do you remember?"

"It was something like..." said Marcus, animatedly using his hands.

"They were saying, 'We're rich... Izabelle's got a big one...'" York closed his eyes. "Wally... Same time... Password is... Password is... It's **GELATO**. I know it."

"That sounds right. Put it in, and let's see."

"Give me your phone," said York. "I need to look at the phone app's number pad."

Marcus handed him his phone and watched York translate '**GELATO**' into numbers.

"435286," said York under his breath, feeling his glasses slipping down his sweaty face.

"Did it work?" Marcus watched York pull his head up and gaze at the metal door.

Access Granted.

"Welcome to The Creamery. Please grab a mask on the wall as you proceed to the nearest available suite. A green light means open, and a red light means taken. For your security, please do not enter The Creamery without a mask. Enjoy!"

Marcus and York stepped back. The once so mighty metal entrance unlatched from all four corners. "Watch your step!" shouted York, putting his hand up to protect Marcus. "Cover your mouth!" He brought his handgun to eye level as a dark, foggy mist oozed from the bottom crevasses of the floor in the next room.

"What do you think?" Marcus's voice was muted. "Is it a trap?" He watched York step forward and examine the diffuser-like haze.

"It's..." York removed his hand from his face. The faint smell of patchouli and cedar flew into his nostrils. "I think it's okay," he said, signaling Marcus to meet him.

As Marcus lunged forward, he was greeted by an aroma that tickled his back shoulder blades. "That smell." He sighed, drifting into a moment of relaxation.

"Look at this," said York.

Marcus saw York pointing at a wall with dozens of animal masks. "I don't believe it."

"Neither can I." York ran his fingers through the fur of a panda mask. "They're so real."

Marcus walked up and reached for a turtle mask. "Grab a one!" he shouted, ripping it from the wall and adjusting it behind his head. "Let's go! We're running out of time."

York saw Marcus's black, restless eyes as the mist near their feet faded. "I'll go with this one," he mumbled, grabbing the panda mask.

"What next?" asked Marcus.

A closed-door latching sound came from the corner of the room as a voice made an announcement.

```
          Masks and bodies detected.
```

The metal door they entered from locked them in.

Marcus looked around the room in terror until a small figure in a bunny mask appeared from the escaping mist.

"Hello, and welcome to The Creamery. I'm Chújú. I'll be

escorting you to one of our available suites." Marcus rolled his eyes to York. "You're in luck! We still have a few open spots. Right, this way!" Chújú motioned them forward and grabbed each of their hands. "The show is starting soon. Please hurry."

Marcus and York didn't say anything—they surrendered and followed her instructions.

84

THE UNMARKED FLOOR: PART 2

Wally's watch finally struck the top of the hour. "Donnie," he muttered. "Where are you?" Taking a heavy sigh, he stood from the couch and paced around the room like a mad scientist, waiting for the final results of their radical experiment. The ember on his cigar continued to burn. "C'mon, Donnie! Fuck you!" he yelled from the top of his lungs, feeling his anger unbottle. "I want it now!" He watched his hands start to tremble. "We need to start. We need to start," he chanted, pulling out his phone and calling Chújú.

"Hello, sir," Chújú said. "Two more guests arrived, and I'm taking them to the next open suite. Give me five minutes... Once I seat them, we can begin."

Wally's eyes bulged. The dim platform looked like an altar. "It's not enough time. We need to start. Our guests are getting impatient." He ran his hand through his slimy black hair. "They'll miss the first auction. I'm sorry. I have to start this without Donnie."

"Understood, sir. We're almost to the suite."

Wally hung up. "Time to make some money," he mumbled, sitting at the intercom system.

85

THE UNMARKED FLOOR: PART 2: II

"Get up!" Derek clawed at the boy's arm and pushed him against the wall. "Do you remember what I said?"

The boy squealed as tiny tears fell down his cheeks.

"Say you remember! Do you understand the instructions?" Derek shoved him toward the platform entrance.

The child nodded and closed his eyes.

"That's my boy!" Derek looked at his puffy eyes. "Say ah!" he said, dipping his finger into his white baggie and putting it near his prisoner's mouth.

"I don't want to." The boy gulped.

"That's too bad!" Derek felt him pull away. "C'mon!" He yanked the boy's arm back. "I'll have some too. Don't you worry," he whispered, taking a tiny lick from his finger. "It's good stuff. I promise." The metallic drip he felt in his throat made his body numb.

"No," cried the boy again.

"You piece of shit." Derek pinched the boy's neck back and jabbed his finger into his mouth. "Don't fuckin' move," he said as his phone vibrated. "You hear that? That must mean you're up." He padded the boy's cheek and threw him to the floor.

I changed the wallet's address to ours.
Nikola and I have the car ready.

Derek felt his eye twitch. Everything he planned was falling into place. He looked down at his hostage. "You're going to make me some money tonight, right?" He hooted at the ceiling. "You can do it. This is what you're meant to do," he said, picking the boy up and sliding him to the platform door. His fantasies about his new life in New York with his uncle were interrupted by Wally's auction anthem loudly playing throughout The Creamery. "Here we go. They're making your announcement... Look how special you are." Derek grinned at the boy and put his hand on his shoulder. "See how special you are?"

"People of the night. People of The Creamery. My kind of people... Without further ado, we're ready to begin our evening."

"Our first auction is a young boy, fearless and clean of heart. Our bidding will start at two hundred and fifty thousand and be bid in increments of twenty five thousand... Let's begin!"

"Fuck, yes!" Derek saw the boy's shoulders shrivel up. "Pull it together. You're the star of the show!" he said, grabbing the boy's hand and leading him through the doorway. "Walk to the center."

The boy squeezed Derek's hand and desperately grabbed his leg. "No! No! I'm scared. I want to go home."

Kneeling to eye level with the boy, Derek hugged him. "Everything's going to be okay. Remember, this is all for you. It's like the game we played." He poked his nose and smiled. "And you remember how fun that was, right? Everyone loves you."

The boy tilted his head.

"Okay, I'll show you how to do it again." Derek walked in front of him and scooted him to the front of the dark stage.

86

THE UNMARKED FLOOR: PART 2: III

Matilda rubbed her eyes and massaged her temples. "He's not answering," she said, looking at the two officers in York's driver-side window. "I'm not sure what to do. I doubt they have service where they are." She lightly tapped York's steering wheel. "Look, I know this is all messed up, but we have to move now. We have the videos for evidence..." Matilda eyed the two officers, nodding in agreement. "And someone's already hurt... York, the officer I told you who's 'undercover' is..."

"We get." The lead officer put his hand on York's driver-side window. "We just need to confirm with our boss. We believe you. It's hard not to... it's just this being the sheriff and all... we have to make sure we have everyone behind us."

"Thank you," Matilda whispered, closing her eyes. "We're coming for you, York."

87

THE UNMARKED FLOOR: PART 2: IV

"Fuckin' Derek... He's a goddamn prick." Donnie stopped walking and hunched over. "What am I doing?" he cried out, feeling his chest tighten. With each second he stood alone in the dark tunnel, the more his vision blurred and caved into his heart. "For Izabelle..." A numbness in his hands made him fall onto the wall for support. "All ready? You started without me?" he grunted, rolling his bloodshot eyes to the speaker system playing Wally's auction interlude. Donnie felt his balance give out. "Izabelle..." he mumbled, thinking about her on the floor.

"Good evening," said a female voice in the distance.

Donnie immediately pulled his head up.

"Good evening!" Donnie waved his hand and examined the two guests wearing turtle and panda masks. "Please," He cleared his throat, "Enjoy the night."

Chújú and the two guests cordially waved as they passed by.

After they turned the corner, out of sight, Donnie grabbed his chest again and yanked off his mask. "Fuck." He felt dizzier with each step toward the exit. Sweat dripped from his forehead onto the golf cart steering wheel. "I'm coming for you, Bella," he slurred, feeling his anxiety numbing his face.

88

THE UNMARKED FLOOR: PART 2: V

"Come, sir." Chújú's coconut body oil melted into Marcus's hand. "We're almost there. Please hurry," she said, tightening her grip and speeding their walk.

Marcus made eye contact with York above her head. "Just go with it," he mouthed, scanning the space. The candle-lit tunnels and excavated auditorium-like city left them without words.

"Right this way." Chújú straightened her back when she saw someone wearing a duck mask, hunched over and catching their breath.

"Good evening," the deep voice said. "Please enjoy the show."

Chújú bowed and pointed Marcus and York toward the next roundabout.

"Donnie?" Marcus mouthed again, watching York nod his head.

"Please, right this way." Chújú opened the suite door.

As they entered the room, Marcus stood in the doorway.

"This is the suite, huh?" York ran his hand across the couch in the middle of the room and looked down at the misted platform with an area spotlight.

Chújú giggled. "Yes, sir. This is your private room." She walked over to the window and pointed. "Down there is our live auction. I don't think you will make it for the first one." She cupped her hands. "We must..."

"How do we bid?" interjected Marcus, breathing out his mouth.

"Yes, sir! I like your attitude." Chújú waved him to a desk in the corner. "We need you to connect your virtual wallet to our system for easy and discrete payment." She opened a screen with a QR code. "Please, sir. Let me connect you to our Wi-Fi." Chújú opened her hand and allowed Marcus to pass her his phone. "I'm sorry, sir," she looked at York. "We can only have one phone connected to our system. It is the rules." She passed Marcus his phone back. "Very good, sir... You are now connected to our Wi-Fi... Please scan this code with your phone, and you'll be ready."

"Right," said Marcus without hesitation.

"Have you been here before?" asked Chújú.

"First time!" shouted York, looking beneath the window. "It's quite the operation. How long have you all been doing this?"

"Many moons, sir. I'm not allowed to say much."

Marcus finished inputting his information and stepped back.

Wallet address initiated.

"Thank you, sir." Chújú looked at the clock above the door. "You're all set on my end. Please enjoy the show." Marcus caught York looking at her lace thong as she left the room.

"A virtual wallet? They have this thought out," said York.

He walked over to Marcus and inspected the small screen he scanned.

"Crypto," mumbled Marcus, pointing at the boy on the platform.

York curled his eyebrows. "I don't know much about it."

"It's not important right now. I'll explain later." Marcus shook his head. "I can't believe..." A robotic, muffled voice cut into the room's speakers.

"Do I have three hundred and fifty thousand?"

"Three hundred and fifty thousand... Once, twice... four hundred thousand from Suite A3... My favorite customer."

"Can anyone beat that... Once, twice... twice and a half..."

"Four hundred thousand from Suite A4... Let the Ice Cream Party begin!"

Flashing red lights from each suite reflected onto the boy's face as he stared into a black hole. "It's an auction," whispered Marcus, looking around at the tinted suite windows. "This is fuckin' unbelievable."

"I'm calling Matilda again." York pulled out his phone.

Marcus dug his hands into his hair and yelled.

"I knew this was fucked. Donnie was selling people all along," said York.

"What do we do?" Marcus frantically looked around the room. "We need to get this video to Matilda."

"I'm already on it." York waved his phone in the air. "The service here is shit. I think I can get a message through."

"ANOTHER GREAT EVENING FOR SUITE A3... FOUR HUNDRED AND FIFTY THOUSAND. PLEASE CLAIM YOUR PRIZE AT THE LODGE."

The boy looked around the room as the lights went dim.

"OUR NEXT AUCTION WILL BEGIN IN FIVE MINUTES. GET READY BECAUSE THIS NEXT PRIZE WILL SATISFY ALL YOUR NEEDS AND MORE."

Marcus stepped back from the window and tossed his mask on the couch. "Fuck!" His anxiety was piercing a thorn through his chest. "God! That poor boy! What is going to happen to him? He looked like he's seen too much."

York gulped. "I know."

"His face!" Marcus grabbed the vase off the table and flung it at the wall. "I can't take it anymore."

York let the room's silence calm Marcus. "It's going to be okay... It's going to be okay," he repeated, examining the chaos lurking between the lights hanging from the tall ceilings. "Look!" York pointed to a door at the end of the platform. "There! That's where the boy went." The light from the next room revealed a person wearing a serpentine mask.

Marcus buried his face between his thighs. "Do you think that's where they have Aleeia?" A dark force pulled him out of his rut. "Is it?" He sprung to his feet and looked where York was pointing.

"I don't know.... We'll solve this, though... Do you think the virtual wallet you linked to their system is what people use to bid?"

Marcus sniffled his nose. "Fuck York! I don't know. I guess, I guess. Why do people do this? What the fuck is this!"

"And that amount someone just bought the boy for." York paused. "You have that much in your wallet?"

"Yes, I have more than that. I got into crypto years ago."

York chewed at his nails. "So, hypothetically speaking, you could buy Aleeia outright, and this would all be over?" He pushed up his glasses and blew air out of his teeth.

Marcus rubbed one of his eyes with his palm. "What're you saying? I buy her from them?"

York shrugged. "I mean, Matilda might have backup on the way, but we don't know. In the meantime, we could walk out of here without anyone getting hurt."

Marcus sucked on his jacket collar. "I mean, money comes and goes. I'll never find another Aleeia. I'd pay anything to have her back right now." He moaned in frustration. "You're right. We need to do it their way. No violence. Just their rules."

"It can't be that easy, right?" said York.

"It's their rules. Not ours. For all they know, we're a regular client." Marcus sat next to him on the couch. "Did you send Matilda the video?"

"I'm just waiting for it to go through. I sent her the password, too."

89

THE UNMARKED FLOOR: PART 2: VI

"It's a pleasure doing business with you," said Derek, handing the young boy off to the highest bidder. "He's all yours. Thank you."

The patron grunted. "No, thank you. He's perfect," the man muttered, yanking the dog leash attached to the boy's neck collar. "A wild dream this will be." He rubbed the boy's back.

"We'll see you next time." Derek waved them out the side door and crossed his arms. "One down... And that's fuckin' money in my account." A hidden lever by the door opened a new room with two metal cages. "How are we tonight, ladies!" Derek put his hands up and began clapping. "You like that?" He knelt and kissed the stripper from Florida's curly hair. "You're stunning, sweetheart. A true uncut gem!" Derek's voice echoed off the walls as he approached Aleeia. "Don't worry! You're still my favorite," he whispered into Aleeia's cage.

"Derek!" Aleeia tried standing. "Marcus will give you anything, please." Dry saliva was accumulating on her lips.

Dancing to his own soundtrack, Derek pulled out his white bag again. "Who would like a little more party?"

"Me. Please." The brown-skinned woman in the cage next to Aleeia stuck her tongue out. "I want more."

Derek chewed on his lips as he walked up and placed his finger in her mouth. "Just like that," he said, feeling her sucking on his finger. "That feels nice... I'd love that somewhere else." He unzipped his pants. "Do you want more?" Derek poured a little substance on his dick and waited. "It's free. All you have to do is lick it."

The woman with tattoos across every inch of her forearms looked up at Derek with big eyes as she quickly wrapped her mouth around him.

"Mmm... That feels good." Derek held on to the metal bar for support. "Keep going."

"You're fuckin' disgusting," shouted Aleeia, crawling back into the corner of her cage. "I hope you rot in hell."

Derek tilted his head back. "Give me one second, darling," he said, zipping up his pants and flicking up the stripper's chin. "You did great. Timing, that's all," he said with a shrug.

Aleeia watched him buckle his pants back up and spit onto the floor.

"Aleeia... Aleeia... Aleeia." Derek crouched down and poked her arm. "We're going to have to be friends... You know that, right?" The faded white in Derek's eye made Aleeia nervous. "Why can't you just accept what's going to happen to you? It's our new life. It'll be perfect..."

Aleeia scoffed.

"I know what type of girl you are." Derek swished his tongue around his mouth. "Let's just say you'll be perfect... You're not like this girl." He pointed at the cage next to her.

Aleeia hugged her legs and closed her eyes. "I'll never do anything for you. You're a fuckin' psychopath! Look at you." Tears fell onto her cheeks. "Look at this life. You're a fuckin' terrorist!" Aleeia tried spitting on him.

A hissing noise came from Derek's mouth. "You'll learn soon enough, baby girl."

Aleeia could see his nostrils flaring.

"Up! Up! Up! You're next. Let's go!" he yelled to Aleeia's cage mate.

The woman tried grabbing Derek's pants. "Please... I want more. I'll give you anything you want," she said, moving her jaw from side to side.

"No. You've had enough." Derek shook her hands off his pants. "After you do your little show, I'll give you a whole bag to take home, just like a party favor." Aleeia heard the cage unlatch. "Do you remember what we talked about? Smile and wave," he said, pushing the woman to the glowing walkway.

"AND NOW... OUR NEXT PRIZE..."

90

THE UNMARKED FLOOR: PART 2: VII

Donnie could feel a fiery heat flooding his blood. "C'mon!" he shouted, watching the floor signal change. His chest was growing tighter and tighter. When the doors finally swung open, he rushed into the living room and fell to his knees. "Izabelle!" he cried. A small pool of blood was by her head. "I'm here. I'm here, Bella," he said, feeling her cold hand.

"Don..." she mumbled.

Donnie watched her try to swallow. "What did I do? I'm sorry," he pleaded. "Please..." Tears fell onto Izabelle's chest. "Stay with me," he said, seeing her eyes fighting to stay awake. "Baby... Don't go! Don't go!" He could feel a faint pulse on her neck. "I promise. We're done!" Izabelle's beauty made Donnie's heart rupture. Each second he took contemplating his decisions felt like an eternity until a knock at the door froze his face. "Who's that?" Donnie looked toward the hallway and pulled out his gun.

"Police. Open up!" shouted a voice outside the front door.

Donnie's eyes twitched. "Izabelle, baby," he said, rearranging her head in his lap. "Don't worry. Everything will be okay." He wiped her face and started hysterically crying.

"Donnie! We know you're in there. Open up!" said Matilda.

Izabelle's stomach was slowly moving up and down.

"Come in!" he shouted, knowing his empire had fallen.

Breaking down the door, the squad of officers stealthy moved down the hallway and surrounded Donnie, cradling Izabelle on the floor.

"I'm sorry," he cried, holding his gun up to his head. "It was never supposed to be like this!" He grabbed Izabelle's hand and pushed it against his chest. "It was never supposed to end like this, Bella."

"Donnie! Drop the gun," said Matilda, moving to the front and putting her gun on the floor. "It doesn't have to be like this, please." Matilda stared at a tortured, grown man staring at the cliffs of hell.

"You're a good person, Matilda." Donnie's hand started shaking.

"Don't do it." Matilda watched him press the gun harder into his head.

"This is how it ends," he said, glancing at Izabelle and cocking the trigger.

"No!" Matilda reached her hand out. "Please, Donnie!" She held her hand up.

"Don't shoot. Don't shoot." The array of officers behind her stood their ground.

"It's over... It's long overdue..." Donnie slowly put his gun down and mumbled, "They're on the unmarked floor," before quickly pushing his gun to his head and pulling the trigger.

"Fuck!" Matilda saw his limp body fall on top of Izabelle. "Downstairs! Find them! I'll be right behind you." She scooted closer to Izabelle. "She's got a pulse. Hurry! Send in the paramedics!"

91

THE UNMARKED FLOOR: PART 2: VIII

"THREE HUNDRED AND FIFTY THOUSAND... ONCE... TWICE... DO I HAVE THREE HUNDRED AND SEVENTY FIVE THOUSAND?"

Marcus shook his head. A woman was erotically dancing on the platform. "This is a fuckin' zoo!" He looked down at the bid button on the small calculator-looking device they found on the desk in the corner.

"Should we make sure it works?" said York.

Marcus hesitantly clicked the button.

"FOUR HUNDRED THOUSAND FROM OUR NEWEST PATRON, A7... HOW ABOUT THAT, FOLKS... DO I HAVE FOUR HUNDRED AND TWENTY FIVE THOUSAND?"

"Fuck!" Marcus threw his hands up in terror. "It works!"

"ANYONE... ONCE... TWICE..."

"Someone else bid already! Fuck!" Marcus looked over at York, covering his mouth as he pulled out his phone and read the top message.

"Four hundred and fifty thousand from Suite A4. Do I have any more bidders?"

"God fuckin' dammit!" screamed Marcus, hitting his chest.

York clenched his jaw. "I know..." He paused and stood next to Marcus. "Matilda responded," he said, looking at the woman shaking her butt in circles.

"And?" Marcus quickly tilted his head.

York sighed.

"Spit it the fuck out, York!" Marcus punched his shoulder.

"Donnie shot himself... And Izabelle's getting medical attention."

"What?" Marcus's eyes flared. "That mother fucker. What a pussy! He couldn't even live with himself. I wanted to fuckin' kick him in the face for everything he's done. That's bullshit."

York put his hands on his head.

"I know he was your boss, but fuck him. Look at all of this!" Marcus stomped his foot and violently hit the glass window. "I hope he rots in hell."

"Yeah," mumbled York, pulling his cigarettes from his pocket.

"I don't believe it. six hundred thousand from Suite A5... Does it get any better than this? Don't you all love our Ice Cream Party? Suite A5, please claim your prize at The Lodge."

York stared at the woman, sensually flashing her body around the platform.

392

"I T LOOKS LIKE SOMEONE IS GOING TO HAVE SOME FUN TONIGHT! DON'T WE HAVE THE BEST ICE CREAM FLAVORS?"

The announcer laughed before cutting to the same interlude music. The same man in the serpentine mask appeared at the platform entrance.

"OUR FINAL AUCTION IS STARTING IN FIVE MINUTES... YOU WON'T WANT TO MISS THIS ONE. SHE'S FUN-SIZED, BLONDE, INTO IT ALL, AND BLESSED BY ALL THE GODDESS'S BEAUTY."

"That's gotta be Aleeia." Marcus clenched his knuckles. "I'm not letting her go out this way. I'll do anything to have her back."

"God's on our side," whispered York. "I know it."

92

THE UNMARKED FLOOR: PART 2: IX

"Thanks so much," said the highest bidder, rubbing their neck as Derek clipped a leash to the stripper's collar.

"It's our pleasure." As promised, Derek put a baggy in the woman's pocket and walked them across the room. "She's all yours."

The woman's eyes fluttered as she moved closer.

"What's in the bag?" the bidder said.

Derek whispered, "It's something to get her to do anything you want. Call us if you need any more."

The guest cheered and grabbed the woman's butt. "And if you could, I was wondering if you could add a friend to the invite list."

"We'll see what we can do. You know we love a good party," Derek said, showing them to the exit. "You enjoy yourself now. Take care." As he watched the patron wrap his hands around the woman's waist, Derek felt his phone vibrate.

"Derek!" shouted Colleen. "I don't believe it! All the money from the auction is in our wallet." She squealed. "We've taken enough. Let's get out of here."

"It's not enough. We still have one *special* auction to go."
He stood above Aleeia's cage and ran his fingers around the
metal rods.

"Derek! You're being greedy. We have enough to start our
own operation with your uncle. What's done is done. Let's go!
Nikola and I have the car ready."

"Don't worry." Derek glared down at Aleeia. "This won't
take long. I promise."

Aleeia pushed Derek's hands away and yelled, "Help!
Somebody!" More tears erupted from her eyes. "Whatever the
amount of money it is, Derek, we'll give it to you. Please!" She
felt his clammy hands pull her out of the cage.

"Come here, you little shit!" Derek's grip pinched Aleeia's
arm.

"No! No! No!" Aleeia tried ripping away, but his force was
too much. The smell of his sour cologne flew into her face.
"Please!" she said, choking from her dry throat.

"I have a better idea." He shoved Aleeia across the room.
"How about... If you go out that door... and smile and wave for
five minutes... I'll let you come with me and not with the creep
that's going to buy you."

Aleeia fell to her knees. "Please, Derek! Marcus has enough
money. Let me go!"

"You'll learn one fuckin' day!" Derek knelt and pulled
Aleeia up by her hair. "I'm trying to do you a favor."

Aleeia screamed, and in a blink of an eye, Derek shoved a
white-covered finger up to her mouth. "Open up, you bitch!"

Aleeia screamed louder.

"Just relax," Derek whispered, finally edging his finger into
her mouth. "That should do it. Smile and wave. Smile and
wave."

Aleeia curled up into the fetal position.

"If you don't do as I say, I'll shoot you; remember that. I'm the boss now." Derek pulled a gun from his belt and shot a bullet next to her ear.

93

THE UNMARKED FLOOR: PART 2: X

"And my people! Tonight's final auction is about to begin. So, without further ado, please turn your eyes and attention to the center stage."

With the flick of a switch, the lights shined on a fragile woman whose eyes shuddered from the brightness hanging from the top of the underground jungle. Translucent beams encompassed her dignity as she gazed at the suites and tinted windows.

"There she is!" Marcus clasped his hands to the bidding system and analyzed Aleeia's beaten look.

"She's a sweetheart, alright... and better yet... she's already warmed up for you... if you know what I mean..."

The dark voice hysterically laughed.

"It's our final auction of the night. And what a

NIGHT TO REMEMBER. OUR BIDDING WILL BEGIN AT FIVE HUNDRED THOUSAND AND BID IN INCREMENTS OF FIFTY THOUSAND. ARE WE READY?"

"You got this," mumbled York. "We got this."
Marcus sighed. "Whatever it takes."

"DO I HAVE FIVE HUNDRED AND FIFTY THOUSAND?"

Marcus clicked a button.

"WHAT A GENEROUS BID FROM SUITE A7. THANK YOU FOR YOUR KIND DONATION. DO I HAVE SIX HUNDRED THOUSAND? SIX HUNDRED THOUSAND FROM SUITE A3... DO I HAVE SIX FIFTY?"

Without hesitation, Marcus plugged in a bid again.

"SEVEN HUNDRED THOUSAND FROM SUITE A7. THIS MUST BE THE PRIZE OF THE NIGHT. DO I HAVE SEVEN FIFTY?"

"I got you, Aleeia."

"EIGHT HUNDRED FROM SUITE A3. DO I HAVE EIGHT FIFTY?"

Marcus cursed under his breath as he watched Aleeia's puppy dog eyes lurk around the corners of the room.

"WHAT A BID FROM SUITE A7. DO I HAVE NINE HUNDRED? ONCE... TWICE..."

The voice paused for a brief moment.

Marcus and York glued themselves to the window.

"We're going to get her back." Marcus held his breath.

"Oh my. Suite A3. Nine hundred and fifty thousand. Do I have another counter? Once... Twice..."

Marcus screamed and released a dormant devil from the insides of his chest.

"One million dollars from Suite A7. It looks like we may have a winner. Once... Twice... Sold to Suite A7. Please claim your prize at The Lodge... And everyone, thank you again for a lovely night. You will be missed. Stay tuned for more updates coming this week."

Marcus dropped the remote control to the ground and opened his mouth in awe. "I got her!" he shouted, falling to his knees and placing his hands into his face. "I got her back."

"You did it!" shouted York.

Tears of joy ran down Marcus's chest. "Fuck this place. We have to get to The Lodge!" Rushing towards the door, he threw his mask back on and looked back at York, holding his gun by his thigh. As they opened the door and crept down the dark hallways, they saw the other patrons funneling out of their suites. No one said a word as they passed by. Everyone was in their own world, a world they didn't want to discuss with anyone.

"Which way is The Lodge?" asked York to the second person he saw walking in the opposite direction as them. They pointed down the hall.

"Freeze!" said a voice behind them.

York's eyes lit up. "Matilda... They made it!"

"We have to hurry!" said Marcus.

As they sprinted down the hallway, they finally arrived at a door labeled 'The Lodge.'

"Fuck this place." Marcus banged on the door and rushed inside.

94

THE UNMARKED FLOOR: PART 2: XI

"You did great, Aleeia." Derek pushed her through the hallway and put a chain around her neck.

"Why!" Aleeia felt her body tingle. "Why me," she slurred, feeling the room spin. "We could give you anything!"

"You know... We're going to be great friends. Just you wait." Derek tugged her towards the exit door. "What did you think was going to happen? I'd let someone buy you from me?" Aleeia saw terror in his eyes as her vision blurred. "We're better friends than that, Aleeia." She heard him gulp. "Do you want to know what someone just paid to have you? One million dollars." Derek cackled, "I just robbed this place."

"What?"

"This place is a joke. I only used you to get more money out of these leeches. I'll sell you the first opportunity I get."

"Stop!" Aleeia's yell was weak.

"Shut up!" Derek covered her mouth as they heard someone knock and open the door.

95

THE UNMARKED FLOOR: PART 2: XII

"Let her go!" shouted Marcus, barging into the room and seeing a man yanking Aleeia away. "She's mine. Let her go!"

York whipped out his gun and pointed it at the man. "Let her go, and no one has to get hurt!"

"You want to play that game!" Derek held his gun to Aleeia's head. "I don't think you've got that good of an aim!"

The room went silent as everyone held their position.

"If you don't put your gun down. I will shoot her," said Derek.

Marcus and York froze.

"Drop it!" Derek cocked his gun and tightened his grip on Aleeia.

"York! Put the gun down," shouted Marcus. "Aleeia! Stay calm. I'm right here." Marcus ripped off his mask.

"Marcus?" Aleeia tried moving forward, but Derek jabbed her stomach.

"What the fuck! Marcus? How did you get down here?" Derek said, inching him and Aleeia backward.

Staring into Aleeia's eyes like the first time they met,

Marcus put his hands up. "Let her go. Please! I bought her. Fair and square."

"Right. Those aren't the rules now..." Derek threw his mask across the room. "You'll be happy to know she'll be safe with me."

"You piece of shit!" yelled Marcus, attempting to move forward.

Derek shot the ground near Marcus's feet. "If you come any closer, I'll pull the trigger on her head," he said, quickly choking Aleeia and jerking her closer towards the exit. "That's it. Take a step back. And another. And another."

Taking small steps backward, Marcus and York watched Derek's every movement.

"If you follow us. I'll kill her. And that's not even the worst of it. I'll make her a glorified hooker before I sell her to some low-life that'll..." He paused and bit his lip. "When we walk out this door, you turn around and arrest the man in suite A1. He's an older gentleman and used to live on 8372 New Heaven Road."

Marcus's jaw dropped. Aleeia stopped wiggling around.

"That's right, Wally, or as most know him, Mikal Wallace, used to live in your house. There's even an old tunnel Wally would use from your basement. He filled that up years ago. Have the police check that out!" Derek pulled him and Aleeia through the doorway.

"Marcus!" shouted Aleeia.

"Aleeia!" screamed Marcus, running forward as Derek unleashed sporadic bullets on the ground.

"Get back!" shouted York.

Marcus jumped to the side for coverage and watched Derek disappear into the next room. "They're getting away," he shouted as they heard a knock at the door behind them.

"They're going to get away!" Marcus lunged forward but tripped when Derek unleashed another two gunshots.

"Freeze!" said someone entering the room.

York looked back at Matilda and a dozen officers by her side.

"Get out of the way! Move! Move! Move!" shouted Matilda.

"It's the police! Drop your weapons!" said one of the men, directing the team to either side of the door Derek went through. They nodded and waited.

"Go after them!" Matilda pushed her way forward. "Go!" she shouted as she entered the empty room. A ladder with an escape hole was on the other side of the room. She peeked her head up. "What?" Marcus heard her gasp. "It's... It's... The Lodge... The breakfast place."

Marcus pulled his eyelids down and pushed past everyone. "Where is she?" he shouted, stretching up the ladder and seeing the cash register from behind the counter. Flashbacks of Colleen's conversation haunted him. 'We have the best pecan bread and *Georgia's favorite ice cream.*' He thought about the announcer's voice. '*Claim your prize at The Lodge. The Creamery. Ice Cream Party.*'

Stumbling into The Lodge, Marcus ran out the front door. "Aleeia! Aleeia!" he shouted, looking around the dark, lonely roads. *I don't get it.* He dropped to his knees. "Where is she?" Where did they go?"

Aleeia was lost to the abyss that lurks in *every city*...

EPILOGUE

After a devastating evening, countless missing person reports, and a dumbfounded police branch, Marcus buried himself in self-pity, heartache, and depression. His life crashed before the rocky cliffs of purgatory, and his purpose melted to the cracks beneath his darkest thoughts—Aleeia was lost. Eventually, he returned to San Francisco to regain his strength and sanity. Not a day went by without the thought of her. As he'd lie awake at night, Aleeia's ghost would visit him and help him recall every interaction with Donnie, Derek, Izabelle, and Colleen.

It wasn't until one early October morning Marcus woke up drenched in sweat, remembering what Derek had said.

'*New York... My uncle has friends in New York... I can't wait to go back soon.*'

Derek's grin punctured an arrow through Marcus's heart as he crawled up from the coffee-stained floor and went to his wall of ideas. He finally found his clue.

"New York," Marcus said, scratching his beard and lighting a cigarette.

IDENTIFYING HUMAN TRAFFICKING

According to the Department of Homeland Security (DHS, 2022), there are many key indicators of human trafficking and how identifying victims **can help save a life.** Some common indicators to help recognize human trafficking are the following:

- Does the person appear disconnected from family, friends, community organizations, or houses of worship?
- Has a child stopped attending school?
- Has the person had a sudden or dramatic change in behavior?
- Is a juvenile engaged in commercial sex acts?
- Is the person disoriented or confused, or showing signs of mental or physical abuse?
- Does the person have bruises in various stages of healing?
- Is the person fearful, timid, or submissive?
- Does the person show signs of having been denied food, water, sleep, or medical care?
- Is the person often in the company of someone to whom

he or she defers? Or someone who seems to be in control of the situation, e.g., where they go or who they talk to?

- Does the person appear to be coached on what to say?
- Is the person living in unsuitable conditions?
- Does the person lack personal possessions and appear not to have a stable living situation?
- Does the person have freedom of movement? Can the person freely leave where they live? Are there unreasonable security measures?

References

Department of Homeland Security. (2022, March 21). Indicators of Human Trafficking. Blue Campaign. https://www.dhs.gov/blue-campaign/indicators-human-trafficking

TO MY FAMILY AND FRIENDS

Thank you so much for your unconditional love and patience with me throughout my writing journey. From my original copy to today, I can't say that I would have completed this project without you.

TO MY EDITORS

Hayes, thank you for reviewing my first draft with care.

Kirsten, you took my writing to the next level. Anyone who works with you is destined to do something great.

To you both, I'm lucky our paths crossed in this lifetime.

And to my unofficial editor, **my sister,** thanks for being my biggest fan and best friend.

MY INSPIRATION

The Unmarked Floor was inspired by a lucid dream I had about a previous significant other. We lived together in a different reality for a week, and when I woke up, I found myself questioning everything around me. Instead of over-thinking my experience, I wrote a screenplay for it.

Years later, I decided to pull out the original, more graphic script and turn it into a digestible read. There's a reason I had that dream. This story has burned a hole through my brain for many moons, and I feel honored for you to have read and experienced this world I created.

Human trafficking is an extremely sensitive subject, and I feel that by having had this moment of clairvoyance, I am to bring awareness to it.

Do not fear what makes you uncomfortable—learn to surrender to the moment, create what you desire, and believe in yourself every step of the way.

The **STOP** can only start with your actions.

ABOUT THE AUTHOR

 Wandering the aisles of a multi-floor Border's Bookstore was part of Lukas's typical afternoon as a kid. Between the mystery and fiction sections, he'd let the old woody and vanilla aromas encompass his mind and get lost in his daydreams. Years later, Lukas still wanders the aisles of bookstores, only this time searching for his name and finding entertainment from authors like Paulo Coelho and Gregory David Roberts.

Lukas lives with his 32-pound French bulldog, Juice, whose snoring and slobber keep him occupied throughout the day. *No, really.* Lukas doesn't know where he finds the time to write between their park walks and snuggles. Maybe, *Juice* is his ghostwriter.

Visit **lukasoswald.com** for more updates.

-LO

 instagram.com/lukasooswald

www.ingramcontent.com/pod-product-compliance
Lightning Source LLC
Chambersburg PA
CBHW031415240626
47154CB00001B/49